ALSO BY MEGAN McCAFFERTY

Sloppy Firsts

Second Helpings

Charmed Thirds

Fourth Comings

Perfect Fifths

Bumped

Thumped

MEGAN
McCAFFERTY

WEDNESDAY
BOOKS
NEW YORK

First published in the United States by Wednesday Books, an imprint of St. Martin's Publishing Group

THE MALL. Copyright © 2020 by Megan McCafferty. All rights reserved. Printed in the United States of America. For information, address St. Martin's Publishing Group, 120 Broadway, New York, NY 10271.

www.wednesdaybooks.com

Designed by Devan Norman

Library of Congress Cataloging-in-Publication Data

Names: McCafferty, Megan, author.
Title: The mall / Megan McCafferty.
Description: First edition. | New York : Wednesday Books, 2020.
Identifiers: LCCN 2020001290 | ISBN 9781250209955
    (hardcover) | ISBN 9781250209979 (ebook)
Subjects: CYAC: Coming of age—Fiction. | Shopping
    malls—Fiction. | Friendship—Fiction. | Dating
    (Social customs)—Fiction. | Buried treasure—Fiction.
Classification: LCC PZ7.M47833742 Mal 2020 | DDC [Fic]—dc23
LC record available at https://lccn.loc.gov/2020001290

Our books may be purchased in bulk for promotional, educational, or business use. Please contact your local bookseller or the Macmillan Corporate and Premium Sales Department at 1-800-221-7945, extension 5442, or by email at MacmillanSpecialMarkets@macmillan.com.

First Edition: 2020

10 9 8 7 6 5 4 3 2 1

TO ALL RIOT GRRRLS,
PAST, PRESENT, AND FUTURE

1

MOST LIKELY TO SUCCEED

*L*ess than five minutes into my triumphant return to the mall, I was targeted for assassination by a rabid spritzer from Bath & Body Works.

Before the ambush, I was as happy as anyone making minimum wage could possibly be. It was by far the best mood I'd been in since the night in late May when I'd landed in the ER with a teeth-chattering, bone-rattling case of mono. After six weeks of quarantine, I was finally reunited with my boyfriend, Troy. We had gone from seeing each other every day to not at all, and I could tell Troy was a bit discomfited by the space forcibly put between us. Luckily for him, I'd spent that time at home alone convalescing and contemplating the state of our relationship. By the end of my confinement, I'd come to a course-altering conclusion:

Troy and I absolutely needed to have sex.

The sooner, the better.

I was barely keeping it together on the short walk from the parking lot to our jobs at the food court.

"I missed you so much!"

I angled for a kiss as Troy turned his head to check his watch. I got a mouthful of earlobe instead of lips.

"Not now, Cassandra," Troy said without slowing down. "I'm late for my shift."

"*We're* late for *our* shift!"

The Parkway Center Mall was home to 105 specialty shops, three department stores, and two movie screens. This 900,000 square foot monument to consumerism was Pineville, New Jersey's, de facto downtown. Never referred to by its full name—always and only "the mall"—this capitalist mecca wasn't the biggest or the best or the newest our state had to offer, but it was the closest. For that reason alone, the mall was the center of the universe for bored hordes of suburban teens with limited spending money and infinite time to waste.

The mall also provided summer employment for roughly half of our high school's working class. The rest took their chances at Casino Pier in Seaside Heights. The pay was slightly better on the boardwalk, as were the odds that you'd lose a finger while operating the Tilt-A-Whirl because that's what happened when hungover minors helmed heavy machinery. Troy and I had taken the safer route by getting hired by America's Best

Cookie: "Where home-baked goodness is as easy as ABC!" The recession had hit other businesses hard, but in times of trouble, Americans evidently comforted themselves with Chocolate Chippers and Fat-Free Fudgies. Troy and I had just completed our new employee training when I got sick.

"I don't know if I'll be able to keep my hands off you when I see you in that sexy apron."

I was half kidding. My boyfriend of two years was wholly mortified.

Troy was not an obvious target for lusty objectification. He was my cherry-cheeked cherub, whose angelic face often caused opponents in Mock Trial and Odyssey of the Mind to underestimate his devilishly clever brain. Also, I'd never been, like, an excessively horny girlfriend. When Troy and I made out, my mind often wandered. *Would the collapse of the Soviet Union end the Cold War? Why did anyone think Urkel was funny?* But forty-three days of social isolation and physical deprivation had taken a major toll. From the moment he had picked me up at my house in his Honda Civic, I'd wanted to grab him by the popped collar of his America's Best Cookie polo shirt, press his body against mine, and break every rule we'd ever set against public displays of affection.

We passed Spencer Gifts, a store that sold smutty merchandise alongside kitschy novelties.

"Pity the naive child who enters Spencer Gifts for fake poop," I joked, "and exits with cinnamon-flavored lube."

Troy said nothing.

"Pity the pure babe who enters Spencer Gifts for a lava lamp," I tried again, "and exits with glow-in-the-dark condoms."

The mall had three main entrances, each located in front of a major department store. My family *always* entered the mall through Macy's, but the first time Troy drove me to the mall, I discovered his preferred entrance was through Sears.

"If we'd parked at Macy's, we'd be there already," I teased, leaning in for a kiss.

He ducked, deftly dodging my mouth for the second time.

"Are you *sure* you aren't contagious anymore?"

I almost couldn't blame him for being so paranoid. He was more traumatized by the extremity of my illness than I was, if only because he could actually remember the details. Troy was the one who took me to the ER. He was there when Dr. Barry Baumann said my spleen had swollen to the size of "a small spaghetti squash," which was an oddly specific gourd to choose from all of the more common vegetables he could have selected. After I was hooked up to various IVs and my temperature finally went down and I wasn't in immediate danger of dying, Dr. Baumann said mine was the most severe case of mononucleosis he'd ever seen in forty years of practicing medicine.

"Overachiever," I'd rasped. "Even when it comes to viral infections."

Each word was more excruciating than the last, as if Dr. Baumann had removed my vocal chords with rusty garden shears, scrubbed them with bleach, and reattached them to the back of my throat with six blindfolded sharpshooter blasts of a staple gun.

"That's not funny," Troy had replied.

I disagreed. It was a little funny. If anyone knew anything about overachieving, it was us. We were *the couple* with *the plan.* The boy and girl Most Likely to Succeed, as voted by our Pineville High School classmates and forever immortalized in the yearbook superlatives. Troy and I studied hard—together—to get into our dream schools—together. I was set to attend Barnard College in the fall where I'd major in biological and biomedical sciences en route to med school. Troy would be right across the street at 116th and Broadway, an econ major at Columbia with both eyes on business school. We thought it very mature of us to attend different schools within the same university system. Our parents would cover tuition, but Troy and I were responsible for earning money for books and any nonacademic purchases very loosely described as "incidentals" that to me were anything but. It was all part of *the plan.*

We passed the One-Hour Fotomat where I would've gotten all my pictures from prom and graduation developed if I hadn't been too sick to attend either of those events. Mono wasn't fun any time, but it particularly sucked in June of my senior year. Troy made me feel better about missing prom by reminding me how anticlimactic it was, as these things predictably were.

"Prom only matters for those who don't have anything better to look forward to," Troy had said. "If you can't go, I won't go either."

Of course, Troy was the type of boyfriend who would offer to stay home on prom night in solidarity. But I wouldn't hear of it. He'd already bought the tickets, rented a tux, and put a nonrefundable deposit on a limo shared with a small group of friends. Plus, we both assumed it was only a matter of time before his own symptoms developed. So I stoically urged him to live his life before he was struck down.

I wasn't disappointed about prom. Graduation was another story. If I hadn't gotten sick, would *I* have been the senior class speaker instead of Troy? I was happy for him, of course, but while my classmates were celebrating in top-down, cherry-red convertibles and skinny-dipping in pristine swimming pools, I was building igloos out of blankets and waiting for my internal organs to shrink back to normal size.

Troy and I slowed down in front of a pyramid of Billboard Hot 100 CDs displayed in the window of Sam Goody. Among all the usual, commercially successful but terrible suspects— Color Me Badd, Poison, Wilson Phillips—I was pleased and quite surprised to see a poster promoting Morrissey's newest release. The shot was taken from below, the photographer on his knees, the Moz all in black, rising up against the backdrop of a cloud, arms outstretched in a way that, for me—and I wasn't religious at all—evoked a priest performing a benediction.

"I'll drown myself in the Wishing Well if we don't get tickets," I said solemnly, referring to the chlorinated fountain where shoppers literally threw their money away. Pennies, mostly. But still.

Troy picked up the pace, easily overtaking a pack of power walkers. My wobbly legs struggled to keep up.

"It would be fun for us to see his show in New York City," I said. "Not, like, *fun* fun, because, you know, *Morrissey*, but, like, depressing fun."

Troy stopped so abruptly, his curls quivered. He looked to the Piercing Pagoda's lone employee for reinforcement, but she was too preoccupied with a paperback Danielle Steel novel to take any interest in the teen relationship drama playing out right in front of her.

THE MALL

At last, his innocent blue eyes met mine.

"Let's just get through the summer."

Those were the final words I heard before taking a violent blast of cucumber-melon body spray

right

to

the

friggin'

face.

2

BAD HUMORS

*I*n the immediate aftermath of the assault, I expected an apology.

Of course, I assumed it was an accident, an honest mistake made by a trigger-happy Bath & Body Works newbie who would thank me profusely for not bitching to her boss because she really, really needed this job. But I was wrong. Oh, so wrong. There would be no apology, no gratitude from the itty-bitty blonde with the crispy bangs. Only this unmistakable battle cry:

"Die, Mono Bitch!"

Followed by two more shots to the face and one to the chest.

The tiny sniper struck all my important orifices—eyes, mouth, nostrils, ears—leaving me gagging and gasping for air.

"Hell, no!" Troy yelled. "Hell, no!"

At least that's what I thought he was saying, but who could tell for certain with all my senses clogged by a cucumber-melon fog. Troy took me by the arm to the relative safety of the break room at America's Best Cookie. I splashed cold water on my face at the Employees Only sink.

"Did you get a good look at the wild animal that did this to me?"

I wiped my nose and blotted my eyes with a rough paper towel. My sight slowly adjusted to the break room's patriotic décor, a kaleidoscopic riot of red, white, and blue. Troy's face was still too blurry to read.

I wish I could say I had figured it out at that point. But this was Troy. My trustworthy boyfriend, Troy, who had dependably called me every day, twice a day, during my quarantine. One call before work and a second call after. Like clockwork. Literally. The phone rang at 9:45 a.m. and 6:15 p.m., and Troy gave me a rundown of his day, regardless of whether he had anything interesting to share or not.

"So random, right?"

"It didn't seem random," I said. "She screamed, 'Die, Mono Bitch.'"

"What?" Troy asked. "Are you *sure*?"

I held my head under the faucet, swished water around my mouth, and spit it out.

"Yeah. I'm sure."

"No, it was definitely: 'Try Melon Spritz,'" Troy replied. "Maybe the mono damaged your eardrums."

I doubted very much that mononucleosis had damaged my eardrums. And that became obvious enough when I very clearly heard the killer right outside the door.

"I know you're in there, Mono Bitch!" And then, most significantly, "I know you're in there, Troy!"

"Troy?"

"Open the door, Mono Bitch!" She pounded furiously on the door. "Open the door, Troy!"

I still hoped against hope that Dr. Barry Baumann had misjudged my recovery. Perhaps I was still gravely ill, unable to distinguish fantasy from reality. An aural hallucination had to be the only explanation for what was happening.

"You thought you could sneak around with Mono Bitch, and I wouldn't find out? Well, guess what, Troy? I'm everywhere!"

"Just give me a second, okay?" Troy pleaded. "I can explain everything."

Before I could process or protest his request, he slipped out the door to face the madwoman on the other side. There were a few seconds of incoherent shrieking, followed by sudden silence. Against my better judgment, I crept to the door and peeked out the small window. I half expected to see a cucumber-melon spritz murder-suicide crime scene. What I saw was worse.

Way worse.

My boyfriend of two years had subdued my executioner by shoving his tongue in her mouth.

My head got hot and fuzzy, like I was coming down with mono for the second time this summer. I definitely would've chosen another trip to the emergency room over this. Okay, maybe I had actually died from the mono and was now living in my own personal hell? Appropriately enough, that was when I heard the creepiest whisper in the underworld.

"Fat-Free Fudgie."

I turned around and would've screamed if I'd had the ability to scream. I was apparently being haunted by a female poltergeist pierced at the eyebrow, nose, and lip.

"Fat-Free Fudgie."

The monotone was equal parts talking calculator and the teacher futilely taking Ferris Bueller . . . Bueller . . . Bueller's attendance on his titular *day off.* Her haunted appearance and affect were so at odds with her *rah, rah, rah* America's Best Cookie apron that I laughed out loud at the ridiculousness of what my life had become. But Ghost Girl didn't flinch. She kept her tray steady, right under my nose.

"They're fat-free. And fudgie." She swirled the tray beneath my nostrils. "Fat-free. And fudgie."

Her tongue was pierced too. And her ink-black hair was swept up in a hairnet, which somehow enhanced the overall creepy occult vibe.

"Fat-free . . ." *Swirl . . . swirl . . . swirl.* "And fudgie."

Troy reentered the room. And he wasn't alone.

"Cassandra, we need to talk."

He and the miniature murderess were holding hands. And by that, I mean all four hands, all twenty fingers tightly interlocked in a way that didn't seem at all romantic, but more like an improvised form of restraint. The assassin smiled at me menacingly, but at least I could see that she was unarmed.

Troy turned to Ghost Girl.

"Zoe, can you give us some privacy?"

"Ms. Gomez," Ghost Girl corrected.

Troy sighed. "*Ms. Gomez*, can you give us some privacy?"

Without further acknowledging Troy, Ghost Girl—aka Zoe, aka Ms. Gomez—set down the tray of samples on a nearby table. Then she floated toward me, pressed a cold hand on my shoulder, and whispered what I'd hoped would be words of wisdom from beyond the grave.

"Fat-Free Fudgie."

I don't know why I expected anything different.

"Cassandra." Troy stood straight and tall, projecting the matter-of-fact confidence I'd seen him use to great advantage as the lead attorney for the Legal Seagulls. "Meet Helen."

My throat collapsed in on itself.

"Helen," Troy repeated. "Like Helen of Troy."

Troy had always loved that our names were heavily featured in Greek myths. Troy was the city fought over in the Trojan War. Cassandra was a princess of Troy, who saw visions of the future.

Clearly, I had not seen this coming.

"Helen," he added, "whose great beauty caused the Trojan War."

I choked. This Helen was not beautiful. She was tiny and terrifying like a feral Chihuahua with a horrendous home perm.

"Why didn't you tell me?" I somehow managed to ask.

"I thought it would be disrespectful to break up with you over the phone."

"So, *this* is better?"

He shrugged and sheepishly looked at his feet. Helen bared her yellowed snaggleteeth. She was a smoker for sure. And her receding gums were common for a non-flosser. My parents would be appalled by her poor oral hygiene.

"So, you expect me to be okay with working next to you two all summer?"

Troy and Helen exchanged knowing looks. They released each other from their four-handed death grip, and Helen slid her palms into the back pockets of Troy's pleated khakis.

"No," Troy replied. "We don't expect that at all."

"Didn't Zoe fire you?" Helen asked.

"She's the assistant manager," Troy said.

I leaned against the wall for reinforcement. Ten minutes into what was supposed to be my triumphant return to the Parkway Center Mall, I'd lost the job, the boyfriend, and—worst of all—*the plan.*

"I can't believe this is happening."

I wanted to return to my blanket igloo and never come out again.

"I'm sure you can get hired somewhere else," Troy said.

"Maybe another Steve Sanders," Helen offered condescendingly. "Or at least a David Silver . . ."

A rush of angry adrenaline shot through me. I seized Troy by the strings of his ABC apron and shook him. Hard.

"You told her? She knows the *90210* Scale of Mall Employment Awesomeness?"

Troy had let Helen in on what was by far one of our best inside jokes. This betrayal was even worse than the kiss or anything else they had surely done together. And by the overly familiar way Helen was massaging his butt right in front of me, I assumed they'd done *a lot*.

"We never meant for this to happen," Troy insisted.

"I had a boyfriend when we met." Helen stopped groping Troy and casually twirled a crusty curl around her finger. "I was only at the Pineville prom because I went with Sonny Sexton . . ."

This was just about the only part of this whole sordid situation that made any sense to me. Sonny Sexton was legendary at Pineville High for being the first twenty-year-old senior in school history. Obviously, we'd never had a single class together. But I couldn't avoid passing him in the halls, this denim-on-denim dirtbag who reeked of weed and Designer Imposters Drakkar Noir even at a distance. Sonny Sexton and Helen made sense. Troy and Helen? I couldn't wrap my head around it.

"It's kind of funny," Troy said. "If you hadn't insisted I go to the prom without you, Helen and I never would have met."

My ex-boyfriend's new girlfriend rested her head on his shoulder, releasing a brittle crunch of Aqua Net dandruff onto his ABC polo shirt.

"We have you to thank for putting us together . . ."

For thousands and thousands of years, going all the way back to the ancient Greeks, four types of body fluids—or humors—were believed to influence personality and behavior. Bad moods were blamed on too much black bile in the spleen. I got off easy with an IV and six weeks of bed rest. In the fourth century BC, Dr. Hippocrates might have treated a "splenic" temperament by surgically removing the bulging, bilious organ without the benefit of anesthesia or antiseptic. I know all this because Troy left a copy of *Apollo to Zeus: Greek Mythology and Modern Medicine* in my mailbox as a get-well gift.

Blame a buildup of bad humor for what happened next.

I grabbed the only weapon within reach—the tray of Fat-Free Fudgies—and chucked it directly at Troy. I only wish I'd felt more satisfaction when it smacked him right between his lying eyes.

3

BEING ALIVE

*T*he Volvo inched toward Macy's. If my legs weren't so shaky, I would've leapt out the vehicle and run the rest of the way. Anything to escape Mom, Dad, and Barbra Streisand.

"*Nothing's gonna harm you . . .*"

The Broadway Album. Track Four.

"*Not while I'm around.*"

Too late, Babs, I thought. *Too late.*

Kathy hit fast forward on the tape deck to get to the up-tempo Sondheim number she preferred.

"Explain to me again why Troy couldn't drive you to work today?"

I earned top grades, respected curfew, and kept myself too busy with extracurriculars to cause trouble. I'd never had incentive to lie to my parents about anything this big before. Without much practice, I did the best I could.

"He got promoted to seasonal assistant manager and had to, um, attend a meeting?" I answered unconvincingly. "Or something?"

"Hmph." Frank tapped the steering wheel. "Why does he get to be seasonal assistant manager and not you?"

I should have predicted Dad would be disappointed in me for not getting a nonexistent promotion for a job I didn't have anymore.

"Because he's worked there for six weeks and I haven't started yet?"

"You should have the same opportunities as him," Dad said. "Your medical condition shouldn't be held against you."

"Uh-huh," I said noncommittally.

The mall wasn't open to customers yet, but the parking lot was already filling up. Shoppers stayed in their cars, keeping the engines and AC running right up to the moment the doors opened at 10:00 a.m.

"I was surprised when you told us you needed a ride," Mom said. "Troy assured us that he'd do all the driving this summer. And when Troy says he's going to do something, he does it."

"You can't expect us to drive you every day," Frank warned.

"I don't," I said, though I kind of did.

I didn't have a license. I took driver's ed like the rest of my class, but I just hadn't bothered to take the road test. It wasn't a priority. Since I was ten years old, I'd fallen asleep with a poster of the five boroughs map above my bed, dreaming of public transit, of attending college, and living the rest of my life in New York City.

Who needed a license when I had Troy? With a September birthday, he was one of the first in our class to turn seventeen. He'd gotten his license early and had chauffeured me around in his hand-me-down Honda Civic ever since. Not that we ventured out very far, very often. By junior year, I was sticking subway tokens in the slots of my penny loafers, a perpetual reminder to prioritize practice tests over parties.

"You can't spell 'Saturday' without SAT," I'd joke to Troy.

"You can't spell 'party' without AP," Troy would joke back.

Though he was technically correct, the wordplay wasn't nearly as funny as mine. Comedy wasn't his forte. But I laughed anyway because that's what I did when we were together.

And I hated myself for it now that we weren't.

"Troy is so reliable, I'm sure he'll come through." Kathy pressed play.

Until yesterday I would've agreed with her. But not anymore.

"*Someone to hold you too close*," sang Barbra Streisand in between sexy sax riffs, "*Someone to hurt you too deep . . .*"

From the back seat, I had zero control over the Volvo's radio/tape deck.

"*But alone*," Barbra Streisand sang, "*is alone . . .*"

Dad hit stop.

"Frank!" my mother shrieked. "She was just getting to the best part!"

"It's 9:49."

"I don't care what time it is!"

Not even Dad could get away with shutting up Barbra Streisand when she was singing Sondheim. Mom pressed rewind, then play to give justice to her impeccable phrasing.

"Not aliiiiiiiiiiiiiiive . . ."

"We're gonna miss it, Kathy!"

Frank stabbed the eject button and another screech filled the car. Only this time, it was the unmistakable sound of *The Broadway Album* being eaten by the Volvo's ravenous tape deck.

"Frank!" Mom yanked the unspooled, unplayable tape out of the machine. "I've told you a million times that you've got to press stop before eject!"

Dad had already hit number one on the radio presets: WOBM-FM. He never missed an opportunity to listen to the local radio station to make sure Worthy Orthodontics and Pediatric Dentistry got the advertising spots they paid for: Morning and afternoon drive time, on the fifties, five days a week. The simple, singsongy jingle was performed by a kiddie chorus who had graduated from high school years before me.

"Braces make happy faces."

And in my parents' case, a happy marriage too. Frank and Kathy fell in love over their mutual admiration of symmetrically aligned cephalometric X-rays, got married, cofounded Worthy Orthodontics and Pediatric Dentistry, and have spent nearly all day, every day, with each other ever since. Whenever anyone asked them the secret to their long-term professional and personal partnership, they made the same joke.

Dad's line: "We're closer than a ceramic bracket to the back of a molar."

Mom's line: "Our bond is stronger than resin-modified dental cement."

"Braces make happy faces . . ."

"Well, they played the ad, just like they've been doing for twenty years." Mom lifted the tangled ribbon of cassette tape for Dad to see. "And Barbra is dead."

Frank tunelessly hummed along to WOBM's hazy, hot, and humid weather forecast as we finally reached the pedestrian drop-off in front of Macy's.

"Okay! Thanks for the ride! Goodbye!"

I tugged on the door handle, only to find that it was on auto-lock. Dad put the car into park, pulled out his wallet, and handed me a twenty-dollar bill.

"When you're on break," he said, "buy your mother a new Barbra."

Then Dad kissed Mom on the cheek, and I was ready to leggo my Eggos all over the Volvo's leather interior.

Not because I was grossed out.

I was jealous.

I mean, I'd always sort of known my parents' seemingly ceaseless enjoyment of each other was unusual for long-term relationships. But I didn't quite understand what an impossibly high standard they had set until I saw Troy's tongue in Helen's snaggletoothed yuck mouth.

I flung open the car door and got out of there before I could incriminate myself.

"Later!" I blew kisses at the car. "Bye!"

I thought for sure I had made it when Mom popped her head out the window.

"Give our best to Troy!" And then—just to make it extra excruciating—she added, "He's a keeper, that one."

I waved goodbye and waited until the Volvo was of sight. Then I walked right past Macy's and kept going, continuing halfway around the parking lot to Entrance Two, J. C. Penney. As the entrance farthest from the food court, it was the location least likely to result in another attempt on my life, and I needed to be alive in order to find a new job.

Make no mistake: I was going to find a new job. I needed somewhere to be every day or my parents would start asking questions I couldn't answer. Not yet anyway, not before I'd come up with a *new plan* that did not involve Troy.

4

UNWITTING WITNESS

*N*o plan.
No boyfriend.
No job.
And worst of all?

The food court was off-limits for the foreseeable future, so I couldn't even wallow in *our* booth. It was perfectly situated, far away from the greasy fast-food grills but still in view of the special events stage where the Silver Strutters dazzled the lunchtime crowds. They were the best of the senior citizen aerobic dance troupes. I'd joke with Troy about the fierce competition among the various nursing homes, how the spryest octogenarian aerobicizers were actively recruited by coaches trying to lure them away from rival assisted-living facilities by offering artificial hip scholarships.

Troy and I had always had the best conversations in our booth. It was there, as we dipped spoons into chocolate-and-vanilla-swirled spires of Froyo, we had decided to attend different colleges in the same city. It was there, as we dunked cheese french fries into mini paper vats of ketchup, we had said things to each other like, "A relationship needs space to help it grow."

Ha. I guess the best joke was on me.

I wandered the mall in a sort of fugue state. After drifting unconsciously around the alphabetized concourses for who knows how long, I found myself in front of Surf*Snow*Skate. As much as I hated Troy for letting Helen in on it, I couldn't help but refer back to our teen-soap-opera hierarchy of employment prestige.

The *90210* Scale of
Parkway Center Mall Employment Awesomeness

1. THE DYLAN McKAYS
These were the unquestionably coolest jobs requiring the least possible effort.

2. THE BRANDON WALSHES
These jobs also held a certain social cache but with just the faintest whiff of dorkiness that knocked them out of the top tier.

3. THE STEVE SANDERSES

These jobs weren't looked down upon as hopelessly
loserish, but were certainly scrubbier than 1 and 2 (see
above). This category was dominated by virtually every
job in the food court, including America's Best Cookie.

4. THE DAVID SILVERS

These were sucky jobs at all the punny stores specializ-
ing in very specific and very boring things beloved by
old farts: Feet First (orthopedic shoes), Sew Amazing!
(fabrics), Deck the Walls (picture frames).

5. THE SAD, SAD SCOTT SCANLONS

The lowest of the low. Woolworths Pet Center dead
guppy scooper-outer. Razzmatazz Family Restaurant
balloon animal-maker/busboy. Trash can gum-scraper.

Surf*Snow*Skate was the Ultimate Dylan McKay.
The HELP WANTED in the window was not merely *a* sign.
It was *the* sign.
At Surf*Snow*Skate, I'd find redemption. I'd show Troy and
Helen and everyone else, I deserved more than America's Best
Cookie. I was better than a scrubby Steve Sanders! I was Dylan
McKay material!
I strutted into the store and found myself face-to-face with
Slade Johnson and Bethany Darling. Voted Pineville High
Class of 1991's Best-Looking Guy and Girl, Slade and Bethany
frustrated all fans of beautiful out-of-wedlock babies by rejecting
the assumed inevitable and not coupling up. Bethany wore a

pink push-up bikini top with high-waisted spandex bike shorts. Slade wore knee-length Jams, but his tank top was cut low around the armpits, almost down to his waist. He was exposing as much suntanned skin as she was, and I was sort of impressed by the store's equal-opportunity, all-genders approach to sex as a sales tactic.

"Hey!" I announced myself. "I'm here for the job!"

Bethany and Slade did double takes.

"Cassie Worthy?" Bethany squinted at me.

Slade didn't take his eyes off me.

"Didn't you like, almost *die*?" Bethany asked.

"I had the worst case of mono my doctor had ever seen," I bragged. "But I'm totally fine now."

"Totally," said Slade. "Fine."

"Well, the mono diet is amazing!" Bethany marveled. "You must've lost, like, twenty pounds."

Leave it to Bethany to celebrate my involuntary starvation. I had to take her word for my weight loss because I never stepped on a scale. But I *had* noticed that my once-snug jeans now slipped past my hip bones. I also had hip bones for the first time in my teenage life, and my belt was cinched at a never-before-seen notch. It wouldn't last long though. Unlike Bethany—whose entire diet consisted of cottage cheese and Diet Pepsi—I liked eating real food like a healthy human being.

"You just need a few hours in the tanning booth," advised Slade.

Bethany nodded in agreement. The two of them were sculpted and bronzed to teenage perfection. Slade was undeniably great looking and totally deserved the yearbook superlative, but I'd never found him attractive. Slade was just so *predictable* with his handsomeness, the quintessence of every uncreative football-playing, homecoming queen–dating, keg-tapping high school stud stereotype. It's as if he'd enrolled in a master class at the Cobra Kai Academy of Asshole Arts and Sciences but took it pass-fail because he couldn't be bothered to put in the extra effort required for a unique spin on teenage cockiness.

"Oh! Okay! Thanks!" I said brightly. "So, you're hiring?"

"We're hiring," Slade said.

"Yeah," Bethany said, "but it's, like, super competitive. We only take the best."

No duh, I thought. *That's why it's a Dylan McKay.*

"We've got a few routine questions we ask all candidates." Bethany pulled on the base of the platinum ponytail anchored high on her scalp. "It's, like, a prescreening to see whether it's even worth our time to give you an application."

"Really? This sounds more complicated than getting into college . . ."

And as soon as I said it, I realized it was a mistake.

"Does that mean you're only going to be here until September?" Bethany asked.

"Well . . ." I hedged. "Um . . ."

"It's our busiest time of year," Slade said. "She'd be a big help."

"June and December are our busiest times of year," Bethany corrected.

"Just ask her the questions!" Slade demanded, going full Cobra Kai. "And let the head honcho decide!"

"Fine," Bethany said testily.

Now for the sake of accuracy, I wish I could provide the exact wording of the merciless quizzing that followed. At best, I can only provide a vague approximation that went something like this.

BETHANY: What are the pros and cons of a longboard versus a funboard for a beginner?

ME: ?

BETHANY: What's a goofy foot?

ME: ??

BETHANY: Have you ever set foot on a surfboard, a snowboard, or a skateboard?

ME: ???

"We can't hire you."

I hated the store.

I hated Slade and Bethany.

I hated Troy and Helen.

But I mostly hated myself for wanting the job so badly.

"You don't know anything about surfing, snowboarding, or skating."

See above for reference and trust that it was a million times worse than that. Bethany was right. I didn't know anything about any of those things.

"I can learn!"

"I'll teach her!" Then Slade got close enough that I could smell the coconut tanning oil that gave definition to the muscles in his shoulders, arms, and abdominals. "I'll teach you everything I know."

In two years of middle school and four years of high school,

Slade had never, ever spoken to me. A peculiar sound escaped my lips that sounded strangely similar to . . . a *giggle?*

"Stop thinking with your wang for once," Bethany snapped. "You'll forget all about her as soon as the next set of tatas comes bouncing into the store."

Slade slowly nodded. I couldn't tell if he was agreeing with her or tracking the up-and-down tata bounce in his imagination. Either way was bad for me.

"Maybe try Sears?" Bethany adjusted the straps on her bikini top. "They look for your kind of knowledge of everything and nothing."

"*Sears?*"

How dare she tell me to settle for a Steve Sanders! There were plenty of Dylan McKays that would be happy to have me. At the very least, I'd be willing to accept a solid offer from a Brandon Walsh but absolutely no lower than that. Sears was desperate, but I sure as hell wasn't.

Not yet anyway.

I knocked over a revolving display of Oakleys on my way out. It was entirely an accident, but I didn't apologize. I kept moving without looking back.

If I had Greek-myth Cassandra's clairvoyance, I would've foreseen the next humiliating hours of my life. Please forgive me for bullet-pointing my embarrassment.

* I couldn't identify a single brand, shade, or formulation of foundation for sale at the Macy's cosmetics counter, and I was shown a $25 bronzer highly recommended for brightening my pasty complexion,

and perhaps I would be interested in purchasing a seven-piece Face for All Seasons Gift Set, which was on sale for the low, low price of $49.99 including the tote bag that came free with every Lancôme purchase, because with my warm undertones I was categorically a "spring" and I couldn't help but consider what that meant on, like, an existential level because maybe my best season in life was already behind me.

* The General Cinemas ticket-taker couldn't believe I hadn't seen a single film all summer, and when I blamed mono and tried to prove my love for the art form by recalling the last movie I'd watched in the theater, the first one that came to mind was *Hudson Hawk*, which was a piece of shit that I'd only agreed to see because Troy bribed me with popcorn and Jujyfruits and promised to come with me to see *Thelma & Louise*, which he never did and obviously never would.

* When asked of my dishwashing experience, I very earnestly replied that I sometimes emptied the Kenmore at home without being asked and quickly followed up by inquiring about a hostess position that kept me far, far away from the kitchen and was therefore a better fit for my vegetarian lifestyle, and I was curtly informed that half a dozen shift leaders were already in line for

that cushy job, and I'd have to work my way up the Ponderosa Steak & Ale organizational hierarchy from dishwasher to busser to food runner to server to shift leader, which could take years and I did not have that kind of time and also I was already nauseated by the smell of roasting animal flesh.

After the Ponderosa rejection, I circled back to the music store to worship at the altar of Morrissey. This, for anyone who knows anything about The Smiths front man turned solo artist, was counterintuitive at best and suicidal at worst. With legendarily morose songs like "Heaven Knows I'm Miserable Now," the Moz was the go-to artist for wallowing in pain, not overcoming it. Perhaps it was for the best that the poster I had admired earlier had been removed from the display.

"You're loitering."

The Asian guy in the Sam Goody tee was technically correct. I was standing aimlessly with no intention to buy. But I also wasn't bothering anybody either. Except, evidently, him.

"You're loitering," Sam Goody repeated. "If you step inside, another one of our sales associates can provide you with all the Marky Mark and the Funky Bunch merchandise your heart desires."

With his pompadour, rockabilly boots, and black jeans rolled *just so*, there was no question who had put the Morrissey poster in the window. Maybe he knew why it had been removed.

"For your information," I said, "I came here looking for Morrissey . . ."

Sam Goody spasmed with laughter.

"Oh, because you're so deep?" he asked facetiously. "Because you're so dark?"

"I am deep!" I protested. "I am dark!"

This only made Sam Goody laugh harder. He removed his thick-rimmed specs and wiped away pretend tears.

"Let me guess," he said. "There's a boy you like who doesn't like you back. Boo-hoo-hoo!"

How did he know? Was the rejection written on my face? Had Troy turned me into such a plainly pathetic cliché? I had no time to ask because Sam Goody wasn't finished mocking me yet. He was about to use the lyrics to one of my favorite songs against me.

"So you go home and you cry and you want to die?"

No ride.

So I couldn't go home.

No plan.

No boyfriend.

No job.

Suddenly everything I didn't want to think about was all I could think about. How dare this smirky jerk weaponize "How Soon Is Now?" to such devastating effect?

I refused to cry. And I didn't want to die.

But as Sam Goody was my unwitting witness, I wasn't too far off.

5

CHICEST AND UNIQUEST

I stood on the edge of the Wishing Well. My weary eyes imprecisely counted the coins that had come to rest on the bottom, each penny a wish that would never come true.

"Don't jump!"

The warning squawk had the opposite of its intended effect. I slipped on the tiled lip and would've fallen in if a manicured hand hadn't pulled me back from the brink. It was only a foot-deep drop so I wouldn't have, like, *drowned*. But walking around in sopping wet penny loafers would've added a whole new and unpleasant dimension to my already sucky day.

"Oh my Gawd!"

The Wishing Well was located on the far border of the food court in Concourse G. In happier times, Troy and I called these crossroads *Unz Unz* Alley, after the thumping bass that originated at Chess King and reverberated across the intersection to the entrance of Bellarosa Boutique. It was at least five years since we'd last spoken, but I immediately recognized my rescuer as the latter shop's owner, Gia Bellarosa. I was less sure if she recognized me.

"Hon, are you okay?"

I had a clear view of Drea Bellarosa, Gia's daughter, in the display window, carefully adjusting a bustier on one of the mannequins. She stretched catlike in her catsuit, evoking the sexy feline villain from the groovy sixties *Batman* series I slept-watched during my recovery. Her real body was somehow even more unrealistically flawless than the fake, a prerequisite for upselling overpriced vulgar couture imported from Europe— though I supposed being the owner's daughter also helped. Watching Drea, it was hard to believe we were from the same species, let alone the same graduating class. It was even harder to believe that once, so very long ago, we had briefly and fiercely pledged to be each other's best friends forever in the way that only fifth-grade girls can.

Gia tried again.

"Are you okay, hon?"

I was too dazed to answer. Instead, I stared at the hand resting protectively on my arm, nails painted bloodred to match a sweater dress that would sell well among Bellarosa Boutique's clientele. It was July, but the retail calendar was already well into fall. Outside the mall, humanity wilted in the muggy swelter of a South Jersey summer. Inside the mall, the temperature was just chilly enough to get shoppers in an artificially autumnal state of mind.

I wished I could fast forward through summer and get to my future already.

"No, I am not okay," I finally replied. "I am not okay at all."

This was the first hint of true kindness anyone had shown me all day. And before I could stop myself, I unloaded.

"I got mono, and my boyfriend of two years dumped me for a foaming-at-the-mouth mallrodent who tried to spritz me to death, and I lost my job, and I might be haunted by a ghost with a pierced tongue, and I don't have any skills, and I doubt I could be hired by a sad, sad Scott Scanlon, and I was mocked by a Morrissey lookalike who accused me of liking Marky Mark and the friggin' Funky Bunch and . . ."

Gia was totally unfazed—a telling testament to the certifiably insane shit she'd seen in her lifetime.

"Come on, hon," she said, gently leading me by the arm.

Without hesitation or explanation, I followed her to Bellarosa Boutique, best described in the ad that ran weekly in the *Ocean County Observer*: "Jersey Shore glitz meets Manhattan glamour since 1984. Upscale sportswear and special occasion dresses for South Jersey's chicest and uniquest clientele."

The *90210* taxonomy did not apply to Bellarosa Boutique. The design and décor were an unapologetic celebration of eighties excess, all onyx and gold leaf, marble and crystal, velvet and jungle prints. It were the only store at the mall operating on a whole different system of measurement—the *Dynasty* Scale—

where it would always and forever reign at the Alexis Carrington apex of fabulousness. By twelve years old, Drea carried herself with the confidence of a nighttime soap opera diva, a junior-high Joan Collins catwalking around the halls of Pineville Middle School in double-wide shoulder pads and starter heels.

It's no coincidence that our friendship ended right around that same time.

"Drea!" Gia brayed as we walked into the store. "Quit getting paid to do nothing and come over here!"

Drea very slowly lifted her head from the *Cosmopolitan* magazine spread out on the counter. She was the very picture of glamorous nonchalance.

Until she saw me.

"Cassie Worthy!" Drea gasped. "I thought you were *dead*."

It was so like Drea to take the rumors about my ill health to a more dramatic and morbid level.

"No, I'm alive," I said.

Barely, I thought.

Drea jumped up and click-clacked her way over to us. With meticulously applied makeup and dark hair sprayed to exhilarating, ozone-poking heights, Drea looked older than she was, Gia younger. If I didn't know better, I would've assumed they were roughly the same age—meeting somewhere in the middle around thirty. Neither mother nor daughter would ever correct such a mistake.

"Cassie here has fallen on hard times," Gia said, giving my shoulder a squeeze. "She needs a job and we're hiring."

"We're hiring?" Drea asked.

"You're hiring?" I asked.

"We need someone on the books," Gia answered. "You know, keeping track of inventory, making sure vendors get paid—"

"What about Crystal?" Drea interrupted.

Gia frowned.

"I'm loyal to family, but enough is enough," Gia said decisively. "I'm done with my no-good brother's no-good wife's no-good brother's no-good daughter."

So that made No-Good Crystal Gia's . . . niece-in-law? Untangling the branches of this family tree was like an Odyssey of the Mind brainteaser.

Drea barely tilted her head in my general direction.

"But you haven't seen Cassie in years!"

"I know! I was all worried about finding someone to replace No-Good Crystal, and there she was! It's fate!"

The Greeks cared so much about the concept of fate that they put not one, not two, but *three* sister bosses in charge of carrying it out for all humankind. I disagreed with the Greeks. I didn't believe in destiny. And Drea didn't either.

"You don't even *know* her!" she pointed out.

Gia took hold of my chin and squeezed my cheeks. My own mother was never this hands-on with me.

"She was always a good kid. And she can't be worse than your cousin."

"Ma, look at her. She *obviously* doesn't care about fashion." Drea fluttered her thickly coated lashes at my Barnard T-shirt and cutoffs. "No offense."

I took, like, half offense.

"Drea's right," I conceded. "I'm probably unqualified for this position."

"I saw your name listed in the graduation program," Gia said. "Didn't you get the math award?"

I nodded.

"Congrats!" Gia applauded. "You're qualified! And I don't have any more time for discussion because here comes the white whale."

Gia gestured toward a fiftyish woman in tennis whites making her way toward the store's entrance. She carried a quilted Chanel handbag in one hand, a cigarette in the other.

"A *whale?*"

This woman was all sinew, gristle, and bone.

"It has nothing to do with her weight," Gia said. "It means, she's a big fish . . ."

"Whales aren't fish," I corrected. "Whales are mammals."

"Fish, mammal, whatever!" Drea threw up her hands in exasperation. "I forgot how annoying you are!"

Gia smacked her daughter in the back of the head.

"Manners, Drea!"

Then she turned to me.

"Mona Troccola is a big spender," Gia explained patiently.

Mona paused at the entrance to take a last, long drag on her cigarette before depositing the butt into the child-size metal ashtray.

"I have to pull some looks for Mona," Gia said. "Drea, you take Cassie to the back office. Show her around."

"But, Ma . . ."

"Do not give me any lip!"

Drea pouted in literal defiance to her mother's orders. Gia rushed over to greet Mona with a nicotine-tinged air kiss.

"Mona! Darling! Mwah!"

"Gia! Darling! Mwah!"

I followed Drea through a mirrored door into Bellarosa's back office. A multitiered chandelier hung over a gold-trimmed desk, behind which sat a zebra-print upholstered piece of furniture that more closely resembled a throne than any chair I'd ever seen.

I was alone with my former best friend for the first time since seventh grade. I didn't know much about what she'd been up to all these years; I mean, other than what we *all* knew about Drea. She'd run through dozens of boyfriends since middle school. Jocks, skaters, punks, metalheads, hicks . . . Drea's exes shared no common denominator other than their inability to resist her many charms.

I was at a total loss for what to say when Drea spoke up.

"You reek." She scrunched her nose. "Like rotten fruit."

"Really?"

I'd barely had the energy to shower that morning and hadn't bothered with shampoo. Maybe the scent was still trapped in my hair?

"It's cucumber-melon body spray," I tried to explain. "I was . . ."

"I don't care if it's Giorgio Beverly Hills! You need to change into something else before you contaminate the merchandise!"

"But I don't have any other clothes with me."

Rolling racks of couture lined the gilded walls. Drea slowly swiveled her head from one side to the other.

"Where, oh where," she asked, "could we *possibly* find you something to wear?"

The idea of wearing Bellarosa's clothes was so ludicrous that I still didn't quite get what Drea meant, even as she started riffling through the new arrivals that would soon be displayed out front.

"Aha! This!"

She brandished a hanger with an electric-blue stretch of Lycra I couldn't quite identify as a specific item of clothing. Was it a skirt? A top?

"Try on this tube dress!"

So . . . it was *both*?

"Um, I don't have the body for it," I said.

Drea stepped back to silently take me in from head to toe. She appraised me for a few seconds, then shared the results of her skillful scrutiny.

"You're European size thirty-two," she said definitively. "You have the body for it."

"But it's not exactly my style," I said.

Drea snorted. "You don't have a style."

With black velvet clinging to her curves, Drea demonstrated why she was voted Best Dressed at Pineville High. She was the authority. Her expertise would not be denied.

"Put this on right now because I can't stand the sight or smell of you for another second." Drea thrust the hanger at me. "Go!"

I entered the private dressing room and tried to make sense of what Drea had just handed me. It would be hard to imagine a less practical article of clothing. I couldn't figure out whether

I should approach the electric-blue tube from the top down or the bottom up. Shockingly, I didn't get stuck. With one tug, the slippery fabric slid right past my knees, over my hips, and up to my bust.

"Come on out, Cassie!" Drea shook the silk drapes. "I don't have all day."

I parted the pink curtains and cautiously stepped forward. "Well?"

Drea always had this unforgettable honk of a laugh. It was the greatest, most gratifying sound if you were in on the joke. It was the worst sound in the world if you were not.

I emerged to the mass strangulation of a million geese.

"OHMYGAWHAWHAWHAWHAWWWWWWNK."

Drea's awful laughter echoed throughout the whole store. Within seconds, her mother came bursting into the back office to shut her up.

"What's going on back here?"

Gia stopped dead in her tracks at the preposterous sight of me in that tube dress.

"Drea! What is wrong with you?"

Drea was unable to catch her breath.

"HAAAAAAAAWWWWWWWWNNNNNNNNNNK."

"I told her I didn't have the body for this!"

"You have the body," said Gia, stroking my hair. "But not the . . ."

"Soul," Drea finished for her.

I thought Drea was making another joke at my expense. But Gia agreed.

"She's right," Gia said. "It fits, but it doesn't fit *you*. And that's okay. As a back-of-store employee, you can be the exception to Bellarosa's dress code."

"Maaaaaa," Drea objected. "We've got a reputation to uphold . . ."

Gia shushed her.

"Let's help each other out, Cassie." Gia extended her palm. "I need a temporary bookkeeper and you need a job."

Could this handshake get my life back on track? I highly doubted it. But I couldn't go home until I had somewhere to be every day for the rest of the summer. And what other options did I have?

Drea rolled her eyes as I took her mother's hand.

"Just show up when the mall opens at ten tomorrow wearing whatever makes you feel comfortable and confident," Gia instructed. "At Bellarosa Boutique, we encourage all women to be the best possible versions of themselves."

"Riiiiight," Drea said. "Which is why Mona Troccola fuels her workouts with vodka, lettuce, and cigarettes."

We turned to look through the opened door at the opposite side of the store, where one of Bellarosa's most dedicated customers rotated in front of a three-way mirror. In a brown suede halter top and matching pants, Mona resembled an anatomy skeleton draped in deli meat.

"If that new outfit brings Mona a moment of peace," Gia whispered, "mission accomplished."

Gia built a successful business on a simple philosophy: Purchases equal empowerment. Bellarosa customers found fulfillment through fashion, achieved self-actualization through accessorization. I'd take the job. But other than a paycheck, I was beyond Bellarosa's help. No article of clothing could transform me into the best possible version of myself. How could it? After the past two days, I didn't have a clue who I even was anymore.

Or if I ever did.

6

NERD OLYMPICS

*A*s much as I looked forward to a carless existence in Manhattan, not all mass transportation systems were created equal. The thought of taking Pineville public transit to and from work every day was downright depressing. A ten-minute drive by car took nearly an hour by bus, so hitching rides with my parents was still by far the best option.

"When does Troy's seasonal assistant management training come to an end?" asked Kathy.

"Soon?"

"You should attend those meetings with him," said Frank. "Show them you're seasonal assistant management material."

"Uh-huh," I said.

The air was already swampy, and I was pretty much soaked by the time I walked all the way around the parking lot and reached the automatic doors to J. C. Penney. The thermostat was set to Christmas, and I was not at all prepared for the drastic drop in temperature. I shivered in the arctic air conditioning—more of a full-blown seizure than an ordinary chill—and vowed to bring a sweatshirt from then on.

One advantage to working at Bellarosa? It was the last place my ex or Helen or anyone would think to find me. Unfortunately, the food court was the congested heart of the mall, located in Concourse D in the dead center of the map. The most direct path to Bellarosa—a straight line from Sears via Concourse C—was not an option because I couldn't risk running into Troy on his way to America's Best Cookie. Instead, I went in through J. C. Penney, took an escalator, traversed Upper Level Concourse B, and came back down in an elevator that deposited me right in front of *Unz Unz* Alley. And I wasn't above ducking behind mannequins and peeking around potted plants whenever I thought I caught a glimpse of the kind of overbleached hair that was, unfortunately, all too popular among Jersey girls in the summer of 1991. I was so focused on avoiding Helen (mostly) and Troy (somewhat) that I was blind to anyone who didn't fit their specific descriptions. So that's why I didn't realize I was being followed until it was already too late.

"Hey, you!" Sam Goody ran up alongside me.

I was annoyed by his face and the interruption. In that order.

"You're the opposite of loitering this morning," he said breathlessly. "I could hardly keep up."

44

"*So?*"

It was 10:05. I literally did not have time for this. I wasn't psyched to start my new job, but at the very least I could avoid unfavorable comparisons to No-Good Crystal by being punctual.

Sam Goody swept a hand through his impressive upswell of hair. Then he gestured toward the words VIVA HATE written across my chest. It was the title of my favorite Morrissey album.

"I guess this proves you're a fan after all." He raised an eyebrow like he expected me to be grateful for his approval. Where did he get off thinking his opinion mattered to me at all?

"I didn't wear this shirt to prove *anything* to you."

Then I walked away without waiting for a response. This bizarre and unwanted interaction was my first hint that 900,000 square feet was not nearly big enough to avoid all the people I never wanted to see again.

Gia was too preoccupied with a busty silver-haired lady to notice my arrival at Bellarosa Boutique. The client posed on a raised platform in front of the three-way mirror, lifting a red-and-black ball gown up to mid-thigh like a can-can dancer.

"Can you make it short in the front but keep it long in the back?"

The mullet of dresses, I thought. *Classy.*

"You ask, we alter," Gia cooed. "Your mother-of-the-bride look will be as chic and unique as you are!"

Drea emerged from behind a rack of zip-front corsets to share her opinion.

"YAAAAWWWWWNNNNNNNNNNNNNNAAAAHHHH."

And it wasn't a subtle yawn either, but the kind that required full over-the-head arm extension and at least three distinct stages of throaty vocalization.

Today's ensemble was even more incredible than yesterday's catsuit. And by incredible, I mean the true definition of the word, as in *impossible to believe.* It was literally impossible for me to believe that someone my age could get away with wearing a rhinestone-encrusted military jacket and matching micro mini. And yet, there Drea was, wearing the hell out of it.

"Cassie! You made it!" Gia trotted over to give me a hug. "Drea will show you the books while I assist Francine here."

"Ma! How about I handle Francine while you show her the books?"

Gia gritted her teeth while Francine watched with gossipy interest.

"How about you do what I say for a change?" She turned to Francine. "Does your daughter give you such headaches?"

"A more ungrateful bride the world has never seen." Francine hoisted her cleavage. "After all the dough her father and I are sinking into this wedding . . ."

Drea cracked her gum and turned toward the back office. I took this as my cue to follow.

"I didn't mention this yesterday, but I'm already familiar with accounting software because I was the treasurer for . . ."

Drea didn't even pretend to listen to my credentials. She dug elbow-deep into the bottom drawer of a file cabinet and scooped out a jumbled armload of loose-leaf paper, unopened envelopes, crumpled receipts, assorted candy bar wrappers, and who knew what else.

"The books," Drea said dryly. "Good luck."

She brusquely dropped the mess on the desk and was out the door before I could let out a gasp of dissent. No-Good Crystal was even worse at her job than I'd imagined. How could I turn this disorganized pile into data I could put into a spreadsheet? I'd have to tell Gia that this was a formidable task for a professional accounting firm, let alone a recent high school graduate with minimal bookkeeping experience.

And yet, as I sifted through the pile, I thought about my Odyssey of the Mind training. Whenever we were perplexed by a particular problem, we were encouraged to take a small, doable step instead of just sitting around and thinking so hard. Ironically, by doing and not thinking, our brains got all stimulated and came up with ideas we wouldn't have thought of otherwise. At least that was the theory.

In this case, I started by isolating and disposing of all the candy bar wrappers. Evidently, Crystal favored Snickers bars (twenty-eight wrappers) but also enjoyed Baby Ruths (thirteen) and PayDays (six) now and then. Tossing them out made a significant dent in the pile.

Next, I moved on to separating bills and receipts from the loose-leaf papers covered in Crystal's scrawls. At a glance, all those numbers and letters and symbols looked like gibberish. Making sense of it was the most daunting task and the one I'd tackle last. It was much easier to track the invoices because they were usually printed on yellow or pink attention-getting paper and, okay, I won't bore you with any more of my methods except to say that I was pretty proud of myself for sorting it all out.

The process took *hours*, an entire shift in fact, only interrupted by a brief lunch break spent eating a cheese-and-tomato sandwich out of a paper bag in Bellarosa's back office. But I didn't mind the work. I hadn't exercised my brain in six weeks, and it felt really good to get it working again. I was sort of disappointed when Gia and Drea came in around six to tell me my shift was over.

"Oh really? I hoped I'd have time to play around with the Mac." I pointed to the beige computer in the corner. "By the way, did you get the memory expansion card?"

"Oh my gawd," Drea said. "You're an even bigger nerd than I thought."

Gia smacked Drea in the back of the head.

"Manners, Drea!" Gia turned to me. "You know how to use this thing?"

"Sure," I said. "You don't?"

"Nah," Gia said. "It was a gift from the manager of Electronics Universe."

"A *gift*?" This computer must have been worth more than two thousand dollars.

"Drea dated him for a while," Gia explained.

Drea picked at nonexistent lint on her sleeve. "He was trying to impress me."

"Did it work?" I ask.

Gia arched an eyebrow.

"Nothing impresses my daughter."

Drea inspected her cuticles.

"Ma made me keep the thing 'cause she thinks it makes the office look more professional."

"You'd be surprised how many people don't take me seriously," Gia said.

I nearly laughed out loud before realizing they weren't kidding.

"I guess I can start a spreadsheet tomorrow." I shrugged.

"You really made sense of this mess?" Drea asked incredulously.

"Crystal created her own code."

"A code?" Drea pulled a face. "It was a bunch of scribbles."

"I thought so at first," I said. "But then I realized Crystal's code had an internal logic to it. Like, once I figured out that the smiley faces meant receivables and the upside-down crosses meant payables, it all kind of came together."

"Why would she make up this wacky code?" Gia asked.

"Cocaine," Drea answered.

"To make herself invaluable to the organization," I replied. "If she was the only one who understood the finances, she thought she could never be fired."

"It also helped make it easier for her to steal from us," Gia remarked.

"Exactly," I replied.

"And you can put all of Crystal's mess into the computer?" She rapped the monitor with the gold rings on her knuckles.

"Sure, that's what it's made for," I said. "Once I enter all the data, you'll be able to use the same template from month to month."

"Fate!" Gia threw her arms around me. "I knew I was right to hire you!"

Then she hustled out of the office to greet an incoming customer. I expected Drea to follow her mother, but she stayed behind instead.

"Your team did good at that Nerd Olympics, huh?"

"You mean Odyssey of the Mind?"

Drea crossed her eyes as a way of saying, *Yes, nerd.*

I cleared my throat and kept going.

"Well, this year's team should have qualified for state but . . ."

"Ahhh!" She waved her hands wildly. "I don't care!"

Drea's reaction wasn't unusual. Very few people were interested in a detailed rundown of the interscholastic power rankings for Odyssey of the Mind.

"I just need to know if you're really good at solving riddles and stuff."

"I guess so."

She broke out into a stunning smile, the kind that could turn any crush into a conquest. Drea Bellarosa was a Worthy Orthodontics and Pediatric Dentistry success story if there ever was one.

"You and I should spend some quality time together," she said. "Like, after I'm finished up here."

"Um, okay," I said. "I think I'm available."

"I *know* you are," she said.

If she weren't right, I might have been offended.

7

THE CABBAGE PATCH

*W*e took the service elevator down, down, down to the second basement. This was a level I didn't know existed. A level not listed on the mall's directory. Level Z.

"Are we allowed to use this elevator?" I asked.

The doors slid open, and Drea took the lead through the narrow underground passageway.

"Are we allowed to go down here?"

She ignored this question too, ducked under a pipe, and pressed onward in the direction of a bassline bump-bump-bumping somewhere in the near distance. We were in the catacombs of the mall, and we weren't alone. Someone had strung up Christmas lights along the ceiling to guide the way, but it was definitely not up to code down there.

"What if there's a fire? How do we get out?"

The music was getting louder and clearer.

"Come on, come on."

Marky Mark and the friggin' Funky Bunch.

"Feel the vibration."

I did. Literally, through the rattling ductwork. And I was close enough to make out the hum of conversation and bursts of laughter too.

"Is there *really* a party going on down here?"

I had barely finished asking this latest question when the skinny corridor opened wide.

"Welcome," said Drea with a sweep of her hand, "to the Cabbage Patch."

A couple in Foot Locker stripes made out on a low-slung tweed couch of dubious hygiene. Packs of Marlboros were being passed around what I assumed was the smoking section, as designated by the cinderblock wall decorated with photos of Naomi, Cindy, Linda, Claudia, and Christy—only the highest echelon of supermodel—posing sexily with cigarettes. Another small crowd gathered around a trash can from which Slade Johnson—yes, *that* Slade Johnson—ladled a questionable beverage into red Solo cups.

"Can ya feel it, baby?"

There *was* a party going on down here. Drea slipped away, and now, here I was, by myself, in the bowels of the mall, being offered a purple drink by Slade Johnson.

Yes, *that* Slade Johnson.

"We meet again."

He held out one of the two Solo cups in his hands. Never much of a drinker, I wasn't about to start with something served out of a trash can.

"No, thanks," I said. "I don't like the taste of alcohol."

He flashed a dazzling smile. Not even my parents could find a single flaw in spacing or symmetry.

"It's Kool-Aid and Everclear," he said. "Not tasting the alcohol is the whole point."

If Slade were Troy and Troy were still my boyfriend, I would have made a joke about Kool-Aid and Everclear being the beverage of choice for our brainwashed generation. But Slade wasn't, and Troy wasn't, so I didn't.

"No, thanks," I repeated firmly.

Slade shrugged and dumped the contents of one cup into the other. Then he said something I couldn't hear. Someone had pumped up the volume on the stereo because Vanilla Ice said so.

"BUM RUSH THE SPEAKER THAT BOOMS!"

To be fair, "Ice Ice Baby" *is* best appreciated at the precise decibel level that causes instant deafness.

"I'M KILLIN' YOUR BRAIN LIKE A POISONOUS MUSHROOM!"

Slade leaned in and shouted directly into my ear.

"Sorry about the job."

"Oh, it's okay," I shouted back. "I got hired somewhere else."

"Oh really?" he asked. "Where?"

"Bellarosa Boutique."

Like Vanilla Ice, Slade didn't miss a beat.

"As a model."

"As a bookkeeper."

He took a drink, then carefully licked his lips.

"That's a shame."

Slade inched even closer to me. The room already felt more crowded than it had moments before.

"It would've been fun to work together," he said. "But Bethany gets jealous of anyone hotter than she is."

I was not used to being talked to like this. And I reacted in the only reasonable way. I laughed right in his gorgeous face. And not a cutesy giggle either, but a guttural *Ha! Ha! Ha!* guffaw.

Slade was undeterred.

"We can still have fun."

I knew what "fun" meant. And most girls would've been flattered by Slade's attention. But I was confused by it. And more than a little uncomfortable too. I looked for Drea to help me, but she was deep in conversation with a mustached guy wearing an orange Electronics Universe T-shirt. Her ex, I assumed. He was one of the few in attendance who looked old enough to drink legally. Maybe that's why he was put in charge of tapping the keg.

"What do you say?" Slade tucked a strand of hair behind my ear. By now, his flirtation was making me downright claustrophobic. He grinned again, only this time his perfect teeth were stained purple.

"You know what? I'll take you up on a drink after all."

Slade didn't hesitate. As he rushed to the trash can, I seized the opportunity to take off in the opposite direction. I couldn't move very far or fast because the Cabbage Patch had filled up with faces I sort of recognized. A makeshift dance floor had formed between the trash-can punch on one side and a keg on the other. Mostly girls but some brave boys did all the sweaty things C+C Music Factory commanded.

"So your butts up, hands in the air, come on say, yeah."

I admired the dancers' joyous, gymnastic gyrations. Their needs were so simple. Total bliss was this basement, some booze, and a booming sound system telling them exactly what to do next . . .

"Troy. Gimme a drink!"

Helen's voice sledgehammered through the wall of noise and smashed me in the chest.

"Gimme a drink. Troy!"

I was totally incapacitated. My ex-boyfriend had arrived at the Cabbage Patch with his new girlfriend, and all I could do was watch.

I watched as my ex-boyfriend and his new girlfriend ladled Everclear and Kool-Aid into Solo cups.

I watched as my ex-boyfriend's new girlfriend straddled him on the couch of dubious hygiene.

I watched as my ex-boyfriend and his new girlfriend broke every rule we had ever set for ourselves about public displays of affection.

I got feverish, dizzy, and barfy all over again. Only this time, I knew for sure it wasn't mono.

I had to get out of the basement without being seen. Troy and Helen seemed pretty oblivious to the world outside their grubby, grabby-handed lust bubble. But what if they came up for air just in time to catch my humiliating exit? I pulled on the nearest door handle and slipped inside. When the automatic lights flickered on, I couldn't quite believe what I was seeing:

Row upon row of creepy babies staring back at me.

Cabbage Patch Kids in their original boxes.

Evidently, I had stumbled into the storage closet that had given this underground party place its name. As marketed, each "Kid" looked different. And the manufactured individuality went way beyond variations in skin, hair, and eye colors. Computers had been used to track freckles and dimples, outfits and facial expressions. Eight years ago, the promise of individuality made them irresistible to millions of kids like me. Like all fads, the frenzy had fizzled as swiftly as it had begun.

I walked up and down the aisle, whispering their names.

"Prentiss Charlemagne. Orville Toby. Rhonda Bess."

For varied as the kids were, each and every ones' arms were outstretched in the exact same way. After all that time—nearly a decade—these unwanted orphans were still waiting for a hug.

It was this excessively maudlin detail that put me over the edge.

I'd tried to convince myself I had it all together when I absolutely did not. I slumped to the ground and finally gave in to my ugliest sobs.

8

OVER AND UNDER

I didn't know how much time had elapsed when the door opened.

"Cassie!"

I was eye level with a pair of shiny black heels.

"Get up off the gawddamn floor!"

A stiletto stomped the cement. I still didn't move.

"Look! I got a present for you!"

An Electronics Universe bag landed on my head.

"It's that memory expansion thingie for the computer you asked about."

Had Drea flirted with Mr. Mustache just to get this for me? On any other day, I would've expressed gratitude for the gift. But full deletion of my heart's hard drive was what I *really* needed, and I doubted Electronics Universe sold any products for that purpose.

"What happened to you?" Drea asked.

What happened to me?

What happened to me?

I'd lost everything I'd worked toward my whole life.

"You never used to cry," said Drea. "And now you're boo-hooing all over the place."

I'd always been so proud of my stoicism. Like, when our team lost our case in the first round of Mock Trial, I was the one who consoled a tearful Troy. Had mono weakened my physical *and* emotional immunity?

"Don't tell me all this drama is about your ex and his new girl."

I sat up.

"You know?" I sniffled. "About Troy and Helen?"

"Well, yeah," she said. "Anyone with eyes knows because they're grinding all over each other out there."

I moaned.

"It's gross."

I moaned even louder.

"Oh, stop it," Drea snapped. "Troy is not worth it."

"We went out for two years!"

"So?"

"How would you know if he's worth it? You've never dated anyone for more than two months!"

Drea's eyes turned to slits.

I almost felt bad about saying it. I mean, I wasn't coming straight out and calling her slutty, but that was the implication. If she smacked me in the back of the head, I couldn't say I hadn't sort of deserved it.

But Drea took the high, nonviolent road.

"You're right. I've never dated anyone for more than a month or two." She cocked her hip defiantly. "But I've never sobbed on a filthy floor over anyone either."

"And neither have I," I replied. "Until now."

Drea opened her purse and removed a pack of Wrigley's spearmint gum.

"Want a piece?"

It wasn't sugar-free. To my parents, she might as well have offered me drugs, but I accepted anyway.

"The way I see it"—she folded the stick of gum into an accordion and popped it into her mouth—"the best way to get over someone is to get under someone else."

Of course Drea saw it that way. What her relationships lacked in longevity, they more than made up for in variety. But *I* was the one on the floor, not her. Who was I to say her choices were worse than mine?

"The thing is." I sniffled. "Um. This is so embarrassing. But . . ."

"But *what*?" Drea pressed. "What could possibly be more embarrassing than wearing an American flag abomination of a uniform?"

I laughed. The ABC apron was almost impossibly unflattering.

"I've never been. Um. *Under* anyone," I admitted. "Not even Troy."

Troy and I had decided to hold off on sex until I could get a prescription for cheap birth control through the university health care center without parental knowledge or permission. The Pill was part of *the plan.*

I braced myself for another one of Drea's honking fits of hilarity. For someone as experienced as everyone knew Drea was, I assumed she'd mock my babyishness just like when we used to be friends.

But she did the opposite.

"Virginity is nothing to be embarrassed about," she said. "Especially when your top prospect was someone who'd need a compass to navigate your nethers. Know what I mean?"

I knew *exactly* what she meant. Troy actually consulted his older brother's *Human Anatomy* textbook for pointers.

"If you want to forget that loser, I can help you with that," she said. "Just like you can help me with the treasure."

"The treasure?" What was Drea even talking about?

"There's a fortune hidden somewhere in the mall," Drea said, "and I'm determined to find it."

"Excuse me, but I'm totally confused."

Drea brushed dust off a cardboard shipping carton and sat.

"Tommy and Vince D'Abruzzi were cousins," Drea began. "Tommy was assistant manager at Kay-Bee Toys. Vince worked the night shift at the Coleco factory . . ."

"This sounds like a Bon Jovi song," I quipped.

Drea sighed.

"Keep your comments to yourself until I'm done."

Rightfully reprimanded, I shut up for the rest of the story. It went something like this:

In late summer of 1983, Vince canceled a fishing trip with Tommy because he had to work overtime on the production line at the factory. He told his cousin how Coleco was going all in on these butt-ugly dolls; the market research predicted they would be *the* craze of the Christmas season. Tommy was a veteran of the toy biz. He survived the infamous Star Wars action figure shortage of 1978, and so he persuaded Vince to smuggle the dolls across state lines. They stockpiled hundreds of them in a secret storage room in the second basement level of the mall, biding their time until the demand far exceeded supply.

"So that's how the Cabbage Patch came to be," I said.

"Right," Drea replied. "But that's not the good part."

As legend had it, in the weeks and days leading up to Christmas, when the dolls were impossible to find at Kay-Bee or anywhere else, Tommy sold them for two, five, *ten* times the retail price. Together, Tommy and Vince made tens of thousands of dollars. Vince used his share to buy a Camaro. Tommy invested his in a cocaine habit. The coke made Tommy paranoid of "the Feds," so he stashed his illegal earnings all around the mall until he figured out how to safely launder the cash later on.

At this point in the story, Drea got as deadly serious as anyone could possibly be in an outfit that was 50 percent leather, 50 percent lace, and 100 percent bimbette.

"Tommy died of a massive heart attack before he got the money out," she said. "The treasure is still somewhere in the mall. And you're going to help me find it."

I wanted to laugh right in her heavily made-up face. Hidden

treasure? A black market for Cabbage Patch Kids? I mean, *come on*.

However.

Here were hundreds of Cabbage Patch Kids on shelves, the unlucky ones that had gotten left behind. And in between sobs, I *had* noticed something interesting. And once I noticed it, I couldn't un-notice it. But this detail only gained significance after I heard Drea's story. What harm would it do to share this information with her?

"About the treasure." I hesitated. "It's probably nothing."

"What's 'probably nothing'?"

From the bottom shelf, I pulled out the Cabbage Patch Kid that had caught my attention. A boy with brown hair, brown eyes, and a single dimple in his left cheek smiled at us from behind the plastic.

"His birth certificate isn't authentic."

Drea eyed me skeptically. "What do you mean?"

"I adopted three Cabbage Patch Kids . . ."

Drea snorted at the word "adopted." Genius toy company marketing ploys die hard.

"I never played with those things," Drea said. "I was way more into designing outfits for my Barbies."

"I remember."

Even at ten years old, Drea was far too fabulous for changing pretend diapers.

"When you compare this one's documentation to all the others on the shelves, you can see the ink isn't the same shade of green . . ."

Drea took a closer look at this boy's certificate.

"And the decorative border is only one line, not two . . ."

Drea chomped harder on her gum.

"But it's his name that really makes him interesting," I said. "Rey Ajedrez."

Between junior high and high school, I'd taken six years of foreign language classes. I was confident in my pronunciation.

And translation.

"In Spanish, Rey Ajedrez means . . ."

I paused to enjoy this moment. I had Drea's undivided attention for the first time since fifth grade.

"Chess King."

Drea stopped chewing.

"That's either one hell of a coincidence," I said. "Or a *clue*."

Drea's face shined brighter than all the sequins in Bellarosa Boutique.

"The treasure is ours!" She pumped her fists triumphantly.

I still doubted hidden riches were ours for the finding at the mall. But I knew I'd be unable to resist Drea's scheme the moment she threw back her head and laughed in the full-throated way that only she could.

"HAAAAAAAAAAWWWWWWWWWNNNK!"

This time she was laughing *with* me. And the magnificent sound of Drea's effusive approval helped me forget—albeit temporarily—why I sought refuge in the storage room to begin with.

"Cassie Worthy," Drea said to me with a smile. "I always liked you."

"I always liked you too."

It was a weird thing to say to my old best friend, but given how different we'd ended up, somehow it made sense to say it out loud.

Drea bumped her jewel-encrusted shoulder pad against my ratty gray T-shirt.

"Let's have a killer summer." She snapped her gum and grinned at me.

I snapped my gum and grinned right back.

9

LUSTIG ZEIT

*T*he next morning, Drea was poised on the edge of my desk in the back office, legs crossed in a way that was intrinsically provocative in fishnet stockings. More notably, she bounced not one, but two Cabbage Patch Kids on her lap. Sometime in the last twelve hours, Rey Ajedrez had been joined by a girl with red braids and a daisy-print pinafore.

"Where have you been?"

I looked at my watch. I wasn't even late.

"I'll tell you where *I've* been." She exhaled theatrically. "I was in the stock room of Chess King, risking life and limb and allergic reactions as I made my way through a treacherous maze of the chintziest rayon-polyester-blend suits I've ever had the misfortune to rub up against."

If Drea saw herself as Indiana Jones, Chess King was her Temple of Doom. When we had opened Rey Ajedrez's box, we discovered that the flipside of the counterfeit birth certificate was, in fact, a map. Crudely drawn in Sharpie and definitely not to any recognizable scale, I'd had my doubts that it would lead to another clue. Drea insisted otherwise.

"The map was legit?" I asked. "You actually found her in a panel behind the shelves?"

"No," Drea replied drily. "I went to Babyland General Hospital in Cleveland, Georgia, and asked Xavier Roberts himself for permission to adopt a sister for Rey Ajedrez because I didn't want him to be a maladjusted only child."

"I'm an only child," I replied. Then, more to the point, "*You're* an only child."

"Exactly! And look how maladjusted we both are! I was up all night searching through old *People* magazines trying to find out everything I could about Cabbage Patch Kids!"

And before I could question whether she was kidding—about the research and our mutual maladjustment—she set the boy and girl aside with more care than I would have expected.

"That map was legit," she said, hopping off the desk. "And so is this one."

She waved another forged birth certificate in my face. When I reached for the document, she snatched it away.

"Oh, so *now* you're all in on the treasure hunt because you know it's for real . . ."

"I told you I was all in last night!"

"But are you *allllllllllllll* in?" she asked teasingly. "Because it won't always be as easy as me flirting my way into the Chess King stockroom."

The entire staff at Chess King was madly in love with her. According to Drea, the store was doomed to go under because Joey and Pauly and Mikey spent more time flexing for her attention across *Unz Unz* Alley than pushing two-for-one mock turtlenecks. Despite the horny gullibility of her first marks, I thought she was vastly underselling her flirtatious powers.

"Quit messing around," I said. "Just tell me the next name."

I sensed that Drea would respect me more if I demanded rather than asked. And I was right. She smiled that devastating smile of hers for the first time all morning.

"Does Loo-steeg Zite mean anything to you?"

At first I assumed it was a matter of mispronunciation. But when she showed me the fake birth certificate, I conceded that she'd sounded it out in exactly the same way I would have. Unfortunately, Lustig Zeit meant absolutely nothing to me.

"It's definitely not Spanish," I replied.

Drea opened her mouth to rightfully inform me just how unhelpful I was being when her mother popped her head through the door.

"Drea! Playtime's over! We've got a banker's third wife out there who somehow made it to thirty without learning the first thing about resort wear." Then to me, "Morning, Cassie! Don't let my daughter be a distraction!"

"I won't!" I promised. "I'm excited to get started on these spreadsheets . . ."

"Thank you, Jesus"—Drea did the sign of the cross—"for bringing us the right nerd at the right time."

"Manners, Drea!" Gia smacked the air because her daughter was out of reach.

"It's not an insult! I'm truly grateful for her expertise," Drea insisted as she followed Gia onto the sales floor.

"You ought to be! A few more months of No-Good Crystal and we could've gone out of business."

Drea nodded at Gia, then surreptitiously turned to remind me of my priorities.

"Lustig Zeit!" she whisper-shouted. "Figure it out before our lunch break!"

▭

I did not figure it out before our lunch break.

"What was the point of taking all those smarty-pants classes if you can't even crack a cokehead's secret code?" Drea demanded to know.

I could've shot back with something about getting into the most competitive all-women's school in the country. But then I would've had to deal with Drea's inevitably horrified reaction to my decision to separate myself from the opposite sex for four years, pretty much guaranteeing that I would die a virgin unless I took her advice and got it on before it was too late.

"I cracked *a* cokehead's secret code," I said instead, pointing to a paper covered in Crystal's scribbles, "just not *this* cokehead's secret code."

"Let's hit the food court," Drea suggested. "Feed that brain of yours."

"I already ate my lunch."

I didn't want to remind Drea why the food court was off-limits. It was simply easier to say I preferred brown-bagging it for vague, post-mononucleosian nutritional reasons.

"A change of scenery, then," she suggested. "Could be just what your brain needs."

As Frank reminded me on the drive that morning, I still had to replace Kathy's copy of *The Broadway Album*. The record store was located on the same floor as America's Best Cookie, but hopefully at a safe enough distance to avoid being spotted by Troy and Helen. While I was in no mood to run into the lusty couple, that possibility was still more pleasant than sticking around Bellarosa's back office and getting harangued by Drea for a half hour.

"I need to go to the record store," I said.

"I'm in!" she said. "I want to hear the new Mantronix remix."

I knew as much about Mantronix as Drea knew about Morrissey.

"Who?"

"House music pioneers, that's who," she answered.

Drea was really into house music—electronic bass-heavy beats that weren't so popular on the radio but played in all the hottest dance clubs in New York City. According to Drea, all the Jersey Shore DJs were "trash."

"Do you go clubbing in the city a lot?" I asked.

"Not as much as I want to." Drea shrugged. "And Crystal

was the one on all the VIP lists. Now that she's on the outs, I'll have a tougher time getting past the bouncers."

Right at that moment, a zitty boy in a Bart Simpson T-shirt walked into a potted palm tree because he was too preoccupied by Drea's cleavage to watch where he was going.

"I find it hard to believe you'd have trouble getting in anywhere," I said.

"Well, shit," she deadpanned. "I *knew* I should've applied to the Ivy League."

By the time I'd decided it was okay to laugh, the joke had hung in the air between us for too long. It was already too late.

Awkward jokes aside, I was grateful for Drea's company. She'd be a good person to have by my side if we *did* run into Troy and Helen. I imagined her removing her door-knocker earrings and getting ready to throw down with a stiletto in each fist.

I slowed down as we approached the record store. The brightly lit shop had a wide-open entrance and glass window displays, so I could stop to check if Sam Goody was working the floor before going in. I breathed a sigh of relief when I didn't see him, and headed straight to S for Streisand. I didn't want to spend any more time in there than I had to. If he weren't so annoying, I might have actually worried about Sam Goody's inevitable hearing loss. The sound system blasted a bouncy adult contemporary hit at an assaultive volume.

"*Looooooove is a wonderful thing . . .*"

Fuck you, Michael Bolton. Seriously.

"What's up with you?" Drea asked just loud enough to be heard above the music.

"Nothing," I lied. "Why?"

"You're acting sneaky," she says. "Like, conspicuously so."

"I am not!"

"Okay, whatever." She rolled her eyes. "You better work on your stealth skills if you're going to be any help to me on the treasure hunt."

I ran my finger along the rows of cassettes, searching for Streisand.

"Lustig Zeit," Drea said. "How is *anyone* supposed to know what that means?"

"It probably doesn't mean anything," I replied. "Lustig Zeit sounds like nonsense to me."

"Why would Tommy go to all the trouble of making a map if Lustig Zeit didn't mean anything?"

"Cocaine," I answered.

Drea arched an eyebrow. "Touché."

"*Looooooove is a wonderful, wonderful thing . . .*"

"Aha!" I called out.

"You figured out what Lustig Zeit means?"

"No," I replied, showing off *The Broadway Album*. "I found what I was looking for."

Drea scowled, equally bothered by my purchase as my lack of treasure-hunting purpose. I took two steps toward the register when none other than my pompous pompadoured nemesis emerged from behind a larger-than-life-size cardboard cutout of Paula Abdul.

"Lustig Zeit is German," said Sam Goody matter-of-factly.

Drea didn't waste a second. "What does it mean?"

"Lustig Zeit." He took in Drea for a moment before returning his attention to me. "Means 'Fun Time.'"

"Fun Time!" Drea whooped. "Fun Tyme Arcade! I told you it meant something!"

Without a moment's hesitation, she gave Sam Goody a wet kiss on the cheek.

"Thanks, Elvis!"

Like I said, Drea knew nothing about Morrissey. She had no way of knowing he idolized Elvis or that The Smiths had used one of the King's earliest promo photos on the cover for the single "Shoplifters of the World Unite." Drea had a talent for knowing the perfectly disarming thing to say to the opposite sex, and Sam Goody was no exception. He blushed at the compliment—and the kiss—in a way that might have been endearing if I weren't still pissed at him. He didn't deserve my thanks. He deserved to be mocked as he had mocked me.

"Of course you'd learn a useless language like German," I said. "Someone so *deep*, so *dark* needs to read *The Sorrows of Young Werther* in its original melodramatic, melancholic tongue, right?"

Then I turned on my heel to make what would've been the perfect exit if I had made it to the register. But I hadn't paid for the cassette, so the antitheft tag set off a security alarm that was somehow even louder and more obnoxious than Michael Bolton.

"Go! Go! Go!" Drea shouted.

In a panic, I hurled *The Broadway Album* at Sam Goody's head and got the hell out of there before I got arrested for shoplifting.

Drea and I ran up an escalator, all the way through Upper Level Concourses F and A, zigzagging past packs of stroller pushers, power walkers, and unaccompanied preteens. If sprint-

THE MALL

ing in stilettos were an Olympic sport, Drea Bellarosa would win *all* the gold medals that she could later turn into earrings and a matching statement necklace. We didn't stop until we reached a satellite kiosk for Orange Julius, far away from the food court. The two of us, bent over, hands on our knees, breathless. Me, with exertion. Drea, with laughter.

"OHMYGAWHAWHAWHAWHAWWWWWWNK."

Orange Julius was manned—or more accurately, *boyed*—by a freckle-faced kid who was barely tall enough to see over the industrial blender he was working with.

"That was hilarious!"

"What part of almost getting arrested was hilarious?"

"All of it! You should've seen the look on your face when the alarm went off!"

Without being asked, the boy behind the counter of Orange Julius offered Drea a large Styrofoam cup that she very graciously accepted.

"Thanks, Dom."

"You're welcome, D-d-d-drea."

The boy could barely say her name, as if he were unfit to speak it.

Drea walked away without paying and took a few satisfied sips of her recovery drink before launching into the next phase of the treasure hunt.

"Fun Tyme!"

She slipped map #2 out of her bra, where it had been nestled between her glistening breasts. If Dom had been around to witness this maneuver, I'm pretty sure he would have died and gone to masturbation heaven.

73

"I should've figured it out." Drea poked a nail at the X marking the spot on the map. "I know exactly where this is! It's the prize cases behind Skee-Ball!"

As I said, the map was very poorly designed. Tommy was not a master cartographer. There was no way I, Drea, or anyone else could determine the location from the drawing alone. But once we knew where to look, the map made enough sense to Drea to fulfill its purpose.

"Here's the plan." She sucked on the straw. "We wait until the arcade clears out at closing. You distract Sonny Sexton while I get the next clue."

While Sonny Sexton's habit of waking and baking would certainly put him on the most distractible end of the attention spectrum, I doubted very much that I was the right girl for this task.

"I think you've got our roles reversed."

"How many days, nights, and weekends have *you* spent at Fun Tyme Arcade supporting *your* boyfriend as he prepared for a *Donkey Kong* tournament?" She tossed the empty Orange Julius cup into a trash can. "Are *you* intimately familiar with the inner workings of Fun Tyme Arcade?"

I had a feeling that word "intimately" was not an accident on Drea's part. I definitely did not want to know the details of what went on between rounds of *Donkey Kong*.

"I can get in and out of there faster than you can," she said. "You won't even have to flirt with Sonny that long . . ."

I stopped dead in my tracks. The withered old man handing out free samples for Hickory Farms mistook this vegetarian for an interested customer.

"Summer sausage?"

Blech. I didn't know what was more stomach-turning. Dead cow or Sonny Sexton.

"I have to *flirt*? I don't know how to flirt!"

I'd seduced Troy with my Mock Trial cross-examination skills. He'd found my Odyssey of the Mind ingenuity irresistible. The closest I'd ever come to a flirty move was "borrowing" his scientific calculator without asking.

"I'll coach you!"

Then, as if to prove her bonafides, Drea lustily licked her lips, pinched a toothpicked mini-sausage from the old man's tray, and plunged it into her mouth.

"Yummmmy," purred Drea.

Hickory Farms' finest was not at all prepared for such provocation.

"Gurgle," gasped the geezer.

What a shame to survive World War I only to be taken out seventy years later by a ruthless temptress young enough to be his great-great-granddaughter.

"You're not as hopeless as I thought you'd be," Drea said as she blithely sauntered away from what was probably a heart attack in progress. "I actually saw a sexy spark when you faced off with that mopey guy in the record store."

"I was angry, not s—" I couldn't bring myself to use the word "sexy" in reference to myself. "I was pissed at him!"

"Well, whatever it was, it was *something* I could work with." Drea let the toothpick dangle between her lips like a cigarette. "Flirting with Sonny will be great practice for when it really matters later on. Because you want to show Troy you're totally over him, right?"

I *did* want to show Troy I was better off without him. But I was also nervous about what that would entail. As I debated, Drea kept chewing on the toothpick, putting her gorgeous smile in jeopardy. Wooden toothpicks were no-nos at Worthy Orthodontics and Pediatric Dentistry. Even when used properly, they were never an acceptable substitute for dental floss. I was relieved when she removed the toothpick from her mouth and chucked it into an ashtray.

"Fine," I said. "I'll flirt with Sonny Sexton. And when I fail miserably at our mission, you'll never ask me to do it again."

"You won't fail because you're an excellent student," she said, "and *I'm* an even better teacher."

Then she carefully refolded the map and stuffed it back in her bra.

10

SEXUAL QUID PRO QUO

*T*hough I was technically still working at Bellarosa for the next four hours, not much accounting was accomplished. Drea kept disrupting my progress by popping in to give so-called seduction instructions between customers.

"Keep the conversation short!"

"Look up at him through your lashes!"

"Play with your hair!"

"Touch him on the arm!"

Her interruptions came every ten minutes or so. My conservative estimate of two dozen flirtation tips was roughly twenty-three too many for me to handle. The instant I was off the clock, she raced to the back office. I think she was afraid I'd escape before completing our mission.

She was right to fear this.

Drea shook a glittery napkin at me.

"Wardrobe!"

I flashed back to the humiliation I felt the last time Drea selected my outfit.

"Ohhhh no," I protested. "Nononononono. I am not wearing that."

"But you can't wear"—she grimaced—"that."

I was wearing black jean shorts and a 10,000 Maniacs T-shirt.

"I am not changing."

Drea must have decided it was not worth the effort to fight me on this.

"Fine." Drea sighed. "At least let me work a little bit of my magic on you."

Then, without permission, she yanked the hem of my shirt.

"Hey! You're gonna stretch it all out!"

I loved that shirt, printed with elephants from the cover of the band's most recent album, *Blind Man's Zoo.* The ethereal lead singer, Natalie Merchant, was a vegetarian, just like my beloved Morrissey, Michael Stipe from R. E. M., the Indigo Girls, and other musicians on T-shirts Drea found equally appalling.

"It's either this or the Parisian special," Drea warned, shaking the hanger at me.

So I let her tie my tee at the waist, exposing my midriff. Then she rolled my jean shorts so they rode high on my thighs.

I was showing approximately 25 percent more skin than I had ten seconds earlier.

She took a step back to observe her work.

"If Sonny were a tougher target, I'd do your hair and makeup," she said. "But he doesn't require that kind of effort, and we don't have that kind of time even if he did."

It should be noted that we had two more hours before Fun Tyme closed. *Two hours* was not enough time, in Drea's estimation, to make me over properly. But it was enough time for me to make some headway on Bellarosa's expense reports—off the clock—while Drea finished her shift.

"It's Fun Tyme!" she announced when the clock struck 8:00 p.m.

As we hurried to the arcade, Drea explained that it would stay open past closing for any player who still had lives left on the quarters already put in the machine. We just had to hope that at least one super gamer was going for his highest score or we'd have to put off our ploy for another day.

The arcade's metal security gate was pulled halfway.

"They're closed!" I said.

"They're open!" Drea said.

As the optimist ducked under, the pessimist had no choice but to follow.

Drea went straight for the Skee-Ball ramps while I stood lookout. The arcade was nearly empty—just a shoulder-length mullet behind the wheel of a stationary Daytona race car—but you wouldn't know it from the noise. A cacophony of screeching tires, gun shots, and laser blasts vied with Guns N' Roses in eardrum-shattering competition.

"Welcome to the jungle, we've got fun and games . . ."

It was way worse than the record store. I didn't know how anyone could spend more than a minute in there without going totally insane. I'd lost all sight of Drea when I felt a tap on my shoulder.

"Heeeeeeey."

It was

Sonny

friggin'

Sexton.

"Heeeeeeey," he repeated.

He didn't give any signs of kicking me out. In fact, he was already drinking something aromatically alcoholic out of a red Solo cup. This certainly contributed to his untroubled reaction to my presence in the arcade past closing. We'd never spoken before. Why would he start now? Maybe he was coming over to apologize on behalf of his diabolical gerbil of an ex-girlfriend?

"Oh . . . um . . . hey."

Even in a slouch, Sonny Sexton stood taller than expected. He had to bend over to talk to me, so he must have towered over Helen when they were together. My gut twisted at the thought of whatever kinky contortions had made their sex fests possible on, like, an *anatomical* level. Over his shoulder, I glimpsed Drea perilously climbing a stepladder in stilettos to reach the upper prize shelves. I just had to stall long enough for her to steal the doll and get away.

"Never seen you in here before," he said.

His eyes were so heavy lidded, it was a wonder he could see *anything*, which would definitely work to our advantage if he suddenly decided to turn around in time to catch Drea sliding open the glass case. She'd told me to flirt with Sonny. But I decided to go in a different distraction direction.

"Your ex tried to kill me the other day."

It was fascinating to watch the effort put forth by the single functioning brain cell that comprised the entirety of Sonny Sexton's intellect.

"Mono Bitch?" he said slowly. "That's *you*?"

"That's me."

He took a long drink from his Solo cup, then wiped his mouth with the back of his hand.

"Well, holy shit."

"I thought you might want to apologize," I said.

"Apologize?" He looked into his cup. "For what?"

Did he not remember me just telling him that his ex-girlfriend had tried to murder me?

"For Helen!"

Blank stare.

"She stole my boyfriend and tried to kill me!"

Drea carefully descended the ladder with the familiar box tucked under her arm.

"You think I got any control over Helen?" Sonny Sexton let out a long, low whistle. "Helen is the wildest girl I've ever been with. And I've been with a lot of girls."

He wasn't bragging. He was merely stating a fact.

"That girl keyed my Mustang and burned my entire record collection in a bonfire on my front lawn! Last week she kidnapped Pink Floyd! Then she mailed me a picture of him in pajamas just to piss me off!"

"Pink Floyd?"

Was Sonny Sexton high on 'shrooms? What did the psyche-delic British band have to do with anything?

"My cat! Cats shouldn't wear clothes! It's not natural."

I was far more surprised to discover Sonny Sexton was a cat person than I was to hear Helen had taken his beloved pet hostage.

"I'm sorry that happened to you," I said, surprised by how genuinely I meant it.

"She's got some anger issues." Sonny shuddered. "Cookie Boy doesn't know what he's in for."

I couldn't help but laugh when he called Troy "Cookie Boy." A lock of lank black hair fell across Sonny's brow, and he grinned like a kindergartener who just learned to tie his big-boy shoes. That smile ruled out the possibility that Sonny Sexton was suffering from post-breakup devastation. Also, what he said next:

"We should have sex."

I nearly fell over. It felt like a lifetime ago that I'd used those same exact words in my failed attempt to seduce Troy. But what else should I have expected from a twenty-year-old Fun Tyme Arcade employee whose God-given name literally couldn't be spelled without *S-E-X*?

"You know," Sonny continued, "to get back at them."

Drea tiptoed between *Ms. Pac-Man* and *Street Fighter II*.

"Like . . . like . . ." I stammered, "some sexual quid pro quo?"

This didn't make sense. But I doubted Sonny Sexton would call me out on my misuse of legal terminology.

"I don't know what that is," he said, "but it sounds kinky."

"Sleeping with me just to get back at Helen is *gross*," I said. "How dare you—"

Drea stealthily slipped under the security gate and motioned for me to follow. I stopped my lecture mid-sentence and darted out the arcade with a hasty goodbye.

"She was hidden in plain sight!" Drea showed off the curly-haired blonde in the box but didn't slow down. "Just another prize on the shelf. No one ever saved up 250,000 Skee-Ball tickets to claim Pieds D'Abord!"

Pieds D'Abord. I slapped a palm to my forehead in disbelief.

"What language is that? French?" It was a rhetorical question, of course. I didn't expect Drea to know the answer. "Who knew a cokehead could be such a polyglot?"

Drea stopped her trot, cocked a hip.

"Who knew a straight-A nerd could be such a hoochie?"

I opened my mouth to protest but was stopped by the sight of myself in the floor-to-ceiling mirrors framing the entrance to Macy's. I mean, if it *looked* like a hoochie and *acted* like a hoochie . . .

"Your point?"

"My point," Drea replied sharply, "is that maybe you shouldn't be so quick to underestimate everyone all the time."

"I don't under—"

"Pieds D'Abord." She jabbed a fingernail at the birth certificate. "Feet First."

Drea, evidently, had taken two years of French.

11

SUMMER STUNNER

*T*he next morning, I arrived for work forty-five minutes late.

"You're not turning into No-Good Crystal, are you?" Gia demanded to know.

"I'm not!" I promised. "My ride left without me! I'm so sorry!"

I'd woken up for work that morning to find both parents—and even more oddly, both cars—gone. Frank and Kathy had not only left earlier than usual, but in separate vehicles. I didn't know if they were passive-aggressively punishing me for not delivering *The Broadway Album* or what. And if I weren't so pissed at them, I might have called into Worthy Orthodontics

84

and Pediatric Dentistry to find out what was going on. But I *was* pissed, so I didn't.

"It won't happen again," I promised.

"I know it won't," Gia replied.

Drea stopped pretending to fold lace camisoles and motioned for me to follow her to the back office. Rey Ajedrez, Lustig Zeit, and Pieds D'Abord sat on the velvet couch, waiting for us with open arms.

"Should we hit Feet First on our lunch break?" I asked.

Drea picked up Pieds and sat between Rey and Lustig. I turned on the computer and prepared to address the stack of invoices that had come in since the day before.

"I don't need your help getting in and out of the orthopedic shoe store," she said. "But you need my help getting laid."

"Drea!"

Sometimes my own prudishness took me by surprise. Drea reacted accordingly.

"Oh, I'm sorry." She placed her hands over Rey's plastic ears. "Not in front of the children."

"Drea! I do not need to get laid!"

She calmly walked behind the desk and pried an envelope out of my white-knuckled grip.

"You're right," she said. "You are totally chill and not at all in need of a release of eighteen years' worth of repressed sexual tension."

"Seventeen," I corrected her. "And I am not repressed."

"Oh, right." Drea rolled her eyes. "How could I have forgotten you skipped a grade?"

Seriously, how could she have forgotten? Drea was

preternaturally mature for her age. But the extra year she had on me widened the pubescent chasm between us. I remembered a trip we took to the mall when we were in sixth grade, watching in shock as Drea shopped—boldly, shamelessly—for underwire bras at Macy's and tampons at Woolworths. At the time, I wore Wonder Woman Underoos and was still three summers away from my first period.

"Even your earlobes are clenched."

I instinctively touched them to see if Drea was right and immediately felt like an idiot for doing so.

"I am not repressed," I repeated for lack of a better argument.

"Prove it," Drea said. "Go to the Cabbage Patch with Slade tonight."

"Slade? Slade *Johnson*?" My legs buckled, and I sank into the throne that served as my office chair. "You think I'm going to hook up with Slade because you dared me to?"

"No," Drea replied. "You're going to hook up with Slade because it will make Troy insanely jealous to see you've moved on with someone so much hotter than he is."

I had to admit that I liked the sound of this revenge in theory, even if I couldn't actually picture myself getting physical with Slade Johnson.

"If I agree to ask Slade to the Cabbage Patch tonight, do you promise to leave me alone for the rest of my shift so I can actually concentrate on getting some work done?" I was already almost an hour behind at that point, and I really hated the idea of letting Gia down. My irrational fear of disappointing authority figures was a key to my academic success.

Drea held up Pieds D'Abord's little stuffed hand.

"We promise," she said.

So I agreed to ask. But I couldn't guarantee Slade would say yes. Despite his flirty overtures at the last Cabbage Patch Party, I was certain he'd laugh me right out of Surf*Snow*Skate. Drea, however, *did* deliver on her promise, though her absence might have had more to do with the high volume of customers taking advantage of half-priced "Cruise and Cabana," which I had learned was boutique speak for swimsuits and cover-ups. I more than made up for my lateness by bringing Bellarosa's accounting totally up-to-date on the computer, an achievement I was eager to share with my boss. I was pleasantly surprised to find that despite No-Good Crystal's lackadaisical work ethic, the store was very solidly in the black.

"Why should that surprise you?" Gia countered upon hearing my report.

I was shaken by her caustic tone. I'd heard her speak to Drea that way, but she'd never used it with me.

"W-well," I stammered, "I've never shopped here, so . . ."

"So what? You assumed no one else did either?"

"Um . . . ?"

From the sour look on Gia's face, it was clear I had achieved the very opposite of the approval I had sought.

"Look, hon. I've been running this business for seven years now. I must be doing something right."

Before I could apologize for the misunderstanding, Gia turned on her spiked heel and walked out of the office just as Drea sashayed in.

"Before you head to Surf*Snow*Skate!"

She shook a hanger at me.

"Nononononononono . . ." I objected.

"Seriously, unclench." Drea yanked my earlobe. "I picked this outfit especially for you."

"That's what I'm afraid of."

Drea brushed off my comment with utmost professionalism. She pressed a denim skirt against my waist.

"See? This isn't any higher than your jean shorts," she said. "But it's a better option because boys like skirts."

"Why do boys like skirts?"

Drea did not dignify my ignorance with a reply.

She held up a cream-colored top with a black satin ribbon woven in and out and around the collar.

"This is basically a T-shirt, just like the one you're wearing," she said. "But you can adjust the tie around the neck so it's almost off the shoulder but not quite."

She coaxed me in front of the mirror. Just draped in front of me and not actually on me, I could see for myself that this was probably the most flattering outfit I'd ever worn.

"I thought you'd feel more confident showing collarbone, not cleavage."

"Thank you, Drea," I said, meaning it. "These picks are perfect."

Drea headed to the supply closet and returned with a purple can of Aussie Mega Hairspray in one hand and two combs in the other.

"You know what would be really perfect? If you let me add just a *little* height . . ."

My bangs fell straight across my forehead. Drea's bangs rose six inches above her eyebrows. Even if we compromised some-where in the middle, three inches of bang would still be too teased for me.

"Ummm . . ." I pointed to the clock. "Aren't we running out of time?"

"There's *always* time for lipstick." She dashed to the closet and came back with a tube of Revlon in Wild Rose.

"Is this too pastel for my complexion?" The pearlescent pink was not what I expected. "The girl at the Macy's cosmetics counter said I was a spring . . ."

"With your light brown hair and hazel eyes?" Drea blew a raspberry in contempt. "The idiot doesn't know what she's talking about. You're a summer stunner, sweetheart!"

I turned to the mirror and couldn't believe what I saw. Drea was right: I *was* a summer stunner. Now all I had to do was prove it.

To Slade.

To Troy.

But most of all to myself.

12

PROTECT THE COOKIE

*I*t was so easy.

"The Cabbage Patch?" Slade asked. "With you?"

A month ago, I would've interpreted those same exact words as a revolted response to a ridiculous question. And I wouldn't have been wrong. But judging from the pool of saliva at Slade's feet, he was anything but repelled by my invitation.

"Yeah," I said, taking Drea's advice to keep the conversation short. "It'll be fun."

I also remembered to look up at Slade coyly through my lashes. I hadn't thought it was possible, but he, too, had gotten even more summer stunning since my disastrous interview. His hair was blonder, his skin darker. Most miraculously, his tank top was cut lower than ever and yet still managed to qualify as a shirt.

"Yeah." Slade ran a hand through his sun-bleached tresses. "It *will* be fun." When he followed that up by touching my arm, I had about a split second to register these as the same exact moves Drea had instructed me to make. Did Slade also subscribe to *Cosmo*?

Without another word, Slade slung his arm around my shoulder and led me across Upper Level Concourse A toward the service elevator that would take us down to the Cabbage Patch. No negotiation or conversation. Just like that. Slade was as easy on the brain as he was on the eyes. So, so, so easy.

His arm was also so, so, so much heavier than Troy's. *Meaty* was the word that came to mind, but that might have been influenced by the collective aroma hovering around the dozen or so members of Ponderosa Steak & Ale's dinner crew who were also ready to party at the Cabbage Patch. My body leaned into Slade's at an angle that was awkward for walking but—based on the startled looks we were getting—awesome for gawking.

"Yo." Foot Locker Boy high-fived Slade.

"Yo." Slade low-fived Foot Locker Boy.

Foot Locker Girl showed no interest in introducing herself to me. The doors to the service elevator opened, and the crowd surged forward. There were far too many of us to fit comfortably.

"Maybe we should take the next—"

When Slade squeezed himself in the last bit of available space, I assumed he was ditching me. I was a joke to him all along, and he'd just been waiting for the best opportunity to humiliate me in front of an audience. Of course. Now this was making more sense.

"Come on, Cassie!"

Just as the doors started to close, he grabbed my hand and pulled me to him.

"Crowded," Slade accurately observed.

"Mmph."

My mouth smushed against his upper pectoral. Troy and I dated for six months before I'd even come close to making similarly intimate physical contact. But there I was, with my lips on Slade's chest, and my God, I didn't know if it was the coconut oil or what but he tasted friggin' delicious. I might have worried we were exceeding the elevator's 2,500-pound weight limit, but I was far too focused on my crotch, which rubbed against Slade's thigh in a not-unpleasant way as the elevator rattled in its descent. As the partygoers chattered about getting wasted, I was already feeling pretty wasted myself. Or, more accurately, what I thought it felt like to be drunk—warm from the inside out, woozy, wobbly—because I'd never actually been drunk before.

"Almost there," Slade said.

He had no idea.

The car convulsed when we hit bottom, and I unintentionally let out a little gasp that sounded more sexual than any noise I had ever made with Troy. So it was a dizzying irony when the doors opened to none other than my ex and his new girlfriend waiting to get on as Slade and I—ahem—got off.

"You've disrespected me for the last time, Troy!"

Troy and Helen were obviously in mid-fight, which explained why they were already leaving the party before it had really started.

"I—"

His defense was cut short when Slade and I literally collided into them to avoid being stampeded to death.

"CABBAGE PATCH! CABBAGE PATCH! CABBAGE PATCH!"

The rowdy Ponderosa crew must have pre-partied pretty hard with pilfered bottles from the restaurant bar. Foot Locker Couple followed close behind, leaving just the four of us to reckon with the awkwardness.

"Yo." Slade held up his hand for a high-five. "I'm Slade."

Compared to Slade, Troy was as pale and soft as a mixing bowl of America's Best Cookie dough.

"I know who you are!" Troy squeaked. "We graduated from the same high school!"

"Ohhhh, yeah?" Slade shrugged. "Sorry, dude."

"We were in the same homeroom for four years!"

Jarvis, Troy. Johnson, Slade.

"Hey," Slade said, holding up his hands. "Chill, dude."

"Chiiiiiiillllllll, duuuuuuuuuude," Troy said mockingly.

The icy looks we were getting from Helen could chill us all back to the Pleistocene epoch.

"You?" Troy pointed a shaky finger at me. "Came here with him?" Troy thumbed toward Slade.

"Actually, *I* came here with *her*."

Slade rested his hands between my neck and shoulders. The elevator door opened, releasing another wave of Cabbage

Patchers representing Jo-Ann's Nut House, Woolworths, and other businesses I couldn't identify because they didn't require uniforms. The last to exit was none other than Ghost Girl—Zoe—herself. I hadn't seen her since she'd offered me Fat-Free Fudgies, but she was as wraithlike as ever in all black.

"Ms. Gomez," Troy said nervously.

He was probably paranoid that his boss would bust him for underage drinking. But she paid him no mind at all. Just as she was poised to pass through our group with spectral indifference, she placed that pale, cold hand on my shoulder for a second time.

"Protect the cookie," she whispered cryptically, with a special emphasis on *crypt*.

As Zoe floated away, Helen made her own message undeniably clear.

"Troy! We are leaving!"

She stepped inside the elevator, but Troy was frozen.

"You . . . you . . ." He spluttered. "You look . . ."

This was my moment. I quoted Bellarosa's philosophy and meant every word.

"I look like the best possible version of myself."

Oh yes, it was happening. I was a summer stunner who'd snagged the yearbook-certified hottest guy in our graduating class. I had made Troy regret dumping me for a girl uglier than me in every possible way. Okay, I knew that wasn't the, like, *feminist* thing to think, but I'd never met anyone whose heinous outsides so accurately reflected her hideous insides. I was a *Cosmo* "After" and I wished Drea were here to see it.

And it had been so easy.

"I swear to Christ, Troy, if you don't get in this elevator with me right now."

"Helen, I—"

Troy's words were mercifully cut off by the closing doors.

Slade turned to me with a bemused half smile.

"You know that chode?"

"He's my ex-boyfriend."

Slade titled my chin so his Pacific-blue eyes met mine.

"You," he said, "are so much hotter than his new girlfriend."

Okay. So it wasn't exactly romantic, but . . .

"Let's skip the party," I suggested. "We can go somewhere private, and . . ."

"Talk?"

"Right," I said, remembering to play with my hair. "Talk."

That's all it took.

So, so easy.

Minutes later, Slade and I were kicking Cabbage Patch kids off the couch in Bellarosa's back office, talking our faces off. And by talking, I mean kissing, and by kissing I mean dry humping as though an American victory in the Gulf War depended on it.

"You're so hot," Slade murmured in my ear.

"So are you," I murmured back.

It all happened so easily, so quickly that it took a few minutes for my brain and body to sync up.

I want this, I thought as Slade pulled his tank top over his head. *I really, really want this.*

But only a few seconds later, Slade was sliding his hand

between my thighs when I suddenly realized that *this* was the reason why boys preferred skirts over shorts.

Easy access.

So, so easy.

Too easy.

An eerie whisper in my ear.

Protect the cookie . . .

"Stop!" I cried, yanking his hand away.

"Stop?" Slade blinked in disbelief. "But I thought you were enjoying yourself."

"I was enjoying myself," I replied honestly. "Until I wasn't."

Slade went back to teasing my earlobe with his tongue. But instead of feeling sensual it just felt . . . slithery. Serpentine. Rey Ajedrez's unblinking brown eyes stared up at me from where he'd been thoughtlessly knocked to the floor. I abruptly shifted to pick up him up, and Slade face-planted into the armrest.

"This is happening too fast." I stood to rearrange my skirt, which had fully rotated from front to back, back to front. "Maybe we should go to the party after all."

I knew as I was saying it that I didn't want to do that either. Location wasn't the problem. Slade was hot, but I wasn't attracted to him. Not really. Or not enough, anyway. And now that Troy had already seen us together, what was the point of pretending Slade was anything more than what he was: a pretty prop in my ploy to make my ex insanely jealous.

"No, Cassie," he said quietly but firmly. "I can't go to the party."

"Why not? Troy and Helen are gone and . . ."

"*No, Cassie.*"

I was taken aback by the sharp rise in his voice. I didn't get where this suddenly unchill urgency was coming from . . . until Slade moved Rey Ajedrez to reveal the magnitude of the bulge in his Jams.

"You can't just leave me here like this."

And for a second time, I reacted to Slade's ridiculous comment in the only reasonable way: I laughed right in his gorgeous face and got the hell out of there.

13

WRECKAGE

*W*hen my parents offered to drive me to work, I thought my family was back to normal.

I couldn't have been more wrong.

I'd spent most of my weekend off thinking about what had happened with Slade. And on the ride to work, I was still thinking about him, and how difficult it would be for me to tell him that we couldn't see each other anymore. No matter how I finessed it, he obviously liked me a lot. He was bound to take it, um, hard.

We're just too different, I'd say. *I'm leaving for college and you're staying at the mall.*

"Your mother and I want to take you out to lunch this afternoon," Frank said as he pulled into the mall parking lot.

The Volvo was rolling along at less than five miles per hour. But my stomach plummeted as if we were speeding over a cliff *Thelma & Louise*–style. Even though I'd never gotten to see it with or without Troy, I still knew how the story ended.

"Lunch?"

My parents never, ever went out for lunch. They always started their work days in late morning and scheduled appointments through lunchtime because it was often the only time of day working moms and dads could get away from their own jobs to take their kids for checkups. It was that high level of patient care and parental accommodation that had made Worthy Orthodontics and Pediatric Dentistry an industry leader for twenty years.

Mom gestured toward the neon red-and-yellow wagon wheel sign.

"Does Ponderosa Steak & Ale serve lunch?"

This invitation had gone beyond bizarre and had crossed over into offensive.

"Are you seriously considering taking your *vegetarian daughter* to *eat* at a *steakhouse*?"

Never mind that their *vegetarian daughter* had considered *employment* at a *steakhouse*. But for all they knew, I was still working for America's Best Cookie and dating Troy, and now didn't seem like the time to correct either one of those assumptions.

"Somewhere veggie friendly, then," Kathy suggested. "Is there still a Panda Express in the food court?"

"Not the food court!"

Kathy sighed deeply. Frank pulled the Volvo up to the pedestrian drop-off and put it in park. Both parents looked at each other, then turned around in their seats to look at me.

"We didn't want to tell you here," said Frank.

"We didn't want to tell you like this," said Kathy.

At that moment, I realized just how infrequently I saw eye to eye with my parents. Like, literally. Back-seat driving was all I'd ever done, so the from-behind perspective was far more familiar to me than the face-first view. Over the years, I'd made myself useful from this vantage point by warning Frank about the deepening sunburn on the nape of his neck or tracking the stealthy gray hairs that had escaped the pluck of Kathy's tweezers.

"We've decided to take a break from each other," said Frank.

"Two decades of living and working together have taken their toll," said Kathy.

The morning sun shined unforgiving light on the lines crisscrossing their middle-aged faces. When had Dad's eyes gotten so droopy? What were those fleshy pouches sagging below Mom's jawline?

"We thought it over very carefully," said Kathy.

"And we've decided that our dental practice is easier to save than our marriage," said Frank.

They were both so calm. So calm that their calmness totally freaked me out.

"What does that even mean?"

They looked at each other again. Kathy solemnly nodded. Then Frank mirrored the gesture. How could this be happening?

They talked about splitting up, yet they were still so totally in sync.

"It means Worthy Orthodontics and Pediatric Dentistry will stay open for business as usual," said Frank.

"But your father is moving out," said Kathy.

And then one of them—I honestly can't remember who—began explaining how Frank had already found another apartment, a *condo* actually, in Toms River, and how I would be welcome anytime . . .

I tugged on the handle, but my parents had locked me inside.

"Let me out!"

"Cassandra . . ."

"Let me out!"

I pulled again, then pushed the door open.

"Cassandra!"

"Cassandra!"

"Cassandra!"

"Cassandra!"

I escaped the wreckage, staggered across the parking lot, and stumbled into Macy's, where I promptly knelt on the floor and puked my guts into the base of a plastic palm tree.

14

CINNABON APPETIT

I arrived at work ten minutes late. Gia was in mid-pitch to a customer in a midnight-blue cocktail dress.

"Now, Vicki, Bellarosa Boutique is a proud member of the International Formalwear Association," she boasted. "We stand by our No Repeat Dress Guarantee . . ."

This girl Vicki was getting a major head start on homecoming. Even in my dazed state, I knew three-quarter-sleeved stretch velvet with a multitiered ruffle skirt was not a summer style. I didn't know who this girl was, but I envied her for setting her sights on such a trivial, easily achieved goal.

"Cassie!"

I expected Gia to chew me out for my tardiness. *Late again? Really, Cassie? You're worse than No-Good Crystal!* Instead, she rushed over and pressed me to her bosom. That was when I should've figured out that I was even worse off than I thought.

"It's gonna be okay, hon," Gia said, stroking my hair.

"How—?"

My question was interrupted by the girl in the dress. With her asymmetrical haircut and mix of silver hoops and diamond studs in both ears, I suddenly recognized Vicki as the Piercing Pagoda's lone employee.

"Toothy!"

Toothy? I had no idea what it meant, but Gia did. Her head nearly snapped off her neck.

"I will not tolerate disrespect in my store!"

Toothy.

My Odyssey of the Mind word association skills automatically kicked in.

Toothy.

Teeth.

Dental.

Dentists.

Parents.

Did *everyone* find out about Frank and Kathy before I did?

"You can forget all about that dress," Gia said to her customer. "I just remembered I promised it to someone else."

"Wha—?" Vicki was on the verge of tears.

Drea arrived on the scene.

"Let's talk!"

She pressed her nails into my upper arm and pulled me into the office. In the bright light of day, it seemed like an unlikely spot for an assignation. It felt like a million years had passed since Slade and I rolled around on that couch. As disappointing as our hookup was, I'd have gone back to that time of blissful ignorance in a heartbeat.

Drea eyed the couch, then me.

"You're taking this worse than I thought you would," she said. "You look terrible."

"How do you expect me to take this? Life as I know it is over!" I supported myself against the desk. "And how does everyone already know when I just found out myself?"

"Word gets around," Drea said. "Look, it's not *that* tragic. Take it from me."

"It's totally different."

Drea's parents split up when she was just a toddler. She had her whole life to get used to D-I-V-O-R-C-E. I couldn't even say the word in my head.

Drea tipped back her head and laughed.

"Name one person at Pineville High who's had more rumors spread about their sexual exploits than me!"

This was true. But I didn't see how gossip about Drea's alleged sluttiness had anything to do with my parents' divorce. Unless . . .

"Wait . . . People know about my parents' sexual exploits?"

"Your parents?" Drea recoiled. "Ewwwww! No!"

"Then what are you talking about?"

"You!" Drea looked at me like I was a simpleton. "And Slade!"

"Me and Slade?"

"Of course, you and Slade! What are *you* talking about?"

"I'm talking about my parents' separation!"

"What?!"

"My dad already has an apartment and is moving out!" Yelling hurt more than it ever had under Dr. Baumann's care. "My parents are splitting up!"

Drea immediately softened.

"Oh, Cassie. I'm so sorry. I had no idea!"

"Neither did I," I croaked. "They just told me on the drive over here."

Drea filled a plastic cup from the water cooler and placed it in my shaking hands. I drank greedily, swallowing down the rawness in my throat.

"But your parents are so good together." Drea shook her head in disbelief. *"Braces make happy faces!"*

"Well, I guess they don't make happy marriages."

Drea hopped up next to me on the desk. "They're really getting a divorce?"

"I don't know. I guess so. I fled the scene before I got the details."

We sat in silence. Me, perfectly still. Drea, swinging her legs back and forth. I couldn't wear any but the thickest tights without getting runs. But Drea's hosiery was of the sheerest denier.

"So, if you didn't know about my parents," I said, "what did you think I was so upset about?"

If I hadn't been watching carefully, I wouldn't have caught the grimace Drea forced into a grin.

MEGAN McCAFFERTY

"I think it's funny, actually!" she said brightly. "It's not a big deal."

"*What's* not a big deal?"

"Slade went back to the Cabbage Patch after you hooked up," she said. "He told everyone . . ."

"Told everyone what? That we barely went past second base?"

"Not exactly."

"Then what?"

"He told them," she said, "that you almost bit off a chunk of his junk."

I seriously thought I might puke again.

"This isn't funny, Drea!" I lowered myself to the floor and locked the trash can between my knees. "So, not only does the entire mall think I'm a slut, they think I'm an *inept* slut!"

Drea laughed because she thought I was joking. But I wasn't.

"You really need to see the upside of this situation," Drea said. "Until now, you weren't hot enough to be someone worth gossiping about . . ."

I couldn't believe what Drea was saying. That only now was I worthy of horrible rumors? That I was too much of a loser throughout high school to even register?

"You are so rude!"

I heaved the trash can at the wall. Drea shrieked in shock.

"Oh my Gawd, Cassie. You could've killed me!"

"You're lucky I didn't aim for your face!"

This was why Drea and I had stopped being friends in seventh grade. Not because she got boobs when I did not. Or a boyfriend when I did not. Or bad grades when I did not.

It was because she made me feel hopelessly . . .

Loserish.

And I was tired of being around someone who made me feel that way.

Then.

And.

Now.

"Come on, Cassie, lighten up!"

I grabbed a stapler and held it up menacingly.

"Get out!"

Drea's eyes widened, and she backed out the door. If she knew what was good for her, she wouldn't bother me for the rest of my day.

⊏⊐

*F*our hours later, the door creaked open and the scent of cinnamon and sugar wafted inside.

"A peace offering!"

I didn't know if I was still suffering from a post-mononucleosian calorie deficit or what. But I went straight to full drool at the inimitable scent of melted butter, caramelized sugar, warm dough, and—of course—cinnamon. I had to give her credit. Not only had Drea paid extra for the Pecanbon, but she had gone out of her way to present this thousand-calorie bomb on a real plate with a cloth napkin.

This wasn't a peace offering at all. This was a weapon of warfare.

She set it down on my desk and stepped back with a flourish.

"Cinnabon appetit!"

I could tell by the way the icing dripped across the swirls and down the curves that the pastry was still warm. Drea was not fighting fair.

"If you think you can bribe me with Cinnabon, you are sorely mistaken," I said.

Then I threw the whole thing—plate and all—into the same trash can I had hurled against the wall.

"Well," Drea said, dropping her smile. "That's a waste."

"I'm done with this stupid treasure hunt."

"But why?" Drea asked. "We're getting close, I can feel it—"

"I don't care! I only care about lying low and making as much money as I can before getting the hell out of here."

I'd been stewing all morning. I wanted to quit so badly, but even in my outrage, I knew the money was too good to give up. Gia was paying me seven dollars an hour—a whopping $2.75 more than the minimum wage I would've gotten at America's Best Cookie. The odds of me finding another job this late in the season that paid nearly as much were nonexistent. Bellarosa was my final pit stop in Pineville en route to my real life in New York City. And now that my family had fallen apart, I had even fewer reasons to look back once I got there.

"Please leave this office," I said, trying to resume an air of professionalism. "I have a lot of work to do."

"Aren't you even the least bit curious about the next clue?"

"No," I said. "I'm not helping you anymore. I'm done."

I resolved to do what I should've done from the start: Focus on the job and forget everything else.

No more treasure hunt.

No more Cabbage Patch.

No more Drea Bellarosa.

"Come on, Cassie," Drea implored.

"I mean it!" I said. "I want those dolls out of here. They're creepy."

"They are not creepy," she said, tickling Rey Ajedrez under the chin. "They're cute."

"I don't like them staring at me from the couch like that," I said. "With their arms out, begging for hugs."

"Where should I put them, then?" Drea asked.

"They're just dolls!" I shouted. "What are you, ten years old?"

Drea's eyes narrowed. All I could see was mascara, liner, and more mascara.

"You want to be a bitch? You get rid of them!"

She walked away with the confidence of someone who knew I would do absolutely no such thing. There was no way I could toss Rey Ajedrez, Lustig Zeit, Pieds D'Abord, and the new baby into the trash. Maybe I was a bitch. But I wasn't a *monster*. Emboldened by her success, Drea turned sharply at the exit to deliver her parting shot.

"Silva Mundi!"

The preemie's name—the next clue—lodged itself deep in my brain. When Drea Bellarosa took aim, she did not miss.

15

THEM AND ME

I sat in the passenger side of the Volvo for the first time in forever. It was weird to see my mom's face in profile. From this side view, her nose looked more beak-like than I had remembered. I wondered if mine looked similarly avian at that angle, then cautioned myself against stepping in front of Bellarosa's three-way mirrors to find out. I'd been through too much trauma in the past few days. I didn't know how much more I could take.

"Do you have enough room?" Kathy asked.

"I'm fine," I grunted.

I knew she was going out of her way to be accommodating.

But I simply wasn't in the mood to make her feel better about her poor life choices. Not when I had my own poor life choices to contend with.

"Are you sure you're comfortable?"

How could I be comfortable knowing Frank was all alone on the commute from his new condo? He got the other, older Volvo, the one they hardly ever drove and had kept in our garage as a backup. From that point forward, I'd think of it as Dad's Volvo, making this Mom's Volvo by default, which was weird because until that day, I don't know if I'd ever seen her in the driver's seat. Frank had always, *always* driven us everywhere. And Kathy had never, *never* objected. That's just how it *always* was in our family, so I *never* questioned it. Just like we *always* entered the mall through Macy's, and *never* through J. C. Penney. There's a reason why our Mock Trial advisor taught us to avoid *always* and *never* statements in our arguments: They were so easy to prove untrue.

Frank and Kathy were always a duo, plus one. My parents always preferred the company of each other to being around me. Oh, they were supportive of my academic and extracurricular endeavors, of course. They were dependable fixtures at Odyssey of the Mind tournaments and Mock Trial courtrooms, but I can barely remember any significant one-on-one time with either parent. In fact, if I even tried to talk to one of them about literally anything—from buying breakfast cereal to applying to college—the inevitable response would be, "Let's wait to see what your father/your mother has to say about this." It wasn't "we." It was "them" and "me" until the end. Just consider the complicated coordinated effort required to separate without me even noticing. Frank and Kathy were the ultimate united front; even in their split I couldn't fathom how either one of them would function on their own. And yet, there Mom was, half smiling, humming along to the radio.

"You don't look comfortable," Kathy pressed. "You're taller than I am. You should move the seat back . . ."

It didn't matter that we were just a few yards away from the pedestrian drop-off. I couldn't stand another second of Mom trying so hard to ease her guilty conscience.

"Fine!" I barked. "I'll move the seat!"

I reached underneath for the handle but felt something soft and crinkly instead. My parents had always demanded the Volvo be kept scrupulously—some might say *pathologically*—clean. So I couldn't quite believe it when I pulled out a crumpled wax bag from Wally D's Sweet Treat Shoppe. What. The. Hell. With this evidence of secret candy binges, Mom had not only abandoned her marriage, but the most basic principles of oral health and hygiene.

"Is something wrong?" Kathy asked, keeping her eye on the road.

I was in no condition to confront her about this. I stuffed the bag even farther under the seat and removed my hand, which was now sticky with a residue that smelled like fudge but looked like shit.

"Don't drop me off here," I ordered. "Keep going."

Kathy looked confused.

"But—?"

"Drop me off at J. C. Penney. Or is that too much to ask?"

I guess Kathy decided it wasn't. She turned the wheel and

continued through the parking lot to Entrance Two without questioning me. My hand was on the door handle when she gently took my arm.

"This will get easier."

I shrugged Mom off and got out of the car without waving or saying goodbye.

Before going inside, I consulted the mall directory to review the ever-expanding list of danger zones. Concourse B—where I stood—was the only letter that hadn't been compromised. Not yet, anyway. The following areas were totally off-limits:

Concourse A, Upper Level (Surf*Snow*Skate)

Concourse C, Lower Level (Sears)

Concourse D, Lower Level (Food Court)

Concourse E, Upper Level (Fun Tyme Arcade)

Concourse F, Lower Level (Sam Goody)

Concourse G, Lower Level (Bellarosa Boutique)

If I were strategic and diligent, I could avoid all but the last. Even at Bellarosa, I could barricade myself in the back office if I had to.

Kathy was right, though. It *would* get easier.

In six weeks, I'd be packing up all my stuff and getting the hell out of Pineville. Away from my parents' midlife marital meltdown. Troy's ratty, rageaholic rebound. Slade's sleazy gossip. Sam Goody's smirky jerkiness. Sonny Sexton's stoner imbecility. Drea's endless drama. But until then, my life at the mall would really, really suck.

It definitely didn't help that Drea had totally outmaneuvered me. As hard as I tried to focus on work, to update Bellarosa's latest debits and credits, I couldn't get her words out of my head.

Silva Mundi

-$775.25 to Muy Cheri Wholesale

Silva Mundi

+$1142.50 from Mona Troccola

Silva Mundi

-$372.75 to Glamorama Distribution

Silva Mundi

+$800.50 from Francine DePasquale

Silva Mundi

Drea knew that a fierce Odyssey of the Mind competitor such as myself would be incapable of letting the clue go unsolved. I managed to hold out for three days before my curiosity finally got the better of me.

Silva Mundi

It sort of sounded like Spanish, but it wasn't Spanish. Portuguese maybe?

I didn't have to give her the double satisfaction of proving her right and providing the answer. I could translate Silva Mundi but keep the answer to myself, thus satisfying my inquisitiveness without perpetuating Drea's obsession with this pointless quest. I'd be doing us both a favor. Maybe if Drea spent less energy on trivial pursuits like the treasure hunt and more on, I don't know, *anything else,* she too would have a future outside the mall.

So when it came time for my lunch break, I followed my Iberian hunch to the only place within the mall where such knowledge might be acquired. Fortunately for me, B. Dalton Books was located in a safe zone. But that didn't stop me from looking over my shoulder every five seconds to make sure I wasn't being stalked, spied on, or snickered at. I wasn't sure if the "toothy" rumors had traveled through Concourse E, but I was in no mood to find out.

I spent four years hauling heavy textbooks around in my backpack. But in direct defiance of the nerdy girl stereotype, I didn't read much for pleasure. I didn't have time, between earning a perfect GPA, extracurriculars, and teaching myself to ace standardized tests that only Troy and I and very few others in our school took at all seriously. In fact, the last item I'd bought at this store was an SAT prep book Troy and I had shared, splitting the cost fifty-fifty. That $15.36 gave me a far better return on my investment than my ex-boyfriend.

After scanning the shelves, the closest I got to a Portuguese dictionary was *The Travel Linguist*, a phrasebook for tourists. Let down, but not totally out, I flipped around to the *S* section of the thin glossary at the back of the book. I found:

Segunda-feira (Seh-GOON-da-FAY-ra): Monday

Sim (SING): Yes

Socorro! (soh-KOH-roh!): Help!

But no Silva Mundi. Silva Mundi wasn't Portuguese after all. Or if it was, it wasn't a common enough expression to justify inclusion in the only Portuguese language book sold by B. Dalton. I was contemplating my next move when I felt a cold whisper on the back of my neck.

"I warned you."

I turned, screamed, and dropped the book on Ghost Girl's Doc Martens.

"Ms. Gomez!"

She smiled serenely. "You can call me Zoe." Then apropos of nothing she added, "He will pay."

If I were a "spring," the Macy's makeup counter girl would classify Zoe's cosmetic aesthetic as "nuclear winter." Like any committed goth, she sought to approximate a translucent complexion that could otherwise only be achieved by death, burial, and disinterment—or, okay, fine, if pressed to offer a less supernatural explanation—a lifelong shunning of the sun. Regardless, I certainly did not want to stick around long enough to find out who she had decided to hex, or why she was telling me about it.

"Coolcoolokaybyebye."

I sounded like an idiot. And, then, in my haste to get away from Ghost Girl, I made sure to make myself *look* like an idiot too, by tripping right over a pair of rockabilly boots and black jeans rolled *just so.*

"Yiiiiiiiiiiiikes . . ."

I would've tumbled right on top of him if an endcap display of self-help books hadn't broken my fall. I was *literally* saved by *Full Catastrophe Living* and *The Language of Letting Go.*

"Hey, Bellarosa," Sam Goody said. "You should watch where you're going."

He was sprawled out on the floor between shelves and offered no apology for obstructing the aisle. So I didn't bother correcting the misconception that I was another Bellarosa cousin hired for the summer.

"Hey, Sam Goody. You're beyond loitering," I said. "You're *lounging.*"

Sam Goody smiled. Not a smirk, but a genuine smile. He had decent teeth. Not perfect—the top row slightly overlapped the bottom. My bet? He'd once had a retainer and lost it. The mental picture of moody Sam Goody wearing headgear actually made me smile.

"I've got an agreement with a guy who works here," he said. "He lets me use his store as my personal library, and I let him use our store as his personal listening booth."

"I should call mall security on both your asses."

Then Sam Goody actually laughed, and I almost relaxed for a second until I realized that he might be laughing *at* me and not *with* me. Had he heard the rumor about me and Slade? Was he two seconds away from calling me Toothy?

"Do you need another German translation?" he asked.

"No," I replied curtly.

"I know some conversational Japanese too," he said. "From my grandma."

"No," I repeated. "I'm fine."

"Oh," he said. "Because I saw you in the foreign language section."

So I supposed it was a good sign that Sam Goody had noticed me but hadn't approached me with a toothy taunt. And since we were talking, I figured I might as well make use of him as a possible resource. It's not like I had any better options.

"Is *Silva Mundi* German?" I asked.

"No." He ran a hand through his pompadour. Sam Goody definitely used more hair product than I did. "It sounds . . . Spanish maybe?"

"It's definitely not Spanish. I thought it might be Portuguese but . . ."

And then I stopped myself because why did I have to explain myself to Sam Goody? I craned my neck to get a look at the cover of the thick book in his lap.

"What are you reading, anyway?"

With zero subtlety, Sam Goody pulled the book away and shoved it under the army surplus satchel at his side.

"It's okay, a lot of guys read *Playboy* for the articles," I teased. "You don't have to be embarrassed."

Where was this coming from? Why was I still talking to this person? I would've walked away if he hadn't decided to show me the hidden book. *Life Beyond the Ivy League: 50 Schools That Will Make You Rethink College.*

"I didn't take German to wallow in Sturm und Drang," Sam Goody explained. "My parents expected me to work in finance. And Deutsche Bank is primed to become a global powerhouse in the wake of communism's collapse."

As a maker and appreciator of plans, that sure sounded like a solid one to me. Far better than mine because it didn't depend on anyone else but himself.

"Well." A hint of envy crept into my voice. "You have it all figured out."

"Oh sure, it was the perfect plan." Sam Goody laced his fingers and cradled the back of his head. "There was only one problem. I hated Wharton and everything to do with finance."

The Wharton School at University of Pennsylvania was pretty much the hardest undergraduate business program to get into in the world. Their students got hooked up with the cushiest summer internships at the top Wall Street firms. So why was Sam Goody wasting his summer working for minimum wage at the mall?

"I didn't take German for Goethe. I took it to please my parents." He knocked the book's cover with his knuckles. "Now that I'm a college dropout, I wish I'd taken Latin, which would've been more worthwhile from a liberal arts perspective . . ."

I couldn't quit Odyssey of the Mind-ing. My brain edited out all the information that wasn't relevant to my quest. I raced back over to the foreign language dictionaries to confirm my suspicion.

"Latin!" I exclaimed, grabbing a Latin volume from the shelf. "That's it!"

Silva Mundi = Wood World

Wood World was the only store at the mall devoted to the boner arts. Ha! Get it? Gotcha! Just joshing! Wood World sold quality woodcrafts but whee! That's how giddy I felt—giddy enough to come up with a dumb dick joke with no one to share it with.

Well, *one* person to share it with.

"Thanks for the tip!" I shouted at Sam Goody.

He was definitely not the person I had in mind.

16

BIMBO DRESS

I was high from the thrill of solving the unsolvable. I did not get the hero's welcome I had hoped for.

"Drea! I got the next clue! Silva Mundi! Is Latin! For Wood World!"

"Oh," Drea said distractedly. "Awesome."

She blatantly looked behind me, not at me.

"Jeez," I said. "I thought you'd be thrilled that I'm back in with the treasure hunt."

"I *am*." She placed her hands on my shoulders and gave me a little push. "It's just . . ."

"Look." I firmly planted my feet because she needed to hear

this. "I'm sorry I was so hard to deal with the other day. You may be used to being the one put through the rumor mill, but I'm not. I mean, the whole mall was gossiping about my terrible blowjob on the same morning I found out my parents' marriage is over. It was just too much for me to handle, and I took it out on you . . ."

Drea pressed her hands to my mouth to shut me up, but it was already too late.

"Cassandra?"

The door to the dressing room swung open and a middle-aged woman came out in a bedazzled spandex bandage that could only be described as a bimbo dress.

"*Mom?*"

The middle-aged woman wearing the bimbo dress was my mother.

"What are you doing here?" Kathy asked.

"What are *you* doing here?" I asked.

To be honest, hers was the more legitimate question. One peek at the collection of short, tight, sparkly options still hanging from the hooks in the dressing room and it was instantly clear to me what Kathy was doing in Bellarosa Boutique.

My mother was putting herself back on the market.

My mother was ready to date men who weren't my father.

My mother was probably going to get laid before I did.

I swear I might have fallen down if Drea weren't *literally* propping me up by my elbows.

"Cassie works here, Mrs. Worthy," Drea answered on my behalf.

"*Doctor* Worthy."

Mom made this correction so often, it was like an afterthought. Kathy shook out her feathered pageboy. She'd had the same hairstyle my whole life. This sensible mom hair did not match this irresponsible bimbo dress.

"Cassandra?"

"Can you please change out of that outfit?" I pleaded. "It's impossible for me to have a serious conversation with you when you're dressed for a special senior citizen episode of *Club MTV.*"

It was a mean thing to say. Kathy was still about twenty years shy of collecting social security. And okay, as much as I hated to admit it, my mother didn't look terrible. Drea had selected a cut and fabric that flattered Kathy's fuller figure, skimming her generous hips and thighs without clinging to any bumps or bulges. My mother actually had the body for this dress. And unlike her daughter, she also had the *soul.*

"Have you been lying to me all summer?" Kathy asked.

Her self-righteous tone put me over the edge.

"Have *you* and Dad been lying to me all my life?"

Kathy's face fell. And the contrast between her depressed expression and this gaudy, good-time dress could not have been more stark.

"Yes, I've been working here at Bellarosa Boutique, not at America's Best Cookie," I admitted. "But before you get on my case, think about who the bigger liar is here."

I'd been fibbing about my employment for a week. My parents had been perpetuating the myth of the perfect partnership my whole life. Who knows, maybe even longer than that? Maybe getting married and having a kid were just boxes to tick off, proof of demonstrable progress on the plan Frank and Kathy had set in motion when they met at dental school . . . ?

"Why did you lie to us?" Kathy asked.

"I didn't want you to know Troy and I had broken up."

Saying it out loud like that, I realized just how foolish I was. Had I really thought I could hide the truth from my parents forever? Or did I believe Troy and I would get back together before they ever found out? Both options were equally dumb.

"You broke up?" Kathy clutched a hand to the rhinestones embellishing her chest. "But you were so perfect together! You had *the plan!*"

All this time I'd thought we'd broken up because Troy cheated on me. But maybe that was just the symptom of a much deeper, possibly genetic problem.

"We broke up," I answered, "because you and Frank aren't the only ones in the family who suck at relationships."

I bolted from the store before I saw for myself how much I'd hurt her.

17

EVOLUTION

I was stabbing pulpy sludge with a straw when someone sat beside me on the bench. Tipped off by the mixed bouquet of Aussie Mega and Giorgio Beverly Hills, I didn't even look up from my cup.

"How did you find me?" I asked.

"With all the people you're avoiding," Drea said, "there aren't many places in the mall for you to hide."

I laughed ruefully. She definitely wasn't wrong.

"Your mom bought the dress I picked out for her," Drea said.

How nice for Drea to make a sweet commission off the dissolution of my parents' marriage.

"Maybe Kathy will go to you when it's time to shop for her second wedding dress."

"Come on, Cassie," Drea said. "Calm down."

Too late. I was all hopped up on syrup, citrus, and resentment.

"Can I get an employee discount on the maid of honor dress when she remarries some old dude who isn't my dad?"

"Are you done yet?" Drea asked.

I chewed on the straw in defiance, putting the soft tissue of my gums at risk and not giving a single shit what my parents might say about it.

"Your mother has known us for years," Drea said. "But she never set foot in our store until this morning. And why do you think that is?"

"Because she's having a midlife crisis?" I guessed.

"At Bellarosa, we prefer to think of it as a midlife *metamorphosis*."

"Of course you do," I muttered bitterly.

"She's changing," Drea continued. "She's not the uptight wife and mom she thought she was. And she came to Bellarosa Boutique because she wanted that inner transformation to be reflected on the outside, through her clothing."

The advertising copy practically wrote itself.

"So for all those years she was married to my dad she was a lowly caterpillar?" I asked. "And now she's a beautiful butterfly?"

"Not exactly," Drea said. "I'm saying that she's evolving from one kind of butterfly into an equally beautiful but totally different butterfly."

"That's not how evolution works . . ."

She slapped her hands against the bench. "Can you shut off your nerd brain for, like, two seconds so I can try to make you feel better?"

No. I didn't think I could.

"Let me tell you a story," Drea began.

Resistance was futile. I uncrossed my legs and made myself comfortable.

"Gia was supposed to be a hairdresser. Her mother was a hairdresser and her mother's mother was a hairdresser. My dad's family were the ones in the clothing business. When my parents got married, my dad's father let him run Main Street Haberdashery, a menswear shop in downtown Toms River."

"Never heard of it," I said.

"Right," Drea said. "Because my dad was as shitty at selling menswear as he was at being a husband and father. It was only as successful as it was because Ma was a quick learner and worked her ass off while my dad got drunk and boinked cocktail waitresses."

This was the most I'd ever heard Drea say about her father. I didn't know where the story was going, but I definitely wanted to hear more.

"Ma got fed up and filed for divorce when I was ten," she said.

"That's when you moved to Pineville," I said. "Switched to my school."

"Right," Drea said, nodding. "At that point, she wanted nothing to do with him. And he wanted even less to do with us. So against all advice from her divorce attorney, she offered to give up any claims for child or spousal support if he signed over full ownership of the haberdashery. He never wanted to sell suits in the first place, so for him it was a win-win."

"Wow," I said. "That could've backfired spectacularly."

"Yeah," Drea replied. "But it didn't. Because the last we heard, my dad had run up a ton of gambling debts and doesn't have a dime to his name. Ma sold the shop and its inventory to Men's Wearhouse, then used that seed money to start her own business."

"Bellarosa Boutique?"

"None other," Drea replied. "Mom named the store after herself, taking her maiden name as a final 'fuck you' to the husband she never should have married in the first place."

A shiny, pink-tracksuited mom dragged her toddler across Concourse B on a leash. She was in a hurry. Her daughter was not.

"Come *on*, Ashley," Tracksuit whined. "I do not have all day for this."

In fact, she looked *exactly* like someone who had all day for this.

"If Gia hadn't married your dad," I pointed out, "she wouldn't be where she is today."

Drea looked me in the eye.

"You almost got it right." She gave me a second to figure it out for myself before proceeding. "If she hadn't married, then *left* my dad, she wouldn't be where she is today."

Okay. So I sort of understood where she was going with this story. But Gia was not Kathy.

"You're out of here in a month, right?"

"Five weeks," I answered. "Orientation starts on August twenty-third."

In exactly thirty-five days, I'd be moving into Sulzberger Hall and meeting my roommate, Simone Levy, from Rochester, New York. So far, she had not responded to the letter I'd sent when I had mono, and I was trying not to hold this slight against her.

"In five weeks you'll finally get out of here and live the real life you've always wanted," Drea said. "Isn't it about time your parents get to live theirs?"

Drea was speaking from experience. And yet I couldn't quite bring myself to agree. I shrugged noncommittally.

"Until then," Drea said, "what do you want to do?"

I shook the cup, removed the lid, and stared into the dregs of my Orange Julius. I wished I had the power to read them like tea leaves. That's how desperate I was to find a new purpose, a new plan to fill the next thirty-five days and help me forget that my family had fallen apart.

"Well," I answered finally. "Do we have time to go to Wood World?"

Drea reached into her bra and pulled out the map.

"Cassie Worthy," she said with a smile, "I thought you'd never ask."

18

THE TRUTH

For as long as there was the mall, there was Wood World. Its lengthy motto was carved in—what else?—wood and displayed in the front window.

WE SELL WOODWORK, WOODWORKING TOOLS, WOODWORKING SUPPLIES, WOODWORKING PLANS, AND WOODWORKING KITS FOR THE PASSIONATE WOODWORKER.

"Please tell me one of your exes was a passionate woodworker," I said.

"Plenty of my exes knew how to passionately work their wood . . ."

I gagged. Drea hawnked with wicked amusement.

The sign was Wood World's only form of promotion. And yet, this funny, fuddy-duddy little shop had survived since 1976, when trendier neighbors—a studio offering disco-dancing lessons that turned into an all-Smurf store that turned into the local headquarters of the Tiffany fan club—had died. It was one of those super niche stores that never advertised because their devoted customers wouldn't shop anywhere else. Three of those devoted customers—all in flannel shirts despite the heat but rolled high enough to reveal their forearm tattoos—were having a very animated discussion.

"As an accent wood, it don't get much prettier than purpleheart," said Gray Flannel.

"Only commercial wood in that color," said Blue Flannel.

"Hard as hickory, but pricey," said Green Flannel.

"That's because it comes from the Amazon," said a heavyset man with a snow-white prospector's beard. His flannel shirt was red. He looked way more like Santa Claus than the guy the mall hired every year to play the part for family photos.

"Sylvester," Drea said as she pretended to examine a birdhouse. "The owner."

"How do you know his name?" I whispered.

"You seem to forget that I grew up here," she said, meaning the mall. "And you don't have to whisper because he can't hear us over the music."

After a few minutes of boisterous discussion, the three men in flannel departed with Wood World shopping bags. That left us alone with Sylvester, who hadn't gotten up from his stool. He hummed along with the John Denver song about country roads that was playing just a little too loud for anyone who wasn't already half deaf, whittling a block of wood with one of the hundreds of knives of varied sizes and sharpness that were available for purchase. If Sylvester hadn't so readily evoked the twinkly eyes, merry dimples, rosy cheeks, and cherry nose of the famous Christmas poem, I would've been terrified.

"So, what's our strategy?" I asked Drea.

Drea admired the smooth curves of a cutting board. "The truth."

"The truth? What do you mean the truth?"

"I mean, the truth," she said simply. "We tell him we want to pry up the floorboards behind the cash register because we're on a treasure hunt."

"Why would he let us tear his store apart?"

"He might not," Drea said. "But he is an elder. He deserves respect, not bullshit. Plus, he has been on this earth long enough to see right through any scam. So, let's just be direct. Unless . . ."

"Unless what?"

"Unless you had your heart set on *seducing* him," she said, wiggling her eyebrows. "But I have to warn you, he's been happily married for fifty-five years . . ."

I poked her with a salad spoon. She poked me right back with a fork. Our jousting got Sylvester's attention.

"Can I help you ladies with something?"

His voice was rich and warm and southern by way of the North Pole. It was sweet potato pie and gingerbread. Hummingbird cake and candy canes. Peach cobbler and eggnog.

"Hi, Sylvester," Drea began, "you don't know me but . . ."

Sylvester might have been half deaf, but he definitely wasn't blind. His eyes got even twinklier when Drea approached his stool.

"Now, you just stop right there, young lady. Of course I know you. You're Gia Bellarosa's girl."

"Drea." She extended a hand and fluttered her eyelashes girlishly.

"To what do I owe the pleasure of your visit? I got a feeling it got nothing to do with y'all taking up woodworking as a hobby."

Drea gave me a pointed look. *See? I told you he was no bull-shit.*

"Well, you see, Sylvester," Drea began, "my friend Cassie and I— Have you met Cassie?"

I stepped forward and extended my hand.

"How do you do?" I swear I nearly curtsied like a debutante at a cotillion.

"Pleased to make your acquaintance, Cassie," said Sylvester, giving my hand a shake.

"We're on a treasure hunt," said Drea.

Sylvester bent forward and stroked his beard.

"Go on," he said.

Then Drea went on to explain how we'd been going from doll to doll to doll, to clue to clue to clue, to store to store to store, until the latest doll and latest clue had led us here, to his store.

"We don't know what's at the end of it," she said. "I think there's fortune to be found. Cassie here"—she jerked her head in my direction—"doesn't think we'll find anything."

"Well, surely you must think there's something to be found," Sylvester said to me. "Otherwise why go on looking?"

"Because she makes me do it," I answered.

"Well, now," Sylvester said, setting his hands to rest on the curve of his stomach. "I don't believe that for a second."

Drea shot me another look. *Told ya. No bullshit.*

She spread the birth certificate on the counter, pushing aside a bowl of key rings carved into shapes of assorted beach creatures. A starfish. A dolphin. A seagull.

"Now, according to this map," she said, "the next clue is located . . ."

Sylvester went behind the register and stomped the floorboard twice with his boot.

"Right here."

"Yep," Drea said.

Sylvester stroked his beard and looked back and forth between us, like he was sizing us up. Then he let loose a laugh that came from way down in the deepest part of his belly.

"Ho! Ho! Ho!"

And, yes, it shook like a bowl full of jelly.

"Let's find some buried treasure!" he said joyfully.

Sylvester had all the right tools for prying up the floorboards with minimal damage. When a big enough gap was made in the planks, he shined a flashlight into the crawl space.

"Whoo-wee!" he whooped. "I'm rich!"

"I knew it!" Drea jumped up and down. "We're rich!"

"Oh, really?" Sylvester said. "Possession is nine-tenths of the law . . ."

Just when I thought we were about to get into a battle with Santa Claus over buried treasure, Sylvester hauled his discovery from the crawl space. And I swear, Sylvester was so pleased to bring this black-haired, brown-eyed boy into the world, you would've thought he was Xavier Roberts himself.

"Another clue!"

Okay. So I was little excited too. And that excitement quickly turned to annoyance when I attempted to read the birth certificate out loud.

"En Tat-wuss Yoo-gain?"

En Tatws Ugain was the funkiest name we'd come across so far.

"That's Welsh," Sylvester said, tapping on the box with a chisel.

"You speak Welsh?" Drea and I asked simultaneously.

"No."

Drea and I sagged together, both of us unreasonably let down by what would've been an unreasonable coincidence. Sylvester let our disappointment sink in for just a second or two more before giving us a mischievous grin.

"I don't speak Welsh," he said. "But my wife, Evelyn, does."

I swear to God, it couldn't have felt more magical, not even if he had put a finger to his nose and swooped up the nearest chimney.

19

SEALING THE DEAL

S ylvester couldn't reach Evelyn on the phone, so we'd have to wait at least another day for the next clue. This was fine by me because I'd had more than enough adventure for one Friday.

"How did you know that honesty was the best way to approach Sylvester?" I asked Drea as we stepped onto the escalator.

"If you sell to people long enough," she said, resting her chin atop the Cabbage Patch Kid box in her arms, "you figure out how to read them."

"Is that how you knew what dress to pick out for my mom?" I asked.

MEGAN McCAFFERTY

"Yep."

When she didn't elaborate, I decided I didn't want to hear any more about what Drea has seen in Kathy that translated to bedazzled bimbo dress.

"Isn't it weird that no one found these dolls before we did?" I asked. "I mean, you can't blame Sylvester for not looking under the floorboards, obviously. But, like, the ones that were barely hidden, or not hidden at all?"

"Nah, not really," Drea said. "People get into their routines. You go into work, do your thing, go home. Get up the next day and do it again."

We stepped around a janitor chiseling gum off the metal platform at the escalator's base. A sad, sad Scott Scanlon. The lowest of the low.

"Work is so depressing," I said. "I'm so glad I'm getting the hell out of here next month—"

And as soon as the words were out of my mouth, I wanted to suck them back in.

Drea slowly shook her head.

"Work *is* depressing," she said, "if you don't love what you do."

That was the first moment I truly envied Drea Bellarosa. She obviously loved what she did and was damn good at it too. Was there any greater joy? I had no clue what I loved to do. I'd joined Mock Trial and Odyssey of the Mind because they were the only extracurriculars available for ambitious kids at our sports-obsessed high school. There were usually two such achievers in every grade—maybe three in banner year—and these eight-to-ten freshmen through seniors met the minimum

136

requirement for fielding teams in competitions. Troy and I were the best and the brightest Pineville High had to offer. Our coupling was inevitable, because what other options did we have?

At least one, as it turned out.

At least one un-housebroken, crunchy-haired option.

"Isn't that Slade over there?" Drea asked.

All at once, I was reminded in the worst possible way that I'd had options too.

"Nonononono!"

The correct answer, obviously, was yes.

Four days had gone by since our disastrous hookup, but I hadn't gotten any closer to confronting him. Avoidance was far easier. So I leapt behind a marble column that served no structural purpose but met my need for hiding—and spying—quite nicely. If I peeked, I had a clear view of Slade leaning on the wall by the pay phone. He was plugged into his Walkman as if passing the time as he waited for a call. I'd bet our buried treasure he was listening to Bob Marley's *Legend*. Greatest hits reggae was so Slade. So cliché.

"Are you gonna rip him a new one or what?" Drea asked.

Drea went off on her enemies—I distinctly remember her announcing to a full cafeteria that a baseball player ex-boyfriend had a micropenis—but I wasn't ballsy like Drea. And I never would be.

"What's the point?" I replied. "It's Slade's word against mine. And it just gives the rumor new life. Besides, I'm out of here . . ."

"In thirty-five days," Drea said drily. "Yeah, I know . . ." Her attention returned to the pay phones. "Oh, look, he's got company."

It turned out that Slade wasn't waiting for a phone call.

"Zoe?"

"Do you know her?" Drea asked.

"Yes," I whispered, which was dumb because there was no way they could hear us at this distance. "I mean, no. Not really. She just kind of appears whenever I least expect it . . ."

I didn't get to review all the times Ghost Girl had entered and exited my life like an apparition because at that moment she was removing a small baggie from her cloak—really, whatever garment she had on could only be called a cloak—and pressing it into Slade's hand.

"It's a drug deal!" Drea gasped.

For once it was comforting to know that Drea was as scandalized as I was.

Transaction completed, they peeled off in opposite directions. Slade toward the bathrooms. Zoe toward the food court. Just before she rounded the corner and out of sight, she stopped. She then very purposefully turned and caught the two of us peeking out from behind the decorative marble column.

"Eeep!" I yelped.

"Eeep!" Drea yelped.

We ducked, but it was already too late. Ghost Girl gave us a wink so cartoonishly exaggerated, it could've been seen from whatever otherworldly dimension she hailed from.

20

DAMAGED GOODS

*g*ia was pissed at us for leaving her alone in the store for two hours, but was *less* pissed when we finally returned. Together.

"You two are lucky these clothes practically sell themselves," Gia said, as she straightened a row of fringed caftans. "By the way, I had a nice talk with your mother after you took off."

"You did?"

"Someone's gotta give her the lowdown on the local divorcée scene," Gia said. "I tell you, in that dress, your mother will be fighting them off left and right on Singles' Night at Oceanside Tavern . . ."

I winced so forcefully, the next thing I knew I was getting crushed in one of Gia's overempathetic hugs.

"Oh, I'm so sorry, hon," Gia said. "I forgot that this is still fresh to you. I know this is hard to believe right now, but I promise you'll all be better off . . ."

As Gia soothingly kneaded my shoulders, it suddenly struck me how maternal the gesture was, and yet not at all something Kathy would think to do for me herself.

I shook Gia off.

"I'll be fine," I said. "I'm out of here . . ."

Drea snorted just loud enough for me to avoid repeating myself.

In thirty-five days.

"Just try to be more supportive of your mother," Gia urged. "Take it from me, it's not easy starting over in your thirties."

"My mom is in her forties."

"Yikes." Now it was Gia's turn to wince.

"Well, maybe she should have thought about that before she and my dad decided not to be married anymore."

Gia opened her mouth, then snapped it shut. She had plenty more to say on the subject but understood I was in no condition to listen.

"There's a package on your desk," she said instead. "*Verrrry* special delivery."

I didn't think much of it, despite Gia's innuendo via inflection. I'd ordered some office supplies and assumed my delivery had arrived a little earlier than expected. Nothing major, just some floppy discs, printer paper, and other stuff that would be used by me for the next month and whoever took over the job after that.

I was wrong.

"What is it?" Drea asked, peeking over my shoulder.

It was a cassette tape.

Barbra Streisand.

The Broadway Album.

I ran my finger along the jagged edge of the case. A chunk of plastic was missing from the corner.

"What is it?" Drea persisted.

I opened it up and found a yellow Post-it note inside. In black ink, blocky handwriting, a message: DAMAGED GOODS. NOT FOR SALE.

"Go on," Gia urged.

"But . . ." I protested.

"You haven't worked all afternoon," Gia replied. "Why start now?"

"But . . ."

"But nothing! As your boss, I demand you go thank that cute boy immediately."

Cute? Was Sam Goody cute?

"Go!" shouted mother and daughter together.

———

So, I went to the music store. Sam Goody didn't notice me right away because he was busy with an aging hippie. I had to get within a foot or two to eavesdrop over the hair band blasting out of the speakers.

"Finally found the love of a lifetiiiiiiiiiime . . ."

This was a song written expressly for senior prom slow

dancing if I had ever heard one. It was even worse than Michael friggin' Bolton. Seriously, I didn't know how Sam Goody endured this daily attack on his senses and musical sensibilities.

"Compact discs have superior sound quality," Sam Goody was saying. "They absolutely will not be replaced by any new form of musical technology any time soon."

"Yeah, yeah," griped the customer. "That's what they said about eight-tracks."

Sam Goody nodded grimly in agreement.

"You know what? You're right. There's always going to be something newer and better to replace what you've already got."

"If it's all the same to you," said the curmudgeon as he shuffled toward the exit, "I'll stick with vinyl."

"What's your opinion on cassettes?" I asked, holding up the cracked case of *The Broadway Album*.

Sam Goody spun around.

"Oh! Bellarosa! Hey! Um. Hi!"

His cheeks flushed with surprise. Gia was right. Sam Goody was cute. And catching him so flustered like this only made him more so.

"*The Broadway Album* is now the least terrible of all musical options when my mom drives me to work every day."

"Aha!" Sam Goody shook both hands through his hair. "Barbra was for your *mom*. That makes so much sense. I was wondering how *The Broadway Album* fit in with Morrissey, 10,000 Maniacs, R. E. M., Indigo Girls . . ."

Aha indeed. It hadn't ended with "Viva Hate." Sam Goody *had* been paying attention to all my T-shirts. Which meant Sam Goody had been paying attention to *me*. He immediately realized how creepy this confession could come across.

"I'm not stalking you or anything! Nine hundred thousand square feet sounds like a lot of space, but it's really hard not to see the same people who work here every day."

Yet I hadn't seen Sam Goody nearly as often as he'd apparently seen me.

"I didn't see you," I replied truthfully. "Until you tripped me at the bookstore."

This made him smile, which made me smile. My parents would've recommended refitting a new retainer, but I liked his mouth just the way it was when it wasn't smirking.

"*You* tripped over me," he said, folding his arms across his chest.

"As Barbra sings on *The Broadway Album*: Po-tay-to, po-tah-to, to-may-to, to-mah-to . . ."

Barbra didn't actually sing those lines on *The Broadway Album*. But I doubted Sam Goody's musical knowledge had that kind of reach.

"I feel bad about how I acted," he said, "you know, the first time we met."

There was just enough hesitancy in his voice for me to know he was telling the truth.

"I'm listening," I said.

"I was having a bad day—a year's worth of bad days, really—and

I decided to take it out on you for some reason. And for that, I'm sorry."

Earlier in the summer, I wouldn't have accepted this excuse for dickish behavior. But I'd had more bad days than good lately. I knew I wouldn't want to be judged by my tray-flinging anger at Troy, my short-and-sick attraction to Slade, or any of the other lows vying for the honor of my sad, sad, Scott Scanlon moment of the summer.

"I—"

"Hold that thought," Sam Goody said.

He needed to help a baffled old lady wandering up and down the Rap/R&B aisle. But I wasn't annoyed by the interruption. For the next five minutes, I watched Sam patiently explain the difference between Prince and the Fresh Prince to this well-intentioned granny who wanted nothing more than to buy the perfect gift for her grandson's birthday. I actually admired how Sam Goody took his job seriously enough to stop socializing and actually do what he got paid to do. Only then did I realize that my lunch break from Bellarosa was well into its third hour. I was bordering on unacceptable No-Good Crystal-level slackery, and I needed to get back to work pronto.

"You've probably seen him on TV," Sam Goody was saying. "*The Fresh Prince of Bel-Air* . . . ?"

"I watch Lawrence Welk on PBS," Granny replied. "Now that's a talent!"

I walked directly in his line of sight and waved goodbye. Sam Goody returned the gesture with an apologetic shrug.

"To be continued," he said, though I had to read his

lips because yet another monster ballad had reached its ear-shattering crescendo.

He knew he'd see me around again, as he'd already been seeing me around so far this summer.

And now that I knew who to look out for, maybe I'd see him around too.

21

RADIOACTIVE

The Broadway Album turned out to be a *double* peace offering. From Sam Goody to me, and from me to my mother. I offered it along with an apology for freaking out on her in Bellarosa.

"Oh, Cassandra!" Mom gushed. "I knew I could depend on you!" Then, after a beat, "Why is the case broken?"

I had insisted we listen to it immediately, you know, to make sure Barbra still played just fine and also to avoid talking about bimbo dresses and Singles' Nights at Oceanside Tavern. We were so unused to speaking one-on-one, and yet I knew when Kathy was girding herself to bring up awkward subjects. I could *see* it—she'd take a breath and square her shoulders and . . . That's when I'd cut her off with an observation about Barbra's impeccable phrasing or Sondheim's lyrical genius. I knew this strategy wouldn't last indefinitely, but it had succeeded in getting me through the weekend and the drive to work.

For his role in this tenuous peace with my mother, I thought Sam Goody deserved a genuine thank-you. Though I had gone to the store with that in mind, I'd never actually uttered the words.

Besides, our last two conversations had not been unpleasant.

Also, I was curious to hear more about what had happened at Wharton.

And how he ended up working at the mall.

And what his next plan would be.

And if there was "life beyond the Ivy League."

For all these reasons, I should've swung by the music store on the way to work. But I didn't. And I'd barely crossed Bellarosa's threshold when Drea hijacked the rest of my day.

"Cassie! Did you get my messages? Why didn't you call back? Do you *want* me to drown you in the Wishing Well?!"

I'd gotten her messages, proving there was no shortage of creative and extremely specific ways to be killed for the crime of ignoring Drea Bellarosa when she had major news. I had the weekend off from Bellarosa, but that hadn't stopped her from leaving a series of increasingly dramatic messages on my answering machine.

"Cassie. This is Drea. I've got news! Why aren't you picking up? I'm gonna be super pissed if you don't pick up. Pick up!"

Her threats got more violent and well detailed with every call back.

"Cassie. This is Drea. If you don't call back, I'll strangle you with a scrunchie!"

"Cassie. This is Drea. If you don't call back, I'll bludgeon you with a thousand-page book on Greek astrology!"

"Cassie. This is Drea. If you don't call back, I'll slash your throat with a Marky Mark and the Funky Bunch CD and make it look like a suicide and everyone will think you did it because you felt so guilty for making fun of me for liking 'Good Vibrations' when you were hiding your secret forbidden love for the lesser Wahlberg brother the whole friggin' time!"

The abuse came to an end only because the tape ran out before she did. So I shouldn't have been at all surprised when she pounced on me Monday morning.

"Seriously, Cassie! Why didn't you call me back?"

"I didn't call you back," I replied calmly, switching on the computer, "because I spent the weekend helping my father set up his new bachelor pad."

When I wasn't avoiding conversation with my mother at home, I was avoiding conversation with my father in his condo. I got seriously nostalgic for the days when I was medically prohibited from talking.

"Ouch," Drea replied. "I'm sorry. That sounds awkward as hell."

Yeah, it was. His marriage of twenty-one years was over, and yet Frank couldn't stop asking about America's Best Cookie.

"Wait," Frank had said as we tore the plastic covering off the mattress he'd bought for the "second bedroom," which he had gone out of his way not to call the "guest bedroom" because I was his *daughter*, not his *guest*. "You're *not* in the seasonal management training program?"

That succinctly summed up the shitty weekend that had left me too emotionally drained to respond to Drea's messages when I got home last night.

"So, what was so important?"

I surveyed the Cabbage Patch Dolls on the couch. Two boys, two girls, one preemie. No new additions, so I assumed she hadn't gotten the next clue from Sylvester.

"Slade Johnson was in the hospital!"

"Oh my God. Is he okay? What happened to him?"

My concern took Drea by surprise. Maybe it's because I'd recently been rushed to the hospital myself, but I felt more sympathetic toward Slade than he probably deserved.

"You really haven't heard?"

I shook my head. And I could tell from Drea's rapturous expression that this story was just getting started and my misplaced sympathy would sort itself out soon enough.

"He's got hypercarotenosis!"

Drea barely gave me enough time to recall the AP Bio definition.

"He OD'd on Brazilian tanning pills and turned orange!"

Yep, that's what I thought it meant: a temporary change in skin tone caused by excessive levels of beta-carotene, the photosynthetic pigment that gives carrots their color. And, apparently, egomaniacal tanning addicts who think if a daily dose is good, then a *dozen* doses in a single day is even better.

"It's been three days, and he still looks like a radioactive Oompa Loompa!"

Then Drea lost all composure and started hawnking her ass off. I found Slade's predicament a lot less funny than she did.

"Why aren't you laughing?" she said breathlessly. "Can you think of a better punishment for such a narcissistic prick?"

No. I couldn't. And that's exactly why I wasn't laughing. It was a little too perfect for comfort. What had Zoe said when she snuck up on me in B. Dalton?

He will pay.

Did she do this to him?

Drea addressed the concerns written all over my face.

"If you're worried about this getting back to Ghost Girl, you can relax," Drea said. "Slade is already on probation for under-age drinking. He can't tell the cops he bought a batch of sketchy drugs or he'd get in as much trouble as she would."

I doubted the "Brazilian tanning pills" were even illegal. More likely, they were over-the-counter megavitamins from General Nutrition Center, making this the perfect *not* crime. I just didn't understand why Zoe would go out of her way to exact revenge on my behalf. She barely even knew me. But I had no time to consider her motivation because Gia poked her head into the back office.

"I hate to interrupt all your *hard work*," she said with sarcastic emphasis, "but you have a visitor out front."

"Who is it?" I asked.

"See for yourself," Gia replied.

Sylvester stood under the crystal chandelier, studying a display of silk scarves as intently as I imagined he'd inspect the grain in a plank of purpleheart. In his coveralls and flannel, he could not have looked more out of place amid Bellarosa's bedazzlery. And yet, he didn't look the slightest bit unnerved by the confused looks he was getting from boutique regulars.

"When you didn't come back to the shop, I thought I'd come to you," Sylvester said, holly jolly as ever. "I hope you don't mind."

"Of course we don't mind!" Drea said. "What have you got for us? What's the next clue?"

Sylvester looked at me. "Is she always such a straight shooter?"

I nodded.

"I like that in a woman." Then he ho-ho-hoed.

"Let's get right to it," Sylvester said. "En Tatws Ugain means—" He paused just long enough to build suspense but in a charming way that didn't feel like he was holding the information hostage. "One Potato Twenty."

"One Potato Twenty?" Drea asked. "What the hell is that?"

I also had never heard of anything called One Potato Twenty.

"That was the baked potato place," Gia replied as she passed by with an array of statement necklaces looped over her arm. "It offered twenty different toppings. Bacon, sour cream, chili, cheese . . ."

"That's right," Sylvester confirmed. "Closed up a few years back."

"So One Potato Twenty isn't around anymore," I clarified. "Where was it located? Do you remember?"

"Of course I remember," Sylvester said good-naturedly.

And before he even spoke, I had the answer to my own question:

"America's Best Cookie."

22

STRUTTERS

The Silver Strutters were putting on one hell of a show.

"Just look at those jazz squares," I observed. "They must have gotten a new choreographer."

"Stop stalling," Drea said.

"Same old Glenn Miller big band songs, though. They could really use a new musical director if they want to maintain their status as Ocean County's premiere senior citizen aerobic dance troupe . . ."

"Stop stalling."

Then she nudged me in the general direction of America's Best Cookie.

"Check one more time to make sure she's really alone," I said.

"Fine," Drea agreed huffily.

Conundrum: I couldn't get close enough to see who was working this shift without also getting close enough to be spotted by whoever was working this shift. Best case? Zoe was working alone. All other scenarios involved Troy or Helen or both and were automatically worst cases.

Drea came back from her reconnaissance flashing two thumbs up.

"Why are you making me do this?" I asked.

"You have a connection with Ghost Girl, not me," she said. "She can give us the lowdown on Slade and help us with the next clue."

"What makes you think she'll tell me the truth about whatever she gave him?"

"The wink." Drea used every muscle in her face to close her left eye, looking almost as ridiculous as Zoe had when she'd done the same. "She *wanted* you to know."

Okay. There was no denying the wink. But I had one last line of defense.

"America's Best Cookie totally renovated the potato place, so I highly doubt the next doll is even there anymore."

"Maybe," Drea conceded. "But we won't know unless we try, right?"

"Unless *I* try."

"Exactly." Drea gave me a firmer push. "Now go!"

The Silver Strutters were marching in a V-formation now, waving American flags to the beat of "The Battle Hymn of the Republic."

Glory! Glory! Hallelujah!

For these World War II vets, Fourth of July wasn't simply a date on the calendar, it was a patriotic state of mind that lasted all month long. I tried to find inspiration in the music, girding myself like a soldier about to enter a war zone. Because despite Drea's promise—that Zoe was by herself at America's Best Cookie—this summer had taught me to expect the worst case even when the best case was supposed to be a guarantee.

I rounded the corner and learned that lesson in real time.

"Cassandra!"

Troy.

Friggin'.

Troy.

And nothing but open, empty space between us. Where was a crowd of pink tracksuits and little girls on leashes when I needed it?

"Cassandra!"

He was waving his arms in the air now, like a Silver Strutter without a flag. There was no way I could pretend I didn't see and hear him calling for my attention. If Zoe had been there thirty seconds ago, she wasn't there now. On the upside, Helen wasn't there either. I turned back to where Drea stood and flipped her the bird.

Glory! Glory! Hallelujah!

My truth was marching on.

"Cassandra!" Troy said warmly.

"Troy," I said coolly.

"You look great," he said.

He looked exactly the same.

"I mean, you look healthy. That's what I mean. I mean, you don't look sick anymore. I mean . . ." He grabbed a Chocolate Chipper with a sleeve of wax paper. "Want a cookie?"

Troy was nervous. And his nervousness gave me confidence to admit that my ex actually looked worse than I remembered. The American flag apron tied unflatteringly high on his waist, giving him an hourglass shape that did not do any favors for his masculinity.

"No, thanks," I said. "And I feel great. Better than ever . . ."

"I heard about you and Slade," Troy said quickly.

Aha. Here it comes, I thought. *The humiliation.*

"Are you two still together?" His full cheeks flushed redder than communism itself. "I mean, are you still hooking up?"

It suddenly struck me: Troy didn't care if I'd botched Slade's blowjob. Good or bad, the quality didn't matter. It only mattered that he thoroughly believed I'd gotten more intimate with Slade in one night than I'd ever gotten with him in two years.

Only it wasn't true.

I turned the question back on him.

"Are you still hooking up with . . . ?"

I stopped short of saying Helen's name out loud, as if it were an evil incantation that would make her materialize from thin air.

"Her?" Troy also seemed reluctant to invoke her name. "No. That's over."

I wasn't at all shocked by the breakup itself. I was surprised by how little I cared. Shouldn't I have been more emotionally invested in my ex's relationships? But short of her threats to my own health and well-being, Helen meant absolutely nothing to me. And Troy just an infinitesimal smidge more than that. My indifference felt, well, a little messed up. Was something fundamentally wrong with me? Had I inherited my drastic romantic detachment from my equally messed-up parents?

"She's not working here anymore either. She got a job on Casino Pier," Troy continued. "I know it's late in the season, and we're leaving for New York in a few weeks . . ."

"*I'm* leaving for New York in thirty-two days."

Troy had lost the privilege of using the collective pronoun "we." My correction was totally lost on him, though.

"Right. Orientation starts August twenty-third. But if you're still looking for a job . . ."

His presumptuousness on all levels was almost too much for me to take.

"Why would I work here for minimum wage when I'm making twice that much doing the books for Bellarosa Boutique?"

Okay, I was exaggerating the paycheck to make my point. But Troy didn't focus on the money.

"You've been working at the mall since we broke up?" He blinked with incredulity. "Why haven't I seen you?"

You haven't seen me because I've been actively hiding.

"I've been busy," I replied. "Living my life."

"Oh." Troy fiddled with his apron strings. "Oh."

I caught movement out of the corner of my eye. Drea was tapping an imaginary watch on her wrist.

"Where's Zoe? I need to talk to her about something."

"Ms. Gomez just stepped out," he said. "Can I help you?"

"I seriously doubt it," I replied.

"Are you sure I can't help you?" he asked. "I know everything she knows. I've been trained as a seasonal assistant manager . . ."

I couldn't stop myself from laughing at this. My imaginary management training program was real. Frank had a legit reason to be disappointed in me after all.

Troy misinterpreted my levity. When he reached for my hand, I snatched it away.

"Does America's Best Cookie still have a walk-in freezer?" I asked.

"It's not really large enough to be a walk-in freezer," Troy answered, "it's more of a stand-in freezer . . ."

"Oh my God! I don't care!" Channeling Drea, I had an acute appreciation for how annoying such superfluous attention to detail could be at the wrong moment. "Do you know if anyone has ever found a doll in the freezer?"

"A . . ." Troy stroked his hairless chin, the way he often did when he collected his thoughts during cross-examination. "Doll?"

"You heard me," I said. "A doll. Has anyone ever found a doll in the freezer. Specifically, a Cabbage Patch Kid."

Troy gave his head a single shake.

"That would be a violation of America's Best Cookie policy," he said. "Freezers are for the purpose of storing America's Best Cookie ingredients only. I'm not allowed to put my *lunch* in there. I can't even imagine what would possess anyone to put a *doll* in there. Why are you asking me such a crazy question?"

On its surface, this was a crazy question. And now that I had kind of involved Troy, it wasn't unreasonable for him to want an answer.

But that didn't mean he deserved one.

"Ugh," I said. "I knew you'd be no help to me."

I turned and put a little extra oomph into my walk—a bit of Bellarosa bounce—knowing full well that Troy was watching me every strutting step of the way.

23

LOW-LEVEL ANARCHY

I strutted all the way to Sam Goody.

And I kept right on strutting up and down the aisles until I finally found him crouched in front of the magazine rack. When I gently tapped him on the shoulder, he sprang backward in a scrambled panic.

"Whew!" he said. "I thought you were my boss."

"Nope," I said. "It's me."

He nodded approvingly at the image of the soldier on my chest.

"Meat Is Murder."

This was arguably The Smiths' most iconic album cover. It

had been proven that Sam Goody was paying attention to my T-shirts. So I had started paying even *more* attention to my T-shirts. But I couldn't let him know that. Instead, I pinched the collar and made a bored face like, *Oh, this old thing?*

"Why are you avoiding the boss?" I asked.

He handed over a stack of zines with titles like *Artificial Insanity, Gray Matter,* and *The Happy Thrasher.* Xeroxed on cheap paper and barely held together with staples, the black-and-white photos and typefaces had gotten fuzzy and fuzzier with every sloppy photocopy and recopy.

"Did you make these?"

"No," he replied. "I'm just a distributor."

He stuck a zine with a bloody cartoon gargoyle on the cover between copies of *Rolling Stone* boasting a geezer rocker wrapped in a leggy supermodel wife half his age. The demon was less grotesque.

"You're rebelling against your corporate overlords by sticking subversive reading material among the glossies?"

Sam arched a mischievous eyebrow. "Wanna help?"

"Of course!"

I stood lookout while Sam shuffled the magazines around on the racks. *Grammar Police*—featuring a doctored cover photo of First Lady Barbara Bush flipping the bird—caught my eye. I skimmed an article about the worst words.

"Says here 'panties' tops the list."

"Really?" Sam asked. "What do people have against 'panties'?"

"It's just a word that makes people feel icky when they say it," I said. "Here's another. Get ready for it. Are you ready?"

"Am I ready?" Sam shook out his arms and legs, jumped up and down, smacked himself in the head a few times, and whooped. "I am ready!"

I took a step toward him, cupped my hand to his ear, and channeled Zoe's creepy, creaky whisper.

"Mooooooiiiiiiiiiiiisssssst."

Sam shivered. I threw back my head and cackled. In that moment, I reminded myself of Drea.

"Moist Panties would make a great band name," Sam joked.

"I loved their debut single." I consulted the worst words list and put two of the grossest together. "'Fetal Smear.'"

Sam grimaced, then grinned.

"Hmmm . . ." He tapped a finger to his temple. "I don't know that one. How does it go?"

I batted my eyelashes in a most sarcastically flirtatious manner.

"Oh no, darlin'," I demurred in a fake southern drawl. "Ah couldn't possibly."

Sam clasped his hands and got down on the floor.

"Pleeeeaase," he begged. "I must hear 'Fetal Smear' by Moist Panties."

"Okay," I said, barely containing how thrilled I was to have brought this boy to his knees. "If you insist."

I closed my eyes and started bobbing my head to the booming drumbeat in my head.

"Fetal Smear!" I shout-sang. "Clogged Slacks!"

I was loud, but not loud enough for anyone but Sam Goody to hear me over the classic rock blasting from the sound system.

"Curdle Slurp! Bulbous Maggots!"

I pogoed up and down.

"Queasy Phlegm! Chunky Roaches!"

The heinous word pairings flowed one into the next, like the best poetry should. The song ended with one last bit of thrashing and a final, primal scream.

"Munch! Munch! Muuuuuuunch!"

I threw my body into a nearby clearance rack, a mosh pit for one causing a tiny avalanche of half-priced cassingles. It was very punk rock. And yet, no one but Sam Goody even noticed.

"That was incredible," he said, applauding. "I'm officially Moist Panties' number-one fan."

I couldn't remember the last time I'd exerted myself like that. But I felt more exhilarated than exhausted.

"Too bad they broke up," I said breathlessly. "Creative differences."

This made Sam Goody laugh so hard, his glasses fell right off his face.

"So," he said.

"So," I said.

I had no idea what to say next. I mean, how do you follow up an act like that?

"Why are you here?" he asked.

It was a good question. This was the first time I'd dropped by the store without a specific purpose other than wanting to see him again. But I couldn't come right out and say that, could I?

"Why am I here?" I mused. "Why are you here? Why are any of us here?"

Sam Goody smiled but didn't take the pseudo-philosophical bait.

"Well, whatever the reason," he said, "I'm glad we're here together."

And for the very first time all summer, the mall was exactly where I wanted to be.

24

MASTER MULTITASKER

*D*rea and I were stuck.

Literally and figuratively stuck.

It had been two weeks since making the connection between One Potato Twenty and ABC and we weren't any closer to getting the next clue. This was the treasure hunt's biggest setback by far. I didn't see how we could possibly continue, but she refused to officially call off our quest. Drea's unrelenting determination led us to the Cabbage Patch catacombs before breakfast.

"We are so close!" she insisted. "I can feel it!"

All I felt was glued to the floor. My loafers and Drea's stilettos were equally ill-equipped to navigate the gummy, scummy linoleum. Moist sucking sounds followed us with every step, a nauseating noise I hadn't noticed over the blare of Vanilla Ice the last time I was down here. And had it reeked so strongly of stale beer and body odor?

"Let's get some lights on down here," Drea said.

She hit the switch. Full fluorescent illumination did not do the Cabbage Patch any architectural or aesthetic favors.

"Ewwww."

Drea took a wide berth around the couch of dubious hygiene. Each cushion showcased a different stomach-turning mosaic of smudges, smears, and stains. I took small comfort in knowing there was no way Troy or his ex had come away from their dry hump without contracting a highly contagious and possibly leprotic disease.

"Let's get in and out of here as quickly as possible," I urged. "I don't want to be the first virgin in history to get a contact STD."

Drea ignored my joke and marched to the storage room as briskly as possible under these sticky conditions. She pushed open the door, and despite knowing what to expect, the sight of row upon row of Vince and Tommy's unadopted Cabbage Patch Kids still struck me as strange and almost unbearably sad. Fortunately, Drea didn't give me any time to wallow.

"We need to open *every* box and check *every* birth certificate," Drea instructed. "There might be another map hidden in here . . ."

I thought her obsession with the treasure hunt had gone too far. But joining Drea down here this one time was a fair exchange for her driving me to work every day for the rest of the summer. I'd do just about anything to avoid spending any more time around Kathy, who had recently taken to reading books with titles like, *Hotter Than Ever: Satisfying Sex You Deserve After Divorce.*

I grabbed the first box (Prentiss Charlemagne) and dug my fingers into the top.

"No!"

Drea slapped my hand away.

"Ouch!"

"You need to open it *carefully*," she said. "We don't want anyone to notice that these dolls have been disturbed in any way. We don't want to draw any attention to ourselves. We don't want anyone getting suspicious . . ."

I was starting to wonder how I'd know if Drea had reached the paranoid point of no return. Then she reached into her bra and removed a knife.

"Whoaaaa!"

"Don't be so dramatic," said Drea. "It's a *letter opener.*"

It was a letter opener that looked *exactly* like a knife. She used it to cleanly slice through the seam on the top of a box belonging to a girl named Rhonda Bess.

"Voila!"

Then Drea reached into her bra to remove a *second* letter opener that also looked exactly like a knife.

"For you."

"What *else* you got in there?" I said through a burst of laughter. "Please tell me it's breakfast."

"You gotta earn your breakfast," she said. "Let's get to these birth certificates."

She removed the pink envelope from Rhonda Bess's box. It looked legit from what I remembered from my own doll's documentation, but Drea wouldn't take my word for it. I swear she muttered a prayer as she cautiously ran the letter opener along the envelope and plucked out the paper inside.

"Gawddammit!"

"No map?"

She didn't acknowledge my dumb question, choosing instead to return to the task at hand.

"Come on!" she commanded. "Your turn!"

I opened the box, copying Drea's precision. The result was the same.

"No map," I replied, holding up Prentiss Charlemagne's birth certificate for her to see.

"Two down," she said. "One hundred and eighteen to go. Between us both, I figure we can open and close two boxes a minute . . ."

"You're *serious* about this?"

Drea plunged the dagger into Orville Toby's lid. She was serious about this. So serious that she blew off all attempts at conversation.

"So, you know how I've been talking to that guy at the record store, right? The one you called Elvis but really looks more like Morrissey?"

"The Chinese guy?"

"Japanese American, actually."

Drea opened another birth certificate and groaned. No map.

"When I first met him, I thought he was one of those bitter genius types. You know, one of those slackers who's naturally gifted and probably did really well on an IQ test in kindergarten, but he never applied himself in school because he was too cool or whatever. And now he's pissed because he's working at the mall and maybe taking classes at community college, which wouldn't be so bad if he didn't have, like, this raging superiority complex . . ."

Drea grunted as she pulled another box off the shelf. Inside was a yellow-haired girl whose name I couldn't read from where I stood.

"Anyway, that's who I *thought* he was. But he's not that guy at all. We've only talked for, like, five minutes at a time so it's not like we were plumbing the depths of each other's soul or anything . . ."

In fact, we hadn't even exchanged our real names. This was fine by me because we'd have no reason to keep in touch when I left for New York City in eighteen days. And yet, what I *had* learned about Sam Goody made me curious to know more. How did he find the courage to drop out of business school when I couldn't bring myself to tell Frank and Kathy I'd gotten fired from the friggin' food court?

"I never thought I'd admire someone for dropping out, but . . ."

"Cassie!" Drea rattled the box so hard, ribbons shook loose from the doll's pigtails. "I'm not listening!"

Drea's lack of interest was disappointing. Worse, her dismissal made me feel silly for wanting to discuss these latest developments in the first place. And the more I thought about it—and I had plenty of time to think about it as I monotonously opened and closed box after box and box—she was right. This wasn't hot gossip. Sam and I weren't hooking up—we were barely even friends. We were two fans of Morrissey and low-level anarchy who'd spoken for a grand total of maybe an hour over two weeks.

And yet . . .

I kept going back every day. I didn't want to spend my breaks with anyone else. Then again, there weren't any better options within 900,000 square feet to choose from. Was I drawn to Sam Goody for who he was? Or for who he *wasn't*?

"Can we at least put on some music or something?" I asked. "I'm pretty sure I saw a boom box back there."

"What about not attracting any attention don't you understand? If someone finds us down here, they could snatch the treasure right out from under us."

"That can only happen if we find the next clue . . ."

"Exactly!" Drea tapped her letter opener twice against my temple. Not so hard it hurt, but just enough to make a point. "Now get to work!"

I didn't understand why Drea was so fixated on this quest. I saw the numbers: Drea wasn't hurting for cash. Her weekly earnings tripled mine and not for nepotistic reasons either. Her mother had an uncanny knack for choosing inventory— the store turned a profit because it never had too little or too much merchandise—but it was still up to Drea to sell it. And she earned an impressive commission doing just that.

With that money, Drea invested in an endless wardrobe,

an unrivaled collection of makeup and hair products, and standing appointments for tanning, highlights, and manicures at Casino Full Service Beauty Salon. Since sophomore year, she'd been living rent-free in what was essentially her own apartment—with its own separate side entrance—on the ground floor of Gia's three-story bayfront condo. Within days of getting her license, she was screeching through the Pineville High parking lot, gleefully terrorizing pedestrians in a shiny Mazda Miata.

I had to admit, when she picked me up in her cherry-red convertible that morning—top up because the wind would wreck her hair—I felt all caught up on the summer I missed out on because of mono. I finally got my *90210* moment, albeit an unaired episode in which rad Dylan McKay takes pity on sad, sad Scott Scanlon and takes him for a spin. But unlike those Beverly Hills brats, Drea wasn't spoiled. I knew for a fact that she had started saving for that car when she was ten years old. What other fifth-grade girl taped a poster of a red convertible above her bed?

"Putting it near my pillow makes dreams come true," she had explained.

"Because that's where you sleep?"

She smiled, showing off several thousand dollars' worth of Worthy Orthodontia.

"I knew you'd get it."

Inspired by that conversation, I hung my NYC subway map in the same prime spot, where it had remained to that very day. Drea, on the other hand, kept new dreams coming. The summer before sixth grade, she replaced the convertible with a color newspaper photo of a wunderkind in short shorts who'd shocked the world at Wimbledon.

"Boris Becker?" I asked. "You don't even like tennis."

"I like *him*."

It was the first time I'd seen Drea go all googly-eyed over a guy. At seventeen, he was the youngest male singles player to win that or any other Grand Slam tournament. Boris was replaced by New Jersey's second most famous rocker, Jon Bon Jovi. After JBJ came Kirk Cameron and a string of even more forgettable boys from even worse sitcoms, followed by whoever happened to be *BOP* magazine's Hunk of the Month. I don't know who she traded up for after the Coreys because that's when I stopped being invited over to her house.

I was still contemplating all this two tedious hours later. Only after every box had been opened and all 120 birth certificates verified did Drea finally speak.

"This blows."

No maps. No clue. No treasure.

"Are you ready to call it off?" I asked.

"No."

"Why do you need this money?" I asked.

Drea cracked her gum. "Who doesn't want money?"

Money was never that important to me. This was the privilege of always growing up with just enough—but not too much—of it. New York City was home to some of the worst rich people on the planet. And yet, with a few thousand dollars, I could live large in ways otherwise unaffordable to a college student on the budget. Like taking a cab downtown instead of the 1 train. Or seeing Broadway shows that were still too popular for half-priced matinees. Maybe even renting an apartment near campus next summer, getting an unpaid internship at Columbia Presbyterian Hospital, and never going back to work at the mall. But it hardly seemed worth even fantasizing about a treasure I didn't believe in.

But Drea very clearly did.

"You must have big plans for the money," I insisted, "or the treasure hunt wouldn't matter so much to you."

Another spearmint snap. I'd struck a nerve.

"You dragged me into this," I said. "The least you can do is tell me why."

Drea nervously drummed her fingernails on a shelf. The *ping-ping-ping* of acrylics on metal was the only sound.

"The witch knows more than she's letting on. She's avoiding us."

Just like you're avoiding the truth about the treasure hunt, I thought.

"Zoe's probably avoiding arrest," I replied instead.

After running into Zoe at seemingly every turn, she had all but vanished from the mall recently.

"If I were her, I'd want full credit," Drea said.

Zoe's role in Slade Johnson's hospitalization was purely speculative on our part. Without a confession from the man himself, there wasn't any proof that she had anything to do with it. Physically, Slade was fine. He was never at risk of dying from too much beta-carotene—only embarrassment. After calling out sick for two weeks, he grudgingly returned to work with a complexion best described as "Dorito dust."

"Speaking of orange," Drea said, hooking her arm through

mine and leading me toward the exit. "You should swing by Orange Julius on your break. Buy one for Sam Goody. Surprise him at work . . ."

"Waaaaaait!" Now I was the one shaking Drea's shoulders. "I thought you weren't listening to me!"

"Of course I was listening to you," Drea replied. "Bellarosas are master multitaskers."

"Then why couldn't we talk about him *and* hunt treasure?" I asked. "Why did we work in silence?"

"Because *I* am a master multitasker," Drea said, stepping into the elevator. "You are not."

Was Drea being insulting? Or insightful?

I was so stymied by the question that I barely got inside the elevator before the doors shut on me.

25

ROMANTIC AND TRAGIC

*B*ellarosa Boutique was busier than ever in the weeks leading up to the Back-to-School Fashion Show. This was the mall's biggest event of the summer and a very lucrative day for the store. I thought Bellarosa's participation was kind of ridiculous, though. The boutique was a popular destination for homecoming dresses and prom gowns, but Drea was the only girl at Pineville High who'd actually worn its clothes to school. That she was voted Best Dressed in a landslide only reinforced how Bellarosa's aesthetic was far more aspirational than practical.

Running the Back-to-School Fashion Show was a huge

174

deal. Gia had to find models who'd walk the runway for free—mostly from the deep pool of Bellarosa cousins, but still, a time-consuming job—pull, style, and make alterations to their looks; choose the music; massage egos ("I'm not trying to make you look uglier than your sister, so put on those jodhpurs and shut your gawddamn mouth!"); and do it all in six-inch stilettos. While Gia focused on these logistics, Drea covered the appointment-only fittings and pop-in business from regulars. As hectic as it got, I never imagined I'd be of any use outside the back office until Gia commanded me to action.

"Cassie! I need you on the floor right now!"

"Me?"

"Yeah, you," Gia said, taking me by the arm. "By special request."

"Special request? Who would special request me? I'm not even a salesgirl."

"This gentleman thinks you are," Gia replied, dragging me away from the computer.

From the tiniest seed of desire, hope half bloomed in my heart. Sam Goody?

"Cassandra!"

All hope shriveled in my chest. I was humiliated by my own imagination.

"Frank."

My father was wearing his typical off-duty attire: plaid shorts and a golf shirt with an embroidered tooth where a Polo pony would normally be. I hadn't seen him in a few weeks. What was he doing here?

"Shouldn't you be at work right now?" I asked.

"My eleven o'clock canceled," he said. "Which gave me the perfect opportunity to slip out to go shopping."

Oh, no no no. I was not getting involved with building another parent's post-divorce wardrobe. No way would I help him select a blazer for Singles' Night at Oceanside Tavern. Frank was on his own for this one.

"I recommend Chess King, conveniently located right across the Concourse," I said. "Or there's always the International Male Catalog . . ."

Frank chuckled.

"I'm not here for me, kiddo." He knuckled my scalp. "I want to get something for your mother."

"For Mom?! Why?"

Honestly, if he were here to get sized for a leather Speedo, I would've been less shocked.

"Well, she was just saying the other day how much she liked Bellarosa's selection and service," he said. "And you get a ten-percent commission on everything you sell, right? So I'd be helping you out too . . ."

I cut him off before he could continue.

"First of all, I'm not a salesgirl, I manage the books," I explained. "Second of all, you and Mom are getting a divorce."

"So?"

"So? You shouldn't be buying her gifts!"

Frank sighed.

"It's her birthday."

I hadn't spoken to Kathy much lately either. We still lived together, but I'd done a bang-up job at avoiding her too—the result of all the practice I'd gotten at the mall this summer. So I'd not only forgotten it was her birthday, but adeptly dodged any hints she might have dropped to remind me. How old was she . . . forty-three? Forty-four?

"She's forty-five years young," Dad answered without me having to ask.

"So what if it's her birthday? If you still care enough to remember her birthday, you shouldn't have moved out."

I knew I sounded like a brat.

And I absolutely did not care.

"It's not that simple, Cassandra," Frank said. "We've known each other for twenty-five years. I'm never going to forget that August eighth is your mother's birthday."

That struck me as simultaneously romantic and tragic.

"We're ending our marriage, but she's still a part of my life," he said. "And remember, I still work with her every day . . ."

"Which is also not normal!"

I knew better to even attempt keeping my job at America's Best Cookie after Troy and I split up. Then again, I could only assume my mom wasn't dry humping any of the dental assistants right in front of my dad. Or vice versa.

Drea emerged from the fitting rooms.

"Oh hi, Dr. Worthy." Drea flashed her biggest smile. "Is everything okay here?"

"Drea! I am so pleased to see that you've obviously maintained an optimal dental care routine!"

"I floss after every meal," she boasted. "And brush for a minimum of thirty seconds in each quadrant."

"Good girl!" Frank clapped her on the back. "You might want to consider an upgrade to our new line of malleable fixed retainers . . ."

Even Drea had to respect my dad's hustle—one salesperson to another.

"What can we help you with, Dr. Worthy?" Drea asked.

"Frank wants to buy a gift for my mom."

Drea's eyes widened. "Are you two getting back together?"

"Oh no," I answered before Frank could. "They're still getting a divorce. My dad is here to buy my mom a midlife crisis outfit for Singles' Nights at Oceanside Tavern, you know, when she's on the prowl for her next husband."

Drea and Frank gawked at me, mouths agape.

"It sounds messed up," I said. "Because it is."

I announced I was taking a mental health break. Let Drea earn another 10 percent. If anyone was going to come out a winner from my parents' dysfunctional relationship, it might as well be her.

26

SEEING RED

I immediately, almost instinctively, headed in the direction of Sam Goody. Lately, that was where I'd gone whenever I needed a little lift during my shift. And he always seemed pretty happy to see me too. But my conversation with Frank had left me feeling a bit off-kilter. Like, maybe I was trying a little too hard? Maybe my visits were getting to be too much for a friendship that would certainly end when I left for college? After all, with the exception of delivering damaged goods, he hadn't reciprocated by showing up at my workplace . . .

I arrived at his store before I had a chance to talk myself out of seeing him.

"So I've been meaning to ask," Sam said, "is your mom still enjoying *The Broadway Album*?"

He pulled the trigger on his pricing gun, slapping a red clearance tag on the solo album by the other guy in Wham! who wasn't George Michael.

"Actually, I don't ride to work with my mom anymore," I explained. "Drea takes me."

Sam looked up and suddenly got way busier with the pricing gun.

"Unnnngh."

The store manager wheezed by us with a box of new releases from Arista Records. Looking gray, sweaty, and generally unwell, Freddy was a fortyish drummer for Boss in the USA, described by Sam as "the third most popular Bruce Springsteen tribute band on the Jersey Shore." He was a decent supervisor, easy to please, except on Mondays when he was brutally hungover after a weekend of gigs. Sam greeted him cautiously.

"Morning, Freddy."

"Unnnngh."

Sam waited until Freddy entered the back office before resuming our conversation.

"Why do you get rides to work every day?" he asked.

He red-tagged the solo album by the other singer in The Go-Go's who wasn't Belinda Carlisle.

"I don't have a license . . ."

"You don't have your driver's license? Are you kidding? I

counted down the days until I could take my driver's test at the DMV! Driving meant freedom!"

I shrugged.

"I never felt like I needed it until . . ."

I didn't *want* to talk about Troy. Again, not because I was still pained by our breakup. It was embarrassing to admit out loud to Sam Goody that I had ever dated him at all.

"Until what?" Sam Goody asked.

"Until my boyfriend dumped me and I didn't have anyone to drive me to work this summer," I said. "But it won't matter much longer. In exactly fifteen days I'll be riding the subway in New York City where only the cabbies need driver's licenses."

I thought Sam Goody would be impressed by my metropolitan attitude.

He was not.

I watched him tag a bunch of other failed solo albums by lesser members of big bands—including the poor schmo from Genesis who wasn't Phil Collins, Peter Gabriel, or Mike (+ the Mechanics) Rutherford—before speaking up.

"What?" I finally asked.

"Not getting your license is a dumb idea," he replied. "You should really get your driver's license."

"I told you," I said, "it won't matter—"

"Right, because in fifteen days you'll be gone," he said. "But what about when you come home? You don't want to rely on your parents or your ex-boyfriend to take you everywhere, do you?"

I hadn't left yet. Why would I already be thinking about

coming home? As if that weren't annoying enough, he took his argument to an even more infuriating level.

"As a feminist, shouldn't you value your independence?"

KA-BOOM. An anger so intense, it distorted my senses. I literally saw red, as if Sam Goody had pulled the trigger on a pricing machine gun and shot a million crimson clearance tags directly into my eyeballs.

"You know what feminists *really* love?" I retorted. "When *men* tell us how to be good feminists!"

"Hey, Bellarosa, I'm sorry," Sam said, "I didn't mean it that way . . ."

He set down the gun and took a step back in a show of surrender.

It wasn't his fault, really. I could see he hadn't intended to enrage me then, just as he hadn't meant to upset me when we first met. Sam Goody pissed me off because he didn't know me. I was starting to think that maybe I was a tough person to know. I mean, Troy and I dated for two friggin' years, and I don't think he ever knew me at all.

My parents were married for twenty friggin' years.

Did anyone ever know anyone?

Standing in the clearance section, the last chance for all the saddest has-beens and barely-weres, I didn't have that answer. But this I knew for certain: The fifteen days I had left in Pineville wouldn't be enough for Sam Goody and me to reach a deeper level of understanding. So why even bother trying?

"Maybe I'll solve the problem by never coming home at all," I said. "It's not like there's anything here worth coming back for."

Sam Goody took off his glasses and pinched the bridge of his nose.

"Well, I guess that solves that."

And then he abruptly excused himself to assist a customer who—like me—didn't need his help.

27

HOSTAGE

I was in a bad mood for the next few days.

And to make matters worse, Drea had zero time to attempt to cheer me up. On this particular day, she was wrangling with an exceptionally challenging bridal party. It's never easy finding a dress that fit and flattered a dozen bridesmaids of greatly varying shapes, sizes, and ages, but the future Mrs. Charles Cappuccio was *really* making Drea work for the commission.

"It's gotta go with the theme," the bride-to-be demanded.

"Which is?" Drea asked.

"Pretty Woman meets *Dances with Wolves."*

Drea—ever the professional—responded with zero hesitation.

"Beverly Hills Heartland."

I was thinking "Frontier Hooker." But I doubt my suggestion would have elicited a downright orgasmic reaction from the future Mrs. Charles Cappuccio.

"Yes! Yes! Yes!"

I lacked Drea's impressive improvisational skills. This is why I worked in the back office and not up front. Drea's impeccable professionalism is to blame for what happened next. If she hadn't been 100 percent consumed by the demands of the future Mrs. Charles Cappuccio, she would have used her body as a human barricade to stop my sworn enemy from trespassing on sacred turf.

"Knock knock."

My ex had already entered the office when he said it. These words—like everything Troy had ever said to me—were meaningless.

"What the hell are you doing here?"

He blinked at me with blue-eyed bewilderment.

"Come now, Cassandra. That's how you greet me?"

Troy was the only person besides my parents who called me Cassandra. The full-name formality equaled familiarity. I thought it was romantic when we were together, you know, because of the mythological connection between our names. But now, my skin crawled at the sound of those three syllables hissing against his lips.

"You have two seconds to get out of here before I call mall security."

I picked up the phone to show him I meant it.

"I have your doll," Troy said quickly.

I held the phone to my ear, refusing to believe what I'd just heard over the dial tone.

"What?"

"I have your doll," he repeated. "From the freezer."

I slowly hung up the phone. Troy assumed the arrogant countenance I'd seen hundreds of times at Mock Trial competitions. This wasn't an act. It was the expression that came most naturally to him and only meant one thing: He had the irrefutable evidence to win his case.

"I don't believe you," I lied.

"Believe me," he said. "I tracked it down."

Then he reached into the back pocket of his khakis and produced a Polaroid as proof.

"This is the doll you're looking for."

A pigtailed girl in purple overalls. No box, which I assumed meant she—unlike the dolls in the basement—had been played with.

Hugged.

Loved.

Thrillingly, a pink envelope rested in her lap. Could I get a good enough look to verify the doctored documentation? Or confirm that this was, indeed, the next clue . . . ?

Troy snatched the photo away.

"You've seen enough," he said.

"You won't give it to me?"

"I didn't say that."

"Then give it to me."

He returned the photo to his back pocket.

"I didn't say that either."

Troy didn't know why I wanted the doll, only that I did. And that was enough for him to hold it hostage. As much as it pained me to negotiate with a heartless terrorist, I didn't want to let Drea down. This was our only opportunity to finish the treasure hunt before I left Pineville for college.

For good.

"Where did you find it?" I asked casually. I couldn't let Troy know how much this doll mattered to me.

"The family who bought the America's Best Cookie franchise found it deep in the freezer when they renovated One Potato Twenty," he explained. "It went to one of the granddaughters."

Troy had always been a tenacious problem-solver. As his Odyssey of the Mind teammate, it was a quality I had always valued, his unwillingness to give up on what seemed like an impossible problem right up to the second he figured out the solution.

"And you tracked down the granddaughter?"

Instead of answering my question, Troy promenaded the perimeter of the office, evaluating the merchandise as if he owned the place.

"I didn't have to find her." He thumbed the ruffle on a blouse. All of Troy's nervousness from our last meeting was gone. "She's my boss at America's Best Cookie . . ."

Troy worked for the granddaughter all summer? That didn't make any sense unless . . .

She was back. Just when I thought she'd ghosted for good.

Zoe.

The granddaughter was Zoe.

Of course the granddaughter was Zoe.

Only nepotism could explain why a phantasmagoric vigilante could rise up the ranks at such an assertively patriotic food court franchise.

"So, Zoe just *gave* it to you?" I asked.

"Not exactly," he said sourly. "There were some conditions involved."

"What kind of conditions?"

"Well, let's just say that I'm on ABC janitorial duty for the rest of the summer."

I bet Zoe would've just given the doll to me if I had a chance to ask. But the thought of her making Troy do all the grossest dirty work pleased me.

"So, are you going to let me have it or what?"

"I too have conditions."

Then he laughed like a mustache-twirling villain. Too bad what little facial hair Troy managed to grow only came in sparse, translucent patches.

"Just tell me what you want so I can get back to work."

"I want," he said, rubbing his hands together, "a second chance."

I don't know what was crazier: thinking he deserved a second chance or bribing me into giving him one.

"How do I know you've even got the right doll?"

"I've got the right doll."

"But how do I know for sure?"

"You don't trust me, Cassandra?"

Before I knew what was happening, a stapler flew out of my hands and struck the wall three inches above Troy's head.

"Cassandra! What the hell?"

"I trusted you not to cheat on me with a homicidal hamster in acid wash Z. Cavariccis," I said icily. "And stop calling me Cassandra."

He was panting, petrified. I dismissed him with a flick of my pinky.

"You can go now."

And when I thought he'd finally run away with his tail between his legs, he demonstrated why he was so hard to get rid of.

"Bellarosa."

At first I didn't understand why he said it. Until I did.

"The doll's name. That's why you want it." His confidence wavered. "Right?"

Rey Ajedrez, Lustig Zeit, Pieds D'Abord, Silva Mundi, En Tatws Ugain.

And now . . .

Bella Rosa.

A shadow of concern passed over his face. Had he just said more than he should have? I summoned everything I'd learned about manipulation and persuasion by observing Drea at work.

"*Of course* it is."

One sunny smile was all it took for Troy's cloud of self-doubt to disappear. My ex was no longer worried that he'd accidentally revealed the very information I was seeking.

When, in fact, that's *exactly* what he had just done.

"One date in exchange for the doll and the birth certificate," I told him. "Deal?"

He smiled.

"One date is all I need."

28

BIG DREAMS

I could hardly wait for Troy to exit the store before sharing the news with Drea. She was at the front counter with the latest issue of *Cosmo,* a reward for selling two thousand dollars' worth of Frontier Hooker bridesmaid dresses. It was the first real break she'd had all week.

"It's here!" I didn't mean to shout, but I couldn't help myself. "The clue!"

"What do you mean it's *here?*"

"Bella Rosa!" I shouted. "The next clue is hidden in the boutique!"

"No."

"Yes."

"No."

"Yes."

"What are you two girls going on about?" Gia asked.

We locked eyes and replied in unison.

"Nothing!"

Then we conspicuously raced to the back office for privacy.

"How do you know?" Drea demanded to know.

"Troy told me."

Drea stuck out her tongue. "What's that loser got to do with our treasure?"

I relayed the whole story, from the trespassing and hostage-taking, to bribery and attempted aggravated assault with a stapler.

"The next clue was here! The whole time!" She spun around wildly. "It could be anywhere! But we can't just go around prying up floorboards and looking for hidden compartments in walls. Ma will *kill* me."

I did not disagree.

"We won't have to," I said. "I'm getting the map."

"How?" Drea asked in a way that implied she already knew the answer.

"I agreed to go on a date with him."

"Agreed" wasn't the right word. Negotiated the terms of a date-like transaction was more accurate: one thirty-minute food court dinner for one Bella Rosa Cabbage Patch Doll with full documentation.

"No!"

"Yes."

"No!"

"Yes."

"You *can't*." She was practically begging. "Let me go in your place."

I wished I could send Drea instead. I was repulsed by the idea of even pretending to give Troy a second chance. And in public! If I managed to make it through an entire Panda Express veggie combo plate without puking all over him, there was always a chance he'd renege on the deal.

"You have to be the very best version of you," Drea insisted as if reading my mind. "I'll put together a look that will make him never, *ever* forget what he's missing out on."

"Okay, I'm willing to make this sacrifice," I told her. "But there's one thing I want to know: Why is the treasure hunt important to you?"

Drea shifted her weight from one stiletto to the other, and back again. Then she sighed in surrender.

"Maybe," she confessed in a hushed voice, "you aren't the only one with big dreams of New York City."

"*What?*"

"Maybe I've always dreamed of attending the Fashion Institute of Technology. Maybe I've always dreamed of designing my own clothing line and selling it in my own stores."

There were no maybes about it. These dreams were too precious for posters above the bed. And I couldn't have been more surprised.

"But you *love* what you do!" I objected. "Bellarosa Boutique is your life!"

"I'm damn good at what I do," Drea replied. "But that

doesn't mean I *love* it. And that definitely doesn't mean my life is Bellarosa Boutique. I've got bigger ambitions than the mall."

Her words came out in a rush now, as if she'd been keeping this secret for a very a long time and couldn't hold it in for a single second more.

"You remember the silk-ribbon chemise you liked so much?"

"The one I wore that night with Slade?"

It was a simple, beautiful top. Too bad it was wasted on such a terrible hookup.

"I made it."

"You *made* it?"

"I came up with the adjustable neckline design, sourced the fabric, and sewed it myself," Drea said with pride.

"You did?" I had no idea Drea knew her way around a sewing machine.

"It wasn't really my style, but I knew it would work on someone else," she added. "And that someone was you."

I was legitimately impressed by her ability to create a look for someone other than herself or the typical Bellarosa customer.

"You're really talented!"

"I know I am!" Drea replied unapologetically. "But I need to be smart about it. Strategic. Like, a lot of talented designers get screwed over and lose their labels by making bad deals. So I really want to study the business of fashion merchandising and management and do it right. I want to be a global luxury brand. And there's no better school for it than FIT!"

I was blown away. This was the closest Drea had ever come to her own *plan*.

"Does Gia know?"

"No!" Drea cried. "Leaving her would be the ultimate betrayal. That's why I can't ask her for any help with tuition or anything else. I have to do this on my own."

"You don't have to do it on your own," I said. "I can help you fill out your application and guide you through the financial aid process and find scholarships . . ."

Drea covered her ears. "See? This is why I didn't want to tell you!"

"This is *exactly* why you should have told me!" I countered. "I excel at this kind of thing! Troy *never* would have been accepted to Columbia if I hadn't edited his application essay!"

By "edited," I meant "totally rewritten." Before me, Troy's personal statement was merely a list of his academic and extracurricular accomplishments in paragraph form. After me, Troy was a future MBA with a soul whose family had suffered great financial and emotional losses in the 1987 stock market crash, who saw himself ushering in a new wave of compassionate money managers dedicated to bridging the income gap and bringing prosperity back to Wall Street *and* Main Street and blah blah blah blah. His first draft was authentic Troy. My rewrite was an idealized version I wanted him to be. It was utter bullshit and the admissions office totally lapped it up. And for two years, I suppose I did too. At the time, I believed such a flagrant breach of academic integrity was thoroughly justified in service of *the plan*. Regrettably, I was wrong. So, so, so wrong.

Had Drea just presented me with the ideal opportunity to make it right?

"Let's play to our strengths! You help me with my revenge makeover, and I'll get you into FIT!"

I extended my hand. And after a moment's hesitation, Drea did the same.

"Deal!"

As we shook on it, I flashed back to the first day of Miss Miscelli's fifth grade. The new girl slid into the seat right in front of me. She wasn't from Pineville. Just moved here from Toms River, the next town over. But she supposedly spent nearly every weekend with her cousins on Staten Island, an outer borough but close, so close, close enough to where I really wanted to be, needed to be, would be someday. Whispers enveloped her, but I was too mesmerized to listen. Her hair was the biggest I'd ever seen, teased higher than the Empire State Building and the Twin Towers combined. I couldn't see the blackboard, and I didn't care. I stared so hard, she felt it like a poke in her exposed shoulder. She spun around, bold in her dress code–breaking tank top.

"So, yeah, I'm Drea, by the way."

She said it as if we'd already started a conversation, as if Miss Miscelli hadn't already warned the chattering classroom to keep eyes and ears open and mouths shut, as if she wanted to know who I was too. The air between us was sweetened by minty gum she was chewing—loudly—but not for long. It too was against the rules.

"I'm Cassie."

Just like that, we were unlikely best friends. And maybe, it occurred to me now, we still were.

29

EDGY AND EFFORTLESS

*W*ith only two hours between the end of my shift and the start of my transactional non-date with Troy, I braced myself for a head-to-toe application of the full contents of Bellarosa's beauty supply closet. Instead, Drea set herself down in my office throne and encouraged me to take the far less regal chair on the opposite side of the desk.

"Let's have a chat."

"A chat?" I pointed to the clock. "We don't have time for a chat!"

Drea sighed heavily. "All the best revenge makeovers start with a conversation."

"What's to discuss? Make me hot!"

Drea shushed me with the jangly flick of her bangled wrist.

"Play to our strengths," she said. "Remember?"

I reluctantly sat.

"What did Troy dislike most about your appearance?"

I was sure I'd misheard her.

"What did he *dislike*? What kind of revenge makeover is this?" I asked. "The goal here is turning Troy on, not turning him off!"

"*Is* that the goal?"

I considered Drea's question. I didn't want Troy to want me. I wanted him to regret not wanting me. Two very different objectives.

"Did he ever tell you not to dress or look a certain way?" Drea pressed.

Troy disliked when I cut my hair above my chin because it was "too severe."

Troy disliked when I bought thrift-store denim because it was "too funky."

Troy disliked when I got my ears double pierced because it was "too punk."

Troy disliked when I pinned a Planned Parenthood button to my backpack because it was "too radical."

So, I grew my hair down to my shoulder blades. Shopped at the Gap. Let the holes in my ears close. Tossed the pins. I told myself these were superficial compromises essential for keeping the peace in our relationship and *the plan* alive. But as I sat across from Drea and answered her questions, I realized how wrong I'd been. Troy's dislikes were about so much more than ridding controversial items from my wardrobe. They were about removing controversial ideas from my *brain*. I wondered how Troy would have rewritten my personal statement if I'd given him the chance.

I was finally starting to see where Drea was going with this.

"You want to make me as *dislikable* as possible?"

"Not exactly." Drea shook her head before making a vital correction. "I want to make you into the girl you should have been all along."

I'd assumed Drea would transform me into a big-haired, spandexed Bellarosa clone. But this strategy was so much smarter. And unexpected.

It was only appropriate for us to begin the revenge makeover journey at Spencer Gifts, the one-stop shop for invisible ink pens and penis ice-cube trays. To accommodate its diverse customer base, it also sold buttons in a full range of offensiveness, from not at all (DON'T WORRY BE HAPPY!) to sort of (FBI: FEDERAL BOOBIE INSPECTOR) to very, very offensive (BUSH/QUALE '92). Drea got us a deal on ten pins for $2.50, all in the "too radical" category.

We followed that up with a quick stop at the Piercing Pagoda. I watched Drea barter like a pro with Vicki, aka The Girl Who Called Me Toothy and Would Not Get Her Dream Homecoming Dress at Bellarosa Boutique, Gawddammit. If she re-pierced the second holes in my ears for free, Drea would put her back on Bellarosa's list and make her blue velvet dreams come true. Vicki agreed without hesitation. By the end of our surprisingly painless transaction, she not only believed the true story about what happened with Slade that night on

Bellarosa's couch, but was determined to tell as many people as possible when she went down to party in the Cabbage Patch that night.

"Now, where can we get our hands on some vintage jeans?" Drea asked out loud.

Unfortunately there wasn't a thrift store to be found within 900,0000 square feet. Recycled goods and clothing undercut the newer-is-better capitalist propaganda that kept the mall in business. But I had a good idea where I could find pre-worn denim—I just had to summon enough courage to get it.

"I believe in you," Drea said encouragingly as we approached Fun Tyme Arcade. "I'm here for backup if you need me."

I found my mark with his head inside an open pinball machine, looking a lot like a mechanic tinkering with a car engine.

"Heyyyy."

I greeted Sonny Sexton like we were old friends. He looked up from the wiry innards with confusion, quickly followed by interest.

"Heyyyy . . ." He pointed a screwdriver at me. "Mono Bitch."

He was wearing *the* jean jacket. It was just as I remembered it: frayed at the collar and faded at the elbows, with a grimy patina resulting from continuous wear and few washings over many, many years. It was superbly gross, and I had to have it.

"I want that jacket."

"You want . . ." Sonny Sexton pressed the screwdriver to the pocket covering his heart. "This jacket?"

"Yep," I said.

Sonny Sexton smiled wolfishly. *My, what big teeth you have . . .* I thought.

"What will you give me in return?"

He wasn't at all interested in hearing *why* I wanted his jacket. It was as if he were routinely interrupted at work by random girls requesting articles of clothing right off his back, you know, like this was just a mildly bothersome consequence of being Sonny Sexton. Unlike Vicki, I didn't know what to barter this time around. I mean, I knew what *he* wanted from *me*. He'd made that abundantly clear in our first conversation. But my virtue was not on the table, the pinball machine, the Skee-Ball ramp, or anywhere else Sonny Sexton was rumored to have scored with gamer groupies defenseless to his scuzzy charms.

So I took a chance on the one thing Sonny Sexton and I had in common: We had a reason to be annoyed with Troy.

"What if I told you your jacket is part of a plan to get back at someone who did us both wrong?"

"Not Helen!" He clutched his chest in terror.

"No! Not Helen! I know better than to mess with Helen."

He pressed two wires together inside the pinball machine. A bell rang.

Ding! Ding!

"Cookie Boy?"

"Cookie Boy."

Ding! Ding!

Thirty seconds later I was walking out of the arcade wearing Sonny Sexton's denim jacket, leaving a cloud of knock-off cologne and skunk weed in my wake. I promised I'd return the garment tomorrow in precisely the same scummy condition I had received it.

"The student has become the master!" marveled Drea.

We had to hustle now. I only had about forty-five minutes before my date-like transaction and one crucial destination left on my make-under journey: Casino Full Service Beauty Salon. I'd never been there before, but it met Drea's standards which was a good enough endorsement for me. I was encouraged by the sign in the window that said walk-ins were welcome. I was less encouraged by the looks of the receptionist.

"Trust me," Drea insisted.

With her frosted, feathered hair and baby-blue eye shadow, she looked like her style evolution had stopped sometime between the end of disco and the start of the Reagan administration. *Maybe that's why she was a receptionist and not a stylist,* I reasoned to myself.

"Do you have an appointment?" She didn't look up from the latest issue of *Celebrity Hairstyles* magazine.

"Sorry, no," I said. "Do I need one for a haircut?"

The receptionist scanned the appointment book with a rhinestoned fingernail.

"Not for Carla," she said. "Carla's wide open."

I was a little nervous to be assigned the stylist who was "wide open," but I didn't have much time to wait for a more in-demand beautician.

"Okay," I said. "Sure. Carla it is."

The receptionist stood and gestured for me to follow her to an empty station. I sat and she spun me around in the chair toward the brightly lit mirror.

"So what are we doing today?" the receptionist asked.

MEGAN McCAFFERTY

"Um, shouldn't we wait for Carla?"

Drea laughed.

"I'm Carla." The receptionist who was actually my stylist draped a plastic cape over my shoulders. "What are we doing today?" she repeated.

My first impression of Carla did not give me much confidence in her abilities. But the clock was ticking.

"She wants it short," Drea answered on my behalf.

"How short?"

"Like . . ." I hadn't quite settled on how much higher above my chin I should go.

Carla flipped through *Celebrity Hairstyles* magazine until she found "5 Fall Trends to Watch Out For." She showed me a photo of the porcelain-skinned, doe-eyed indie movie princess captioned, "Edgy and Effortless." It was *exactly* the look I wanted. But I hadn't known it until Carla pointed it out to me.

"Did you recently go through a breakup?" Carla asked. "A cut like this usually means a breakup."

"See?" Drea elbowed me in the ribs. "I *told* you."

Carla's intuition cleared away any doubts I'd had in her. She'd seen some things in her two decades of salon service. She *knew* things. So in Carla I trusted.

And Carla did not let me down.

When she finished cutting, I had a glossy, earlobe-skimming bob that put my double piercings on prominent display. It was a beautiful, piss-off-my-ex twofer.

"What do you think?" Carla asked, removing my cape with a flourish.

"I love it! It's perfect!"

I tipped Carla twice as much as I normally would, spending down to the last dollar in my wallet. By the time my spree was over, I'd blown a good chunk of my paycheck.

"This is the best money you've ever spent," Drea promised.

And she was totally right.

30

WHAT A FEMINIST LOOKS LIKE

*T*roy nearly dropped my veggie combo on the food court floor. "What happened to you?"

His hands were shaking. Oily lo mein noodles trembled.

"I have no idea what you're talking about."

"Hair . . ." He was at a loss for all but the most basic words. "Ears . . ."

He unsteadily set the tray on the table and slid into the opposite side of the booth. *Our* booth. That had been one of my concessions. I'd negotiated him down from an hour-long dinner by agreeing to sit in our old spot. The stage was empty, though. No performances to distract us from ourselves.

"You're not the same person from this morning!"

"I am absolutely the same person from this morning." I rubbed my chopsticks together. "I'm the person I've always been."

He grabbed my knapsack to get a better look at the buttons I'd affixed to the outside flap.

Silence = Death
Keep Your Laws Off My Body
This Is What a Feminist Looks Like

He tossed it back over to my side of the booth and sniffed in disgust.

"Is this what a feminist *smells* like? Bong water and butthole?"

He wasn't wrong about the jacket's stench. But I was not going to concede even the smallest point.

"As the future president of College Republicans at Columbia, how will you explain to your fellow conservatives why you're familiar with either one of those scents?"

He sat back in the booth and gave me a long, hard look. The change in my appearance had definitely thrown him off his game. And he was studying me now, trying to make sense of what it all meant, urgently calculating how he could possibly retain the upper hand. I looked at my watch. Eight minutes down. Twenty-two minutes left in this date-like transaction to go. A length of a sitcom, minus the commercials. I wondered if I could persuade Troy into reenacting an episode of *The Golden Girls* until our time was up. I could be Dorothy and Blanche. He could be Sophia and Rose.

"Cassandra!"

"What?" I snapped. "And I told you to stop calling me that!"

"Cassssssssie," he overenunciated. "Did you ever hear from Simone Levy?"

Wow. An attempt at pleasant conversation. Well, fine.

"I finally got a letter from her last week," I replied. "She wants to study art history and philosophy."

"Her family must be loaded," Troy said knowingly, "because that's a double major designed for poverty."

And as much as I hated to admit it—even to myself—I'd thought the same exact thing.

"Honestly," Troy continued. "Can you think of a more pointless use of tuition? What a terrible ROI."

Return on investment.

That's how Troy determined the worthiness of his time, energy, and attention. He always wanted to get more back than he ever put in. I recognized in that moment that I had ended up being a very poor ROI and that was probably the only reason Troy wanted to get back together with me: to salvage what would otherwise be a colossal loss of his high school years.

I had felt the same way not too long ago.

"Not everyone has to go to college to be a Wall Street Master of the Universe," I said. "I know someone who dropped out of the Wharton School of Business and has never been happier."

Troy didn't deserve to know about me and Sam Goody. But I didn't want him *not* knowing about me and Sam Goody either. Alluding to Sam without mentioning him by name was my way of getting around this conundrum.

"That person," Troy said with total conviction, "is an idiot."

And that's exactly why I didn't want Troy to know I was maybe interested in someone new. What bothered me most about Troy's comment? Knowing that eight weeks earlier, when I was still in full thrall of *the plan*, I would've absolutely agreed with him.

I checked the time. Fifteen minutes down. Fifteen to go.

"Can you stop looking at your watch?"

"There's nothing in our contract that says I can't look at my watch."

"There's nothing in our contract that says I can't do the Lambada right on this table, but you won't see me doing that throughout our meal."

I choked at the thought of Troy gyrating his hips to the "forbidden dance." At this point, he was as sexless to me as a Cabbage Patch Kid.

"Why don't you just give me the doll and the documents, and we can just put an end to this awkwardness?"

I swirled a spring roll in a puddle of duck sauce and bit it in half. Troy steepled his fingers. It was one of his "power moves."

"Is that the technique," asked Troy with a snide smile, "you used on Slade?"

A few weeks ago, a comment like this from Troy of all people would have made me burn red with humiliation. It brought me great relief to know for certain that Troy didn't have that kind of influence over me anymore.

No, I would not flee the food court in shame.

No, I would not give him the last word in this closing argument.

No, I would not let him treat me like an Odyssey of the Mind problem that needed solving.

No, I would not erase who I really was to become who he wanted me to be.

"Oh, Troy." I popped the rest of the roll in my mouth and chomped down. Hard. "That's something you will never, ever know."

Then in one swift movement, I picked up my untouched lo mein and dumped the soggy heap of soy noodles right over his head.

"What's wrong with you?" Troy spluttered, shaking the wormy tangle from his hair. "No way I'm giving you that doll now!"

"I don't need the doll from you," I replied. "I don't need anything from you."

I hated disappointing Drea, but I could not, would not let Troy think he was doing me any favors. Not now. Not a week from now. Not ever again.

I'd found fulfillment through fashion. Achieved self-actualization through accessorization. An article of clothing transformed me into the best possible version of myself. Adopting a new look didn't make me superficial or stupid. On the contrary, I felt empowered and emboldened enough to tell Troy exactly what I thought of him and *the plan*.

"There are over seven million people in New York City," I said. "Let's not run into each other when we get there."

I left the table with a renewed sense of purpose. Was Sam Goody working a double shift? Would he be at the store until closing? Would I have to wait until tomorrow to make up for how I'd acted? I started out in a trot and increased speed as I got closer and closer to my destination. By the time I hit Concourse F, I was in a full run, dodging oldsters and ducking youngsters who weren't in a hurry to get anywhere. When I burst through the entrance to the music store, I nearly took out a huddle of preteens giggling over a New Kids on the Block fanzine.

I spotted Sam at one of the listening stations with his headphones on. His back was to me, so I crept up behind him to sneak a peek at what he was listening to. I'd never heard of the album or the artist—*Nevermind* by Nirvana—but getting the newest music before anyone else was one of the advantages of working in a record store. Sam cranked the volume way up, but I could barely make out screaming vocals, thrashing drums, and hard, fuzzy guitars through the headphones. Nirvana was no competition for the NKOTB remix Freddy the manager played to please the store's most faithful customers.

I gently tapped Sam Goody on the shoulder.

"Hi."

He turned around, took me in, and grinned.

"WOW," he shouted. "That's a great look on you."

I laughed and he laughed, and a blush heated up my cheeks. If I saw red earlier, I was *feeling* red now. But, like, in a good way. Sam turned off the music and slipped off his headphones.

"I've been thinking about what you said," I said, "about independence."

Sam Goody nodded cautiously. "I'm listening."

"Will you teach me how to drive?"

31

ALL THE FUSS

*T*he mall had only closed fifteen minutes earlier, but the lot was already mostly empty. Sam Goody assured me it would be a safe space for my first driving lesson.

"Here it is," he said, sweeping his hand over the hood of his car.

"Oh," I said. "It's . . . oh."

It was an aggressively ugly car. A fecal-brown Chevy hatchback, with rusted-out patches around the wheels, a crooked back bumper, dented front fender, and too many side-door dings to count. I didn't know if I should be relieved by the sorry state of this automobile—I couldn't mess it up that much more than it already was—or worried that I was being taught to drive by anyone who could do so much vehicular damage.

"I got it like this," he said, sensing my apprehension. "I have a spotless driving record. Not even a speeding ticket."

He chivalrously opened the driver's side door for me. Or, at least he tried to.

"Sorry—" He yanked on the handle. "It sticks sometimes."

He had not bothered locking the door because no one would steal this car. After a few more tugs, it finally swung open with a creaky whine.

"After you," he said, gesturing at the driver's seat.

Upholstered in a phlegm-colored vinyl, the Chevy was equally ugly on the inside as it was on the outside. It was, however, scrupulously clean. The immaculate interior was especially remarkable considering the impromptu nature of the lesson. I mean, it's not like Sam Goody had any time to quickly clean his car in the effort to impress me. This was its natural state.

And I was impressed.

Until I got a better look.

Sam had put the rear seats down and loaded the hatchback with ropes, metal clamps, a kinky sex-harness type thing . . . ?

Oh my God, a serial killer travel kit.

I knew next to nothing about Sam Goody! What had I been thinking when I followed him to this dark, deserted parking lot? Murders were at a record high in Manhattan, but it was just my sucky luck to fall for a hometown killer.

Sam Goody saw me eyeing the serial killer travel kit and laughed.

"Rock-climbing equipment," he explained.

"Rock-climbing equipment?" I replied incredulously. "You're a rock climber?"

I *really* knew next to nothing about Sam Goody.

"Since I was thirteen," he said. "A hippie cousin took me out for the first time when we were visiting family in Oregon one summer. I loved the challenge of it—like figuring out where to grab and grip and get myself up there. I was always a cautious kid, not much of a risk-taker, but rock climbing was my way of, I don't know, being a bit of a daredevil." He popped open the hatchback and removed a *J*-shaped metal device. "I guess you could say I was . . ." He held the clamp up in the space between us. "*Hooked* right away."

"That pun," I groaned, "was way worse than the possibility you were a serial killer."

"Believe or not, I wasn't exactly the sporty type in high school." He swept his hand through his hair and reconsidered. "Actually, that's not true. I *was* athletic, but I *wasn't* sporty." A wistful smile crossed his face. "I was the king of the Presidential Physical Fitness Test in elementary school. Remember those?"

I grimaced at the memory of this annual assessment of our athleticism—or lack thereof.

"I could do more pull-ups and climb the rope ladder faster than the jocks—you know, the *real* jocks—the football, basketball, baseball meatheads," he said. "And they hated me for it. Especially when I refused to join any of their teams because I wanted nothing to do with all that macho gorilla rah-rah locker-room chauvinism."

He grunted and pantomimed like a primate—or a typical Pineville High linebacker.

"No high school rock-climbing teams," I said.

"No championship tournaments," he added. "No varsity letters."

"Not much rock climbing in the City of Brotherly Love either, I imagine," I said, referring to the home of the UPenn campus.

He gave a regretful nod.

"I didn't think about that when I applied or when I was accepted," he said. "But I thought about it all the time after I got there."

This made me wonder what I wouldn't know I'd miss until after I got to Barnard.

"Let's get this lesson started, shall we?"

I lowered myself into the driver's side bucket seat. He walked around the front of the car, opened the passenger door—no sticking this time—and got in next to me. Separated by the center console, it was still the closest we'd ever been.

"What's that smell?" I asked.

He reeled back, alarmed.

"You smell something bad?" he asked. "I try to keep this car clean . . ."

"Oh no! It's a good smell! It's like . . ." I sniffed. "Lavender?"

"It's my Yardley Brilliantine hair pomade." He seemed slightly embarrassed to admit this. "It's British."

Sam Goody's hair was longer than it was when we first met. The pompadour still crested off his scalp, but in a shaggier, less sculptural way. I liked this looser look on him. He wore it well.

"Well, it's a good smell."

"Thank you," he replied.

Mercifully, he did not comment on the funk emanating from my borrowed denim.

From me.

Just to be safe, I took off Sonny's jacket before pulling my seat belt across my chest.

"So," Sam Goody said.

"So," I said.

He dug into the front pocket of his jeans.

I wanted my hand to join his.

I wanted to dig deeper.

I wanted . . .

He extracted a set of keys on a simple silver ring and dangled them in front of me. I liked that he wasn't someone who expressed his individuality through quirky keychains. When he dropped them into my outreached palm, I felt a palpable disappointment that our fingertips hadn't touched. Maybe I had misread Sam Goody yet again. He wasn't interested in me in the way I was starting to think I was interested in him.

"You've really never driven before?" he asked.

"Nope. I passed the written test but never got behind the wheel. So, how do we get started?"

"Key in the ignition," he instructed.

I did as I was told. The dashboard controls lit up.

"Step one." He held up a cassette. "The right soundtrack."

He popped *Nevermind* into the tape deck. Watery guitars washed over us.

"Okay," I said. "What's step two?"

Sam slowly and deliberately looked me up and down. I didn't experience the overwhelming urge to cover up as I had when Slade or Sonny ogled me. Just the opposite. I wanted Sam to keep looking. I wanted Sam to see more. I wanted to reveal, not conceal.

"Your feet aren't touching the pedals," Sam said. "You need to move the seat up."

"Oh," I said, trying not to sound as deflated as I felt. "Okay."

He wasn't objectifying me after all. He was just crossing off all the boxes on the pre-drive safety checklist. I felt underneath for the seat adjuster. I pulled the lever and I thrust my pelvis to make the seat move forward. It stayed put. After a few jerky attempts, Sam offered to help.

"Do you mind?"

I shook my head. *No, I don't mind. I don't mind this one bit.*

He leaned across my lap, reached down between my legs and pulled.

"Ohhhh!"

I bucked as if we'd gone from zero-to-sixty in under a second.

"Sorry!" He lurched backward. "Was that too much?"

I shook my head.

"No," I said with a slight catch in my voice.

"Oh," Sam Goody said with a slight catch in *his* voice.

And in the next instant, our chests crashed and our mouths mashed over the center console.

We kissed to tortured and distorted, melodic and melancholic music unlike anything I'd ever heard before. As Sam Goody kissed me—eagerly, hungrily—I had an acute awareness of what I can only describe of anticipatory nostalgia. For the rest of my life, I knew I'd always remember kissing Sam Goody whenever I heard this song, these words.

"Come as you are, as you were, as I want you to be."

"Can I have another lesson tomorrow?" I murmured dreamily.

"I wish I could," Sam said, kissing me again. Only this time sweetly, softly, tenderly. "But I'm taking a road trip. I'll be gone for a week."

He explained that he was taking time off to spend with his younger brother before driving him to college for freshman orientation.

"I didn't know you had a brother my age," I said.

"He graduated from Eastland this year," he replied. "Do you have any siblings?"

"Nope."

Yep, we'd totally made out before exchanging even the most basic biographical details.

"Where's he going to school?"

I was curious, of course, but also more than slightly concerned that the Chevette might not make it to whatever campus and back.

"Harvard."

We both winced as he said it.

"So much for 'life beyond the Ivy League' in your family, huh?"

"Well." Sam smiled ruefully, adorably. "At least it takes the pressure off me to be the successful son."

And before I knew it, we were going at it all over again. I didn't learn the first thing about driving that night. But I finally, finally, *oh my God* finally understood what the fuss over kissing was all about.

32

BOO

*D*id you get the map?" Drea asked before I'd even slipped into the passenger seat the next morning. "Why didn't you call me back?"

Sam Goody had left me too dazed to return any of her phone calls.

"Cassie! This is Drea! Did you get the map? Call me back!"

"Cassie! This is Drea! You better have that map. Call me back!"

"Cassie! This is Drea! You better call me back! Call me back!"

So, the immediacy of her interrogation came as no surprise.

I didn't look forward to telling Drea about the outcome of my date-like transaction with my ex. But maybe I could cheer her up with the news that Sam and I hooked up?

"I made out with Sam Goody!" I gushed.

Drea tapped the brakes. "You did?"

"I did!" I bounced up and down like a candy-addled toddler.

"Congratulations! It's about time you got some!" Drea double high-fived me. "He's cute!"

"He *is* cute!" My voice was all squeaky in a way I was unused to hearing. "And he loved my new look."

"Sam is the anti-Troy. Of course he loved it as much as your ex hated it."

Then Drea literally and figuratively shifted gears.

"So. Did you hook up with Sam Goody before or after you got the map?"

I fiddled with the silver hoop in my ear instead of answering right away.

"About that . . ."

Drea snorted and took a speed bump about ten miles over the speed limit.

"I'm so sorry, Drea," I said. "I realized, like, halfway into the dinner that I wouldn't want to take the map from Troy even if he offered. I don't want to be indebted to him in any way."

Drea sighed and drooped wearily on the steering wheel.

"Couldn't you have waited to take the moral high ground until *after* you got the map?"

"I—"

It was too late. Drea put the top down and the volume on the stereo way up. Between the synthetic throb of house music and the roar of the road, there was no way she could have heard my explanation even if I'd offered one. She preferred ruining her hair over listening to my excuses for letting her down. When we arrived at the mall, Drea swiftly exited the Miata, and I hurried to follow.

"I really wanted to find the treasure," I said. "But not at any cost."

"I get it," she said curtly.

"I can still help you with the application to FIT."

"Without the money, what's the point?"

"We don't even know if the treasure is real, Drea," I reasoned. "But you shouldn't let that stop you from applying. I *promise* I can get you financial aid and all that . . ."

If I perfected Drea's application to FIT, she'd forget all about how I'd botched the treasure hunt.

"Are you one hundred percent sure you can help me get in?"

Any Mock Trial coach would tell you to avoid answering any questions requiring 100 percent certainty. There was no such thing. But . . .

"Yes!" I lied.

Drea didn't want to let me off the hook that easily, but a barely there smile betrayed her gratitude.

"Fine," she finally agreed with an overly casual shrug. "But you'll have to work around my schedule. I've got two bridal parties *and* a bat mitzvah scheduled for this morning. You know I'm covering all the appointments while Ma works on the Back-to-School Fashion Show."

I was only half listening as I unlocked the office door and switched on the light. In the battle for my attention, Drea's academics were no match for sexual fantasies about Sam Goody.

"Of course! Of course!" I babbled, imagining what he looked like with his shirt off. "Whenever and whatever you want . . ."

We were so focused on ourselves—Drea on her busy day ahead of her, me on my busy night behind me—that it took a moment to register we weren't alone in the office.

"Boo."

33

GHOST GODDESS

*G*host Girl was back. Unfortunately, she was empty-handed.
No doll. No map. No clue.

"I'm sorry."

Zoe didn't offer an explanation as to how she got in the office without a key, or why she was waiting for us in the dark. Honestly, asking for such petty details would've been an insult to her supernatural instincts. Do you ask a vampire why he bites? A werewolf why he howls at the moon?

I did, however, want to know why she was apologizing to us.

"I wouldn't have given Troy the doll if I'd known you wanted it," Zoe explained. "Did I think it was weird that he was asking me for my Cabbage Patch Doll? Sure, but who am I to judge what's weird? I'm saving up for a coffin and want an ankh tattooed on my tongue."

Drea sucked sharply on her teeth. Not in disapproval, exactly. More like, disbelief. Why would anyone voluntarily do that to herself?

"I didn't care why he wanted it," Zoe continued. "I just saw it as my chance to take that entitled prick down a few notches by making him my garbage bitch for the rest of the summer."

"I can't get mad at that," Drea said admiringly.

"Please tell me you put a curse on the doll before you let him have it," I said.

A close-mouthed smile spread across her lips.

"The biggest curse I put on him," Zoe replied, "was putting him on the schedule with Helen."

I laughed hard.

"I have to know," Drea said. "Why'd you go after Slade? Those tanning pills were genius!"

Zoe looked directly at Drea, then shifted her attention my way.

"I'm tired of guys like him being shitty to girls like you," she said. "Or me."

"Go on . . ." I urged.

"Well, I saw what Troy did to you at the start of the summer. And then the way Slade spread those rumors. And I know how that humiliation feels. Like, personally."

Wait, was Zoe saying what I thought she was saying? Thankfully, I had Drea to put it all out there, dispensing with any subtleties.

"You hooked up with Slade?" she asked. "*You?*"

It was a fair question. Slade was the tanned, taut embodiment of sun and fun. Zoe looked like she wandered away from a mausoleum.

"Not Slade, but close enough," she explained. "See, I wasn't always like this."

She withdrew a photo from the inner pocket of her cloak. In it, a beaming french-braided girl posed with pom-poms on her hips in the green-and-yellow cheerleading uniform for Eastland High, Pineville's crosstown rival. Drea and I examined the picture, then Zoe. The picture. Then Zoe again. A quadruple take was absolutely necessary.

"That's who I was before."

"Before what?" Drea and I asked.

"Before I was hurt by a boy just like Slade," she said simply. "They're all the same."

I was instantly incensed. "What did he say about you?"

Zoe lifted her chin, literally holding her head high.

"It's not what he said," she said. "It's what he *did.*"

Her words knocked me right off my feet.

Until that moment, I hadn't considered the possibility that maybe I'd gotten off easy with just a rumor. Lots of girls have dealt with a lot worse at parties just like that one.

"From that point on, I vowed not to let any boys fuck with me," Zoe continued. "Or anyone else."

Drea literally bowed down in worship.

"Amen!"

She, too, was now fully indoctrinated in the Cult of Zoe, a new religion for feminist vigilantes.

"Don't go anywhere!" Drea hustled out of the office.

Once we were alone, Zoe beckoned me forward.

"Next time you're down in the dumper," she whispered, "take time to look up."

Was this a joke? Had Zoe gotten this koan off a greeting card? I almost laughed in her face. But when I looked into her tranquil, kohl-rimmed eyes, I knew she wasn't messing around. Despite sounding awfully close to a Hallmark store cliché, her word choice was just strange and specific enough—the *dumper*?—to be persuasive. Zoe knew what she was saying. I just hadn't, like, *evolved* to the point of understanding what she meant.

"Okay," I said, trusting her words would make sense in time. "I'll do that."

Drea rushed back in with a crushed velvet scarf draped over her arm. It was extra-long and all black save for an interlocking vine design along the edge. The embroidery shimmered in a silvery thread that matched Zoe's piercings.

"I want you to have this," Drea said. "It's from our fall collection."

Zoe accepted Drea's offering without protest.

"Thank you."

She wrapped the scarf around her shoulders and pulled the ends tight across her body. This sumptuous embrace was so much worthier of a warrior goddess than the pathetic hug she would have received from me.

"I knew it was perfect for you."

As always, Drea was right.

After Zoe glided away, Drea turned to me.

"Your mom's out front."

"Actually! I'm right here!" Kathy swept into the room and gasped at the sight of me. "Cassandra! You cut your hair! When did you cut your hair? *Why* did you cut your hair?"

We lived together, but hardly saw each other. If she hadn't invaded my workspace, it's possible Kathy wouldn't have found out about my haircut until she drove me and my belongings to Barnard for orientation.

"I think it's chic," Drea said. "Don't you?"

"It's just . . ." Kathy forced a weak smile. *"Different."*

I could've said the same about the brassy highlights in her hair, but I didn't.

"Mo-om." My tone was whinier than intended. "What are you doing here?"

She held up a Bellarosa Boutique shopping bag.

"Unfortunately, I need to make a return."

She'd finally come to her senses. Mom was returning the bimbo dress because she was a sensible middle-aged dentist, not a horny divorcée . . .

Kathy held up a cashmere sweater in a pumpkin-orange shade known locally as "Slade."

"Thankfully, Frank didn't cut the tags," Kathy said. "And kept the receipt."

Wholesale, Gia got it for $150. It sold for $240. Fifty percent markup was the industry standard. Leave it to the Bellarosa ladies to push it up by ten percent—and convince shoppers they were getting a bargain.

"I knew this would happen," said Drea. "I tried telling Frank that you're a summer, like Cassie here, but he insisted on buying that sweater in orange."

Because orange is her favorite color, I thought.

"Because he thinks orange is my favorite color," Kathy said.

"It isn't?" I asked.

Orange is your mother's favorite color. I thought back to all the orange gifts I'd given her over the years: coffee mugs and beaded necklaces and potted marigolds . . .

"Nope," Kathy answered. "Never has been. My favorite color is blue."

Blue and orange are opposites on the color wheel. Like, you can't get more different than blue and orange.

"I think we've got one in your size in cerulean . . ." Drea said.

For the first time since they announced their separation, I didn't feel sorry for myself. I actually felt bad for them. Maybe I'd go out of my way to see her tonight at home. Maybe we could talk through everything that'd been going on for the last few weeks. Maybe I'd even tell her about what had happened between me and Sam Goody . . .

"Oooooowwwww!" I howled.

Kathy let go of my earlobe.

"Cassandra! Put some peroxide on that," she commanded. "It looks infected."

Or maybe not.

34

PROS AND CONS

For hours, I failed to stay focused on reconciling Bella-rosa's bank statement. All I could think about was Sam Goody. How had I survived seventeen years without his luscious mouth . . . ? How could I last another week . . . ?

So, it was a relief when Drea came bursting through the office, mid-scheme. I didn't have to put up the pretense of working anymore.

"Gia's in a meeting! We need to get started before she gets back!"

"Get started on what?"

"On what?" she asked incredulously. "On getting me into FIT!"

"Right, yes, of course," I said, refocusing.

She sat attentively in front of my desk, pen uncapped, yellow legal pad flipped to a blank page, ready to take notes.

"Okay," I improvised. "Let's assess the pros and cons of your applicant profile."

Drea's pen hovered over the first line.

"Okaaaaaay."

"Nothing too complicated," I said as reassuringly as possible. "Just the basics of your academic history."

The basics, as it turned out, were even worse than I imagined.

PRO

* Lifetime of experience in the retail fashion industry

CONS

* 1.7 GPA

* No SAT score

* No portfolio

* No extracurricular activities

* No letters of recommendation

I sighed. This should not have come as any surprise to me. And yet, I was *still* stunned by the lack of just about *anything* colleges seek in a candidate. I knew Drea wasn't a dummy. But there was very little for her to demonstrate otherwise to admissions officers. And no "rewrite" of mine could ever change that. Drea's prospects were bleak. I'd overestimated my abilities. I'd promised the impossible. I did not see a fat envelope from FIT in Drea's future.

Drea was watching me expectantly, waiting for the expert guidance I'd literally guaranteed her. There was no way to get out of this without hurting her feelings . . .

Or was there?

"Do you have the application?"

"No."

There it was. My out.

"Well, we can't really get started without it," I said, hoping Drea couldn't detect the relief in my voice. "That's the only way of knowing exactly what FIT is looking for."

"Of course." Drea nodded in complete agreement. "I should have thought of that."

"Contact the school and ask them to send you an application and a course catalog," I said, "and we'll go from there."

This was a brilliant first step. Getting the application required actual effort on her part, and I doubted Drea's ability to follow through. And even if she *did* complete this task, it would take a few weeks for the materials to arrive in the mail. I'd be gone by then. By mid-September I had no doubt Drea would have already moved on too. No harm, no foul.

"You *really* think I can get in?"

Her voice was the most vulnerable I'd ever heard it. I'd

never seen Drea so eager for my approval. For *anyone's* approval. There was only one right answer. And it was a lie.

"Yes."

Then Drea's eyes twitched, and I wondered if both sets of fake lashes had gone rogue simultaneously. Only when rivers of black mascara started running down her cheeks did I grasp what was happening.

Drea Bellarosa was crying.

Correction: She was *ugly* crying. If Drea's *laughter* sounded like a genocide of waterfowl, her crying . . .

"WAHWAHWHWHWHWAHHHHHHHHNNNNNK."

. . . was a mega multispecies mass extinction event.

I was so stunned by her raw show of emotion that I didn't have the wherewithal to respond with common decency.

"Gimme some tissues, already! Or do you want me snotting all over the merchandise?"

I rushed over with the box of Kleenex. She took a tissue with one hand, and my own hand in the other.

"No one has ever helped me like this." Drea dabbed her eyes. "Seriously, Cassie. You're the best friend I've ever had."

Most days I wasn't fully convinced Drea even *liked* me.

"I am?"

Drea honked into the tissue.

"Don't go getting a big head about it," she said. "I'm really shitty at picking best friends."

I couldn't tell if she was mocking herself—or me—until she cracked a slight smile.

"That was a joke."

"Oh," I replied. "Ha-ha."

Her smile faded.

"Girls don't like me, but you did," she said. "Until I gave you reasons not to."

This was the first time Drea had ever directly referred to our elementary school friendship. I sat beside her on the couch, wondering. Waiting. Did Drea want to talk about it? Did Drea want to dredge up the middle school drama that led to us not speaking to each other for more than five years? Did Drea want to apologize for abruptly deciding in seventh grade that I was neither hot nor cool enough to associate with anymore? Did Drea want to express regret for choosing dozens of boys over the one girl who liked her for who she was?

Drea did not.

She opened up a mirrored compact and gagged at her reflection instead.

"Ugh. Tammy Faye Bakker." She groaned. "I didn't know this was gonna be a waterproof mascara kind of day."

Whatever had triggered Drea's moment of vulnerability, it was over now.

I followed her into the staff bathroom, which was spotlessly clean but small and strictly utilitarian by Gia's design. Unlike the boutique and the back office, the bathroom was utterly lacking in Bellarosian frills and flourishes because Gia wanted her employees to get back to work. From the drop ceiling to the linoleum floor and the nondescript toilet/vanity/sink set in between, this was a bathroom that discouraged socializing.

I watched Drea wipe away the surface layer of runny mascara with a tissue. Then I continued to watch her at the sink as she swiped away the next layers of bronzer and concealer and foundation. And I watched as she used an astringent-soaked cotton ball to scrub away the most stubborn layers, the stay-put liners for lips and eyes.

"Ugh."

I watched Drea grimace at the face she was born with.

It was not an exaggeration to say Drea was four inches short of a *Cosmo* cover. And she knew it too. It was why she never, ever, *ever* wore flats. She nearly failed gym for violating the athletic department dress code. If she hadn't designed and customized a wedge-heeled sneaker, she wouldn't have gotten enough credits to graduate high school.

No, she was not FIT material. But I wasn't going to be the one to break it to her.

Not now.

Not ever.

35

PINKY PUSH

*W*hen Drea picked me up for work six days later, I was stunned to see an application for FIT resting in the passenger seat.

"Surprise!"

"How . . . ?"

The United States Postal Service didn't work that fast. Drea quickly explained that Crystal—*No-Good Crystal*—had picked it up for her when she was in the city for a club crawl. She would've gotten the course catalog too, but it wasn't available yet. It was just my luck for a Bellarosa cousin to decide to be dependable for the first time in her entire friggin' life.

"Now we can *really* get started!" Drea gushed. "Let's hit the library tonight after our shift."

"The *library*?"

Never in a billion lifetimes did I ever expect to hear Drea suggest a trip to the library.

"Ma will be busy with the fashion show, so it's perfect timing!"

I smiled so hard, I wore the enamel off my molars.

"Great!" I replied insincerely.

The tonnage of that two-page application weighed heavily on my mind all morning. The pressure to make good on my impossible promise only got more unbearable as the hours ticked by. On my lunch break, I was so nauseatingly stressed that I skipped food altogether in favor of a free chair massage at Electronics Universe.

It wasn't working.

I closed my eyes and surrendered to the pulsating waves. My body quivered from head to toe, but a million invisible robot fingers weren't enough to soothe me. All "tension, stiffness, and tiredness" did not "melt away" as advertised.

"What do you think?" asked Doug.

He was Drea's ex who had given her the memory expansion card for the Mac. He'd shaved the mustache since the last time I'd seen him, and he was a lot cuter without it. He could have passed himself off as the younger brother of Rob Lowe if only he weren't cuter than the actual younger brother of Rob Lowe. I felt sorry for him, though. The massage chairs were lined up near the entrance to draw customers into the store. But had any of these free demonstrations turned into an actual sale? Doug went through with the pretense anyway because that's what he was paid for. And I upheld my end of the charade because it was the courteous thing to do.

"It's quite an investment," I said. "I'll have to think about it."

Doug gave me his card and brought his five-star customer service over to an unaccompanied ten-year-old who was repeatedly ramming a remote control monster truck into a stack of cordless phones.

I sighed, shut my eyes, and settled back into the now-still recliner. No, I would not be shelling out for the Miracle At-Home Massage Chair. What I really needed was another trip to bliss in Sam Goody's Chevette. All week I'd found myself wandering past the music store, even though I knew he wouldn't be there. He wouldn't be back for another day, but signs of him were all around the store if you knew where to look. The zines hidden in the magazine rack or the Pixies CD he'd snuck into the Billboard Top 40 window display. I nearly swooned at the sight of red clearance tags on soundtracks no one wanted to listen to from sequels no one wanted to see: *Ghostbusters II. Short Circuit 2. Caddyshack II.*

Sam Goody could be anywhere between Pineville and Cambridge. And even if he were home, I couldn't call him anyway because I didn't have his phone number. That's right. I was officially the type of girl who made out with someone I didn't know well enough to exchange digits.

My eyes were still closed, but I sensed someone standing over me. For the briefest, most beautiful moment I believed it was Sam Goody. He'd come to the mall a day early to surprise me, to put this vibrating recliner to its most arousing use . . .

"Cassandra!"

I got the exact opposite of what I wanted. I kept my eyes closed, though I knew it would do me little good.

"I told you to stop calling me that, Troy."

"Fine, Cassie," he huffed. "Why do you want my SAT prep book?"

"*Our* SAT prep book," I corrected.

"You want a joint-custody agreement?"

Even with my eyes shut, I knew he had a shit-eating grin, the one smeared across his face whenever he thought he was being particularly witty.

"No," I said. "I don't want it at all. I have no idea what you're talking about."

"Then why did Drea Bellarosa of all people come to my workplace and demand that I hand it over?"

Whoa. A trip to the library *and* an SAT prep book? Drea was even more serious about FIT than I could have ever imagined. I clutched the arms of the massage chair and held on for dear life. But I would not give him the satisfaction of opening my eyes.

"She's applying to the Fashion Institute of Technology," I said, "and I'm helping her."

Troy was overcome by piggish snorts of laughter.

"Drea Bellarosa? In college?"

Another round of bovine hilarity.

"Didn't she fail gym? I mean, fashion school isn't even real school, but I don't think they would lower their standards that far."

It should be noted that some of the "lesser Ivies" didn't meet

Troy's definition of a "real school." If pressed, I'm sure he had chauvinistic opinions of Barnard as "okay for a girl school." And yet, he wasn't wrong about Drea's prospects. It was that thin-envelope inevitability that had led me to this massage chair nightmare in the first place.

"Drea Bellarosa is a Pineville lifer," Troy said definitively. "She'll never be college material. The mall is her pitiful destiny."

I wouldn't have used those exact words. But Troy was saying out loud what I'd kept to myself since agreeing to help her. I squeezed my eyes even tighter as if to prevent—and protect—me from seeing the truth of this situation I'd put myself in.

"Look," Troy continued. "You can pretend all you want that you're not interested in talking to me . . ."

"I'm not pretending."

It was true. But it suddenly seemed very silly to keep my eyes closed. So I opened them slowly. And when my vision adjusted to the light, I was rewarded with the sight of Troy kneeling at my footrest. And he actually looked . . . apologetic?

"Okay, Cassie, here's the truth: I'm sorry for how much I hurt you. Both you and I know that we are the only high-IQ intellectuals this lowbrow town has ever produced. There is an unbreakable bond between us."

Troy intoned this with great gravity. I pictured him rehearsing in the mirror at home. Was there any truth to it?

"I know you feel totally lost without *the plan*." His voice was escalating. He was building up to his final argument. "Let's get back to building our future. We are a power couple, stronger together than we are apart."

Troy took my hand in his. His touch felt cold and rubbery

and lifeless, reminding me of the fetal pig we dissected in AP Biology. As a vegetarian, I should have refused to experiment on animals for ethical reasons. Instead, I picked up the scalpel without complaint. Why? Because Troy was my partner in the lab and—according to *the plan*—in life. I couldn't let him down. For two years I chose him over my convictions, but I would not repeat that mistake. Not with Troy. Not with any other boy. Not ever again.

"I'm not lost!" I snatched my hand from his and stood. "In fact, I've already *found* someone new. And he is nothing, *nothing* like you." I poked the center of his chest. "Goodbye, Troy."

With the tiniest push of a pinky, I sent my ex sprawling backward into the massage chair where—for all I know—he might still be to this very day.

36

MIRACLE

*N*ine hundred thousand square feet wasn't adequate for the distance I needed to put between me and Troy. I needed to be as far away from him as possible. I needed to breathe un-recycled air. I needed to escape the mall and go. . . . where?

The nearest exit brought me to the sidewalk abutting the Macy's upper level parking lot. The sun was shining, but the damp air was fragrant with impending rain. I closed my eyes, tilted my head to the sky, and filled my lungs as the first droplets of water splashed off my forehead, my nose, my chin. I don't know how long I stood there, but when I opened my eyes, I was rewarded with the most majestic sight:

240

A double rainbow stretched across the firmament, a turd-brown hatchback idling underneath.

I wasn't religious, but Sam Goody's arrival felt like a miracle, an act of God. The passenger side door was open wide, and I didn't hesitate to get in beside him.

"I came back a day early," he said.

"You came back just in time," I said.

Without another word, he threw the car in gear and sped to a more secluded section of the parking lot.

"I missed you," he said.

He kissed my forehead, my nose, my chin.

"I missed you too," I said.

He kissed my mouth.

---

*M*y mind left me as I kissed Sam Goody. But not in a distracted way. I wasn't thinking about the fall of communism or unfunny sitcoms. I wasn't thinking about getting even with my ex, making peace with my parents' split, or telling Drea the truth about her dismal college prospects. I wasn't thinking about anything at all, not even how easy it would be for a straggler shopper to see two half-naked teens going at it, that is, until we fogged up the windows to completely obstruct the view.

As we kissed in the front seat and did even more on the hatchback floor, I wasn't thinking about how strange it was for me to lose my virginity to someone I had met a little over a month ago, to strip down to next to nothing and unabashedly share my body with this person I barely knew yet trusted completely, a person who, in tacit alignment, made himself equally available—and vulnerable—to me. With only the drumming of rain on the roof as our soundtrack, I let him discover places I hadn't allowed anyone else to go to. I sought out parts of him too, an eager skin-to-skin exploration I never before needed to pursue. In the back of that busted, rusted Chevette, cognition surrendered to sensation. I was completely immersed in Sam Goody's scent, taste, and touch. There was no past, no future, only the exquisite present.

I was fully in the moment for the first time in my life.

37

FRESH STARTS

*K*athy drove me to the mall early on the morning of the Back-to-School Fashion Show. If she had any idea her only daughter wasn't a virgin anymore, she didn't let on. And I certainly wasn't going to tell her.

"Being alive," she sang along with Barbra. "Being aliiiiiiiiiiiiiiiiiiive."

I was so giddy, I nearly joined in. I didn't want to go there with Kathy, but I couldn't wait to share the big news with Drea. She'd be so proud of me! I'd proven I was over Troy by getting under someone else! Maybe I could hit her up for some techniques.

Surely someone who'd subscribed to *Cosmo* for over a decade had a tip or two to share.

I was already fantasizing about our next tryst. I was counting on Drea and Gia being so caught up in fashion show chaos that they wouldn't even notice if I disappeared for an hour . . . or two . . . or long enough for Sam to drive the Chevette somewhere we couldn't be caught with our pants down in broad daylight. Having sex in the parking lot was reckless and risky in a way neither one of us was accustomed to. But achieving an uninhibited level of solitude wouldn't be so easy. Jersey was already the most densely populated state in the country even without the influx of a billion out-of-state bennies every Friday through Sunday in the summer . . .

"Cassandra!"

My Sam Goody fantasies were making it tough for me to concentrate on making minimal conversation with my mother.

"What?"

"We need to go shopping before you leave for school next week," she said. "Get you all the dorm room essentials!"

"Not necessary," I said. "Dad and I already took care of it."

She slowed down as she approached the pedestrian drop-off.

"When?"

"A few weeks ago, when we were buying stuff for the guest room at his condo," I said. "I just made it easy by getting two of everything."

I'd picked a jewel-toned paisley bedspread because it was more sophisticated than the pastel florals I'd grown up with. Simone Levy from Rochester, New York, was a little irritated that I hadn't waited to consult her on our shared room's aesthetic, but that was her own fault for waiting over a month to write me back.

"So, your dorm room at school will have the exact same decor as the guest room at your father's?"

Two bedspreads, four decorative pillows, two area rugs, two desk organizers, two trash cans.

"More or less."

"No!" She accidentally honked the horn, startling us both. "Your dorm room will *not* be a facsimile of your father's guest room . . ."

Honestly, she seemed more upset about my duvet than she did about the divorce.

"But you'll like it, Mom," I said. "It's *blue*. Which, *apparently*, is your favorite color."

Kathy was too exasperated by the shopping trip with Frank to pick up on my sarcasm.

"I hope he kept the receipts, because it's all going back," she said. "You need a fresh start at school, Cassandra. You need to put the past behind you and move forward toward an uncertain future . . ."

When her voice quavered, I realized we weren't really talking about duvets anymore.

"If we put history totally behind us," I said, "how do we learn anything about ourselves?"

For two years I was with someone who never laughed at my jokes. Sam Goody—who, again, was nothing, *nothing* like Troy—laughed at *all* my jokes. But if I had ignored history and pretended like I hadn't spent two years with a boy who *never* laughed at my jokes, I might have set myself up to make the same mistake again. What a tragedy it would be if Kathy called it quits after twenty years only to end up with another well-intentioned but clueless man who thought her favorite color was orange.

"At forty-five, I thought I already knew everything I needed to know about myself," she said. "But I was totally wrong."

When she laughed at herself, I knew it was okay to laugh with her. Was it a coincidence that my parents and I were embarking on new phases in our lives at the same time? Or was it my impending departure that inspired them to start over again? The Volvo had come to a stop, but I didn't want this conversation to end. I was ready to finally ask these questions, but I guess Kathy wasn't ready to answer them.

"Just don't settle for the first duvet that comes your way," she said. "Even if it's really comfy."

"I'm not settling," I said, thinking of Sam Goody. "I promise."

Kathy angled closer to me. I braced myself for the insult, thinking for sure she was about to chastise me for not putting peroxide on my piercing. Instead, she planted a light kiss on my cheek.

"Your father and I love you very much."

I was almost too overwhelmed by this unusually affectionate gesture to assure her I loved them too.

38

THE CROSSROADS

I arrived at Bellarosa an hour early to spill all the details to Drea about my devirginization. Evidently, this was already too late.

"Where have you been, Cassie?" Gia brayed. "The show starts in less than three hours, and I need to make sure everything is in order! Get dressed *now*!"

"Get dressed?" I asked. "What are you talking about?"

She pointed to the electric-blue tube dress.

Yes, *the* electric-blue tube dress.

"We're already seeing more traffic this morning," Gia explained. "I'm counting on you to work the sales floor with Drea while I'm going over all the last-second details for the fashion show."

"No, no, no! There's no way it will fit! I've gained all my mono weight back!" I protested. "If it gets stuck on my head, I could asphyxiate myself! If it cuts off my circulation at the knees, I could bust a blood clot!"

I looked to Drea for backup, but she was on the opposite side of the store pulling looks for a customer in the dressing room. Gia placed a hand on each shoulder and brought her face so close to mine, our noses touched.

"If you don't put that dress on right now," she said in the calmest possible voice, "I will choke you myself."

Like mother, like daughter.

I took the infamous dress into the changing room. Without thinking too hard about it, I stepped into the tube feet first, figuring I could always shout for help if I got stuck.

But I didn't get stuck.

"Come on out, Cassie!" Gia shook the curtain. "I don't have all day."

With one tug, the slippery fabric slid right past my knees, over my hips, and up to my bust. Again. But this time felt different than before. Now the tube dress fit like a second skin and I was not sure how I felt about it.

Gia was far less ambivalent when I finally emerged.

"Why have we been hiding you all summer?"

She slapped her cheeks. Then she slapped mine.

"Whaaa—?"

"A body like yours in a dress like that should not be wasted in the back office is what I'm saying!"

Drea and her mom exchanged superficial compliments all the time, constantly reminding each other how hot they were and how their hotness was great for sales. But Gia had never so blatantly objectified my body before. I was definitely not used to my ass being a business asset.

"Now you're just being silly."

"I am not being silly," Gia insisted, shoving me in front of a mirror.

Gia was right. This was not an outfit for a behind-the-scenes bookkeeper paid to track inventory, income, and expenses. I looked like a heavy metal video vamp whose only responsibility was getting doused by the singer's phallic fire hose. It was the same exact dress I didn't have the soul for earlier in the summer. And now that I was back to my pre-mono weight, I shouldn't have had the body for it either.

And yet.

Now.

It fit?

Perfectly?

Gia held out a pair of strappy flat sandals in gold leather.

"You're ready for the dress, but you aren't ready for stilettos," she said. "Not yet."

"I don't think I'm ready for any of it," I said.

Gia ignored this and buckled me into the shoes as Drea made her approach. She made a very deliberate show of fluffing her bangs in the mirror instead of saying good morning to me.

"Ma, you know I'd never question your brain for business or eye for style," she began. "But are you aware that our back office accountant is leaving for college in less than a week? I doubt she wants to waste her energy by putting in some actual hard work on the Bellarosa sales floor."

Drea was only reinforcing my own argument. And yet, it didn't feel like she was backing me up. It felt like she was putting me down. I managed to withstand a few seconds of Drea's unrelenting glare before grasping why she was so irritated with me.

"The library!" I slapped my forehead.

In my postcoital haze, I'd forgotten all about our plans to work on her doomed FIT application last night.

"What's she talking about?" Gia asked.

"Absolutely nothing of any importance," Drea replied. "Right, *Cassandra*?"

Her snappish reaction took me by surprise. And maybe her too. Because she quickly changed her tone and the subject.

"Relax," Drea said. "I'm just *joking*."

"Right." I laughed uneasily. "Of course."

Here's the thing: I knew Drea wasn't joking. But she wasn't 100 percent serious either. Her tone was pitched at the crossroads, and I honestly couldn't tell which was closer to the truth. One thing I knew for sure: Now definitely wasn't the right time to tell Drea about what happened in the hatchback.

"I'm already in the dress," I said. "I might as well help you on the floor!" And then without thinking I added, "I mean, how hard can it be?"

Drea opened her mouth, then quickly and very uncharacteristically shut it.

If she had spoken up, I might have defied Gia and stayed in the back of the store where I belonged. I might have returned to my blanket igloo and hibernated for the last week of summer. Instead, I sat and let Gia fix my naked face and unstyled hair. There was no way she would let me out on the sales floor without a seasonal makeover.

"No offense," Gia said, spackling my face with what I think was bronzer.

At least she agreed with Drea. I was a summer. This was supposedly the most subtle of all the cosmetic color palettes, and yet Gia had applied no less than four shades of eye shadow, three coats of mascara, two layers of foundation and one very, very purple lip color she swore up and down was "plum." How did any girl smile under the weight of so much subtlety? When she was finished, the three of us stood in front of the mirror and marveled at what Gia was already calling her "five-minute miracle."

Gia, Drea, and I looked like . . .

Family.

"Don't forget! You need to get yourselves to the food court no later than eleven thirty, do you hear me? Eleven thirty!"

Then she kissed us both and left, passing an incoming customer on the way out. I waited for Drea to say something complimentary about my new look.

"Make yourself look busy," she said coldly.

I sighed. There was no way Drea could maintain this level of irritation for long. I was certain she'd come to her senses before the fashion show and laugh the whole thing off as a particularly powerful bout of premenstrual bitchiness or hypoglycemic hysteria, both conditions quickly cured by a complimentary Orange Julius. I'd tell her about Sam and my devirginization and we'd be back to being BFFs.

I was wrong.

39

FEROCIOUS AND FIRED

For the next hour, I stayed out of Drea's way and did a solid job of making myself look busy. I took the same half dozen halter tops on and off their hangers and successfully managed to avoid making contact with any of the customers. Drea was preoccupied with a plastic wife of a plastic surgeon who was shopping for a full calendar of benefits and charity balls.

"Can this neckline go any lower?" she asked, presumably to show off her husband's pneumatic handiwork.

"You ask, we alter," Drea cooed. "Your look will be as chic and unique as you are!"

I assumed she'd totally forgotten that I was technically

supposed to be helping her on the sales floor. As it turned out, Drea was just waiting for the right opportunity to test my nascent customer service skills.

"Aha!"

Drea excused herself from the face-lifted philanthropist and pulled me away from the halter tops.

"Here she comes! The White Whale is back!"

Mona Troccola.

By that point, I was very familiar with Mona Troccola's American Express account number. She lived in Toms River, a few zip and income tax codes over from Pineville. Toms River boasted its own country club with tennis courts, an Olympic-sized pool, and a golf course. Only nine holes you had to play twice, but still. *Fancy.* Mona also owned a thirty-two-foot motorboat that she often referred to as her "starter yacht" in a way that was supposed to sound like she was joking when in fact she was deadly serious. Divorced for two years, she was one year and eleven months behind on locking down husband number two. Decades at the club and on the open water had left Mona's skin the color and consistency of beef jerky.

"You take Mona," Drea said. "Earn your final paycheck."

There it was again. That *tone.* If I were more confrontational, more like Drea herself, I might have called her out right then and there.

"Just tell her every third look is slimming and she'll buy it."

Mona paused at the entrance to take a last, long drag on her cigarette. Regulars knew Gia didn't allow smoking in the store out of respect for the delicate fabrics and luxurious materials Bellarosa Boutique was famous for.

"Every third look?"

"You can't tell her everything she tries on is slimming because she won't believe it," Drea said. "Only recommending certain looks—and not the most expensive ones—builds up a sense of trust. She thinks I'm the only one who tells the truth."

"You're not telling the truth?"

What a dumb question. Of course Drea wasn't telling the truth to a woman who looked like the Crypt Keeper in everything she tried on. Mona flicked her butt into the ashtray. Without missing a single beat, Drea went in for the nicotine-tinged air-kiss.

"Mona! Darling! MWAH!"

"Drea! Darling! MWAH! Who is this gorgeous new girl you got working for you now?"

I was the only person standing there, and yet it still took us both a moment to realize whom Mona was referring to. In the silence, an orchestral cover of Lionel Ritchie's "All Night Long" ended, followed by a jazzy take on Stevie Wonder's "Part-Time Lover." Bellarosa Boutique's soundtrack was familiar and comforting by design. And yet it did little to ease the tension.

"Um, I'm Cassie?" I said, as if I were in doubt of that fact. "I've worked here all summer?"

Mona couldn't believe what she was seeing.

"Cassie?" She blinked her spidery lashes. "*Cassie?*"

I couldn't blame Mona for not recognizing me.

"I can't believe this is Cassie!"

I have to 20/20 vision but, I could hardly recognize my own

reflection in the mirror. Based on the blurry blobs of color I could make out, it was probably better that way.

"It's me," I said, "in the flesh."

"You better watch out, Drea! You've got some competition!"

Drea and I gawked at Mona with incredulity. No one had *ever* said I was in the same league as Drea looks-wise. Makeover or not, her position as "the hot one" was undisputed. It would've been equally absurd to suggest Drea was "the smart one." Mona obviously consumed too much vodka and not enough lettuce for breakfast that morning.

"We already pulled perfect looks that have your name all over them," Drea said. "You'll find them waiting for you in dressing room number one."

I, of course, had no part in this.

"Perfect," I repeated.

I threw a panicked look at Drea, but she just shrugged and used my own words against me.

"How hard can it be?"

I had a few minutes to center myself as Mona tried on her first outfit.

"Taaa-daaa!"

Mona struck a pose in a yellow drop-waist off-the-shoulder sweater and graffiti-print stirrup pants. It was an obnoxious outfit in every way.

"Whaddya think?"

It suited her perfectly. But then I remembered, *Every third look.*

"Hmm. It doesn't do much for you," I said as tactfully as possible. "Let me see you in something else."

Mona smiled and went back behind the pink curtain. Gia claimed the color threw off a creamy glow that complemented all shoppers' skin tones, though Mona's charred complexion was more challenging than most. Fortunately, Gia also insisted on installing top-notch lighting all around the store, especially in the dressing area. The investment had paid off. Customers were always saying they felt more beautiful at Bellarosa than anywhere else in the whole mall, which in this tiny corner of New Jersey meant the whole friggin' world. That's what I was thinking about when Mona asked the fateful question.

"Working here full-time now, sweetheart?"

"No! NO! *NO!* I leave for college next week!"

The horrified escalation of each "no" was as true-to-heart-and-soul as anything that had ever come out of my mouth. It was one thing to *look* like a lifer at the mall, but to actually be one was an entirely different matter. I was insulted by the assumption.

And by the ferocious look on Drea's face, I wasn't the only one who was insulted.

With a sudden, stomach-turning clarity, I realized how I must have sounded to Drea. Her ample chest visibly heaved beneath her leopard-print bustier. Appropriately enough, her eyes flashed white like a jungle cat before it lunged for the kill. I'd seen Drea lash out with animal rage countless times before. But never, ever at me. It was terrifying.

"I can't take it anymore!" Drea roared. "You're fired!"

"Fired? You can't fire me! I've only got . . ."

"Six days left! We know! Everyone knows you can't wait to get the hell out of here. I'm just making it easy for you!"

"Drea, calm down," I said. "You're being overdramatic."

"And you're being an asshole," Drea shot back.

This rejoinder thrilled her audience. Mona and Madame Plastic applauded, and I swear Drea took a bow because she thrived on this kind of attention. She wanted me to skitter away timidly, to wait until she decided she wasn't mad anymore. But what would happen if I didn't play along like she wanted me to? What if I decided to call the shots in this drama? I was dressed and made-up to look like Drea. Maybe I'd take a cue from my makeover and act like her too. Let *her* be on the receiving end of over-the-top histrionics for a change.

"Fine! Fire me!" I shouted back. "Good luck balancing the books without me!"

I didn't really mean it. But I must have been convincing enough because Drea's expression went unnervingly calm. Cool. And when she spoke, it was in a low rasp that was all the more chilling for its utter lack of heat.

"We were just fine for seven years, we'll be fine now," she said icily. "And we'll be fine after you leave."

Then she turned her back on me to receive hugs from Mona and Madame Plastic. This wasn't really happening, was it?

"Drea . . ."

"Just go!"

Now it was *my* turn for guilt-free bad behavior. I'd never outdo her in the art of highly choreographed not-giving-a-shit, but I could try. So I intentionally knocked over a carousel of costume jewelry on my way out to make my exit more dramatic in a *Dynasty* kind of way. I thought I would feel exhilarated by my liberation, by the anticipation of Drea's inevitable apology for overreacting. But when I looked back to see Drea on her hands and knees, scrambling across the gold marble floor to pick up every overpriced, faux stone bauble, I didn't feel victorious. I just felt confused. And sad.

Very, very sad.

Alexis Carrington never looked back. Drea never looked back. And next time neither would I.

Correction: There wouldn't be a next time.

40

GOOD LUCK

I made the best of a sucky situation by heading straight to Sam Goody.

Now that we'd done it, I thought it would be kind of fun for him to see me dressed like a *Cosmo* cover model. Like, maybe I could lure him away from the sales floor to try out some sexy role play or something. Just a few minutes alone in the stockroom would be sufficient to erase what had just gone down at Bellarosa.

I was ecstatic to see him stacking cassettes near the cash registers. I sauntered over to the counter and elbow pressed my boobs together until my cups nearly runneth over. It was one of Drea's classic moves.

"Did you miss me?" I purred.

"Bellarosa!" Sam Goody gaped at my cleavage for a few seconds. "Whoa!"

"Do you like my new look?"

"I like *you*," he answered.

He propped himself up over the counter and kissed me. For a few idyllic seconds, all ill feelings toward my ex–best friend melted into dreamy oblivion. Sam pulled away before I did, his mouth smudged purple.

"Well, I'm glad *you* like me," I said, wiping the wayward gloss from his lips with my thumb. "Because Drea hates my guts . . ."

I wanted to sound like I couldn't care less. Unfortunately, I failed hard at flippancy. The analgesic effects of Sam's kiss had already worn off, and I felt as hurt by Drea as I had when I stormed out of the boutique. Before I could stop myself, my eyes were welling up.

"Hey, there," Sam said with alarm. "What's wrong? Are you okay?"

I brushed away my tears and pretended Drea's dismissal had no effect on me.

"Nothing's wrong," I croaked. "I'm fine."

I was relieved when Sam silently took my hand and led me to the stockroom. Less crying, more kissing. Yes! That was exactly what I needed! I wrapped my arms around him, but he limply returned the hug. This was a crueler rejection than a stiff-armed rebuff.

"I *like* you," he repeated.

It sure didn't feel like he liked me.

"I like you too," I said.

"But this"—he broke from me and swiped a hand in the space that separated us—"is weird."

"It's just hairspray and about ten pounds of bronzer!" I insisted. "I can take it off if you want." Then I lowered my voice to my best approximation of a sultry rasp. "I can take it *all* off if you want."

I didn't wait for an answer before launching myself at him for a lusty kiss. But without my glasses, I misjudged the blurry inches between us and clocked Sam in the chin with my forehead instead.

"Whoa!" he cried out. "Let's slow down here!"

"Slow down?" I objected. "We don't have time to slow down!"

"Seriously," Sam said in a watchful tone, "before one of us gets hurt."

He was rubbing his jaw, but that wasn't the pain he was referring to. This stockroom seduction was not going at all the way I had planned.

"You sure know how to ruin a mood," I griped.

Sam took off his glasses, wiped the lenses on the bottom of his T-shirt, then put them back on again, as if to double-check that the girl he was talking to was really me.

"Look, I don't know what sex means to you, but it's special to me," he said. "Before you, I'd only ever done it with my ex, and we dated for two years first."

This speech was all very sweet and sensitive and wholly unnecessary.

"But the hatchback was fun, right?" I asked. "We had fun."

Sam blushed and nodded in agreement.

"I'm leaving in six days," I argued. "What's wrong with having the most fun right now?"

"I guess I'm not a *right now* kind of guy."

He spoke in such a low voice, I had trouble hearing him over the snarling guitars playing over the store's sound system. It wasn't Nirvana, but similar. The mumbly singer was crystal clear on the chorus: "*Why go home? Why go home? Why go home?*"

"I can't be with you *right now* without thinking about a week from *right now* when you're at school and I'm here," he continued. "Or a year from *right now* when you're in New York and I'm in Portland or Seattle."

Portland—home to his hippie cousin and countless rocks to climb—was understandable. But Seattle? Why would Sam or anyone move to Seattle?

"Isn't Seattle the rainiest, most depressing city in the world?" I asked.

"There's a whole progressive scene happening in Seattle right now—politics and art and music." He pointed to the air, filled with the mumbly singer's moans. "Pearl Jam is from Seattle. Nirvana is from Seattle. Well, Aberdeen, actually, but . . ."

Now I was the one who was totally confused.

"You're moving to Seattle to follow bands?"

"No, no, no," he said. "And this isn't about Seattle, specifically. It's about the future, generally."

"What about the future?"

Sam's eyes widened. "What *about* the future? Exactly!"

He plowed his hands through his hair, making it poofier than I'd ever seen it before.

What about the future?

I didn't have an answer for him. I'd had fun with Sam Goody—more fun than I thought I was capable of having—and that was enough.

For me.

For right now.

"I've planned too much of my life, and it hasn't worked out that well," I said. "I don't want to make more plans I can't keep. So, why can't we just keep having fun while we can . . . ?"

I placed my hand on top of his. Sam shook me off.

"That's not my idea of fun."

Sam was refusing me as I had refused Troy, as Troy had refused me. I thought I'd avoided the vicious cycle of romantic mistakes, but I was no better off now than I was at the start of the summer: rejected and dejected. How could such a smart girl be so dumb?

"Good luck, Bellarosa," he said, walking away.

What Sam Goody really meant was: "Goodbye."

41

THE END OF THE RUNWAY

I wanted to be anywhere but the mall.

I called the office of Worthy Orthodontics and Pediatric Dentistry and told the receptionist to put me through to whatever parent was able to come to my rescue.

"Cassandra! It's your mother. What's wrong?"

"Cassandra! It's your father. What's wrong?"

Both picked up. Simultaneously. On separate lines. I told them I would explain later, but I needed a ride home immediately. I hung up, leaving it up to them to decide between themselves who would get to be my hero for the day. I figured it would take at least thirty minutes, more than enough time to stop by the fashion show to say goodbye to Gia. She had treated me decently all summer and deserved at least that much.

Despite observing weeks' worth of Gia's painstaking preparation, I'd still underestimated the popularity of the Back-to-School Fashion Show. Was there really so little to do in Pineville that the mall was *the* cultural destination of the late summer season? The answer, evidently, was yes. The food court was a frenzy of activity. The Silver Strutters never attracted an audience like this. All booths, tables, and chairs were already occupied and standing-only crowds flanked both sides of the runway jutting away from the stage toward the Wishing Well. Long lines extended from all purveyors of food and beverages, including America's Best Cookie, where I might have caught a quick glimpse of a sweaty, red-faced loser running around with a tray, trying to keep apace of the customer demand for free samples of a new cookie that was supposed to taste like pumpkin pie.

"It's such a good vibration . . . It's such a sweet sensation . . ."

Marky Mark and the friggin' Funky Bunch. Sam's boss, Freddy, was DJing the event and though his tastes skewed heavily toward classic rock, he was obligated to cater to the Hot 100 crowd. I guessed Sam would be put in charge of the store while he was gone, which meant I wouldn't have to worry about another awkward conversation.

I wended my way through the throng to the chaotic back-stage area, where scores of amateur models jostled for position in front of a dangerously inadequate supply of full-length mirrors. I could barely see through the thick haze of hairspray and was about to give up my search for Gia when she came racing toward me way faster than anyone in six-inch stilettos should reasonably be expected to run.

"Cassie! You're a lifesaver! I was having a quadruple heart attack over here!"

Well, at least one person at the mall was happy to see me.

"What's going on?" I asked.

"Drea didn't show up! And you're taking her place!"

"In the fashion show?" I asked incredulously.

"No, on President Bush's cabinet," Gia deadpanned. "Yes! The fashion show! What else would I mean?"

"Drea didn't tell you?" I asked. "She fired me this morning."

"What is *wrong* with that girl? She better be dead because I'm going to kill her!" she ranted. "She can't fire you! Only I have the authority to fire you! You are not fired!"

If Gia knew about our fight, would she feel differently?

"I need you in this right now." Gia pointed to a fuzzy, cowl-neck dress in a deep-wine color. "It's the last look we'll send down the runway . . ."

"I can't," I objected.

"You can."

"I can't."

"You *will*," Gia insisted. "Or . . ."

"Or you'll smother me with this mohair sweater dress and make it look like an accident?"

Gia broke out into a wide grin.

"Are you *sure* we aren't related?" She squeezed my shoulders. "Come on, Cassie. You can do this."

Gia was the only person who had come through for me this

summer in the exact way she had promised. She offered me a job and delivered on it. No more and no less. This was my final responsibility as an employee of Bellarosa Boutique and I would not let her down.

"Fine," I said. "I'll do it."

"Mwah!" Gia air-kissed me so as not to wreck my makeup. "Mwah!"

I took the dress and slipped between a set of curtains comprising the makeshift changing room. I didn't understand why it was so important to Gia for me to be a part of the fashion show when a seemingly endless stock of primping, preening Bellarosa cousins were already lined up and ready to hit the stage. Surely another one could have taken Drea's place. Why me?

"Cassie Worthy! You look incredible!"

I turned to see Bethany Darling representing Surf*Snow* Skate in a wetsuit-style bikini. What swimwear had to do with back-to-school, I had no idea. But she and about half a dozen other barely dressed models were lined up to hit the runway anyway. The store's owner made an executive decision to overrepresent surf in the fashion show, which would give the audience a lot more skin to ogle than snow or skate.

"Vicki told me the real story, that nothing happened between you and Slade," Bethany said. "I should've known he was full of shit."

There was nothing about her demeanor to give me reason to believe she was anything but 100 percent sincere about this. It would've been easier for her to pretend she hadn't seen me, to let me go off to college without ever offering this apology I didn't need, but appreciated anyway. A Beach Boys song erupted from the speakers, Surf*Snow*Skate's music cue.

"That's me! Gotta go!" And before she bounced away, she added, "We should hang out sometime!"

Why—with less than a week left in Pineville—was it suddenly so easy to get along with people I never cared about? And so difficult with anyone I did?

I couldn't actually watch the fashion show from backstage. I could only hear the music and the crowd's response to the various models—which, encouragingly, seemed to be entirely positive. Every single girl—and we were all girls, with the exception of Joey and Mikey and Pauly, resplendent in their Chess King rayons—exited ebulliently from the runway, gushing about how much fun they'd just had and how sad they were that it was already over.

"*Waiting on . . . my feelings, feelings! Waiting on . . . my feelings, feelings!*"

A female soul singer repeated these lines over and over again over a house groove. It was one of Drea's favorites and Bellarosa Boutique's cue.

"*Waiting on . . . my feelings, feelings! Waiting on . . . my feelings, feelings!*"

Bellarosa cousins surged in and out the curtains, entering and exiting, bringing me closer and closer to my sixty seconds in the spotlight. When it was my turn, I took to the stage doing a dead-on impression of Drea's hip-swiveling strut I'd unwittingly committed to muscle memory.

"*Waiting on . . . my feelings, feelings! Waiting on . . . my feelings, feelings!*"

I stomped to the beat, all arrogance and attitude. Who needed stilettos? I was a fashion warrior in gold gladiator sandals, demanding—no, *commanding*—the audience's full attention and getting it. I wish I could say time slowed down, but it didn't. Before I could believe it, I was at the end of the runway, the turning point. I paused to slap my hand on a dipped hip—just like I'd seen Drea do a million times— when I was flattened by

a barbarian horde,

a stampede of horse-drawn chariots,

a starving pride of coliseum lions,

all rolled into one

and

taking the form of an ex–best friend hell-bent on revenge.

42

THE DUMPER

I had to credit mall security for how swiftly they got the situation under control.

It took four full-grown men to stop Drea from trying to drown me in the Wishing Well. In their defense, their training course hadn't covered common protocol for two teenage girls wrestling each other to the death, so it must have been challenging for them to separate victim from perpetrator. If Gia hadn't intervened, Drea probably would have been hauled off kicking and screaming to the county jail. Only someone with years of experience in breaking up domestic disturbances could have successfully herded the two of us back to Bellarosa.

"What the hell has gotten into you?" Gia screeched at her daughter.

We shook in silence, sopping wet and still in shock. Rivulets of black mascara ran down Drea's face, as I imagined it must've run down mine.

"WHAT. THE. HELL. HAS. GOTTEN. INTO. YOU?"

Gia hadn't touched her, but Drea rebounded as if she'd been smacked in the back of the head.

"I was defending Bellarosa's reputation!"

"By making us look like trash?" Gia asked. "Do you have any idea how close you were to getting arrested? You're lucky I keep up with my annual donations to the Policemen's Benevolent Association!"

"That rat"—Drea thrust a talon in my direction—"has no respect for our store and did not deserve to represent our family on the runway."

I was still livid with Drea. I only felt guilty about Gia. She worked too hard to get all caught up in our drama.

"Gia," I began, "I'm so sorry—"

Drea shut me up with a lethal look.

"Where's *my* apology? For using me to get what *you* wanted when you knew you'd never help me get what *I* wanted? For leading me on about FIT?"

"FIT?" Gia asked. "As in the Fashion Institute of Technology? In the city?"

Judging by her puzzled expression, this was the first Gia had heard of her daughter's ambitions beyond the boutique.

"Don't worry about it, Ma, I'm not going anywhere," Drea

said. "Some of us, like *Cassandra* here, are *college material*. But I'm a *Pineville lifer*. The mall is my *pitiful destiny*."

College material . . .

Pineville lifer . . .

Pitiful destiny . . .

My insides twisted in delayed recognition of Troy's words.

"Your boyfriend's voice carries," Drea explained without me having to ask. "Doug heard you all the way across Electronics Universe. He recorded you two lovebirds on his portable tape recorder and played it back for me."

"Troy is not my boyfriend," I replied defensively. "And I didn't say any of those things about you."

"That's right! You didn't say anything! You didn't defend me against his attacks because you agree with him. Just admit it. You knew all along FIT would never *lower its standards* to accept a *lowbrow townie* like me." She used more of Troy's words as weapons. "And that's why you didn't show up at the library. You couldn't bother pretending anymore but didn't have the balls to tell me to my face."

Drea stared me down for a few interminable seconds. Water dripped from her gloppy bangs onto her nose, but she didn't flinch. Even when she was more bedraggled than bedazzled, there was still no fiercer force to be reckoned with.

"I'm—"

"You know what? Keep your apologies," Drea said. "Because the only thing you regret is wasting your summer slumming with a slutty dummy who will never do any better than the Parkway Center Mall."

When she turned and walked away, I felt in my gut it would be the last time I'd watch her go. Drea Bellarosa was the undisputed queen of dramatic exits and always would be.

It was impossible to meet Gia's gaze.

"When you let my daughter down," she said frankly, "you let me down."

Then she handed me a clean towel and left me alone.

I dragged myself into the bathroom. I needed to get out of these wet clothes, but I couldn't muster the energy to undress. When I felt brave enough to look in the mirror, I gasped at my own reflection, which was far worse than I could have even imagined. At some point during my near-death experience, I must've smacked my mouth against the concrete. My upper right front tooth was beyond chipped—roughly half of it was gone, presumably swallowed or sitting among the pennies at the bottom of the fountain. I ran my tongue along the jagged diagonal. It was a bloodless—but traumatic—injury.

I put the lid down on the toilet, sat, and sobbed.

Why did it matter if Drea hated me? This summer at Bellarosa was just a placeholder until I could start my real life in New York City like I'd always dreamed. Once I got there, I wouldn't ever have to see her or any of the other pathetic Pineville lifers ever again. At Barnard, I would finally find my people. I'd be surrounded by thousands of young women like Simone Levy who were ambitious and bright and would never settle for a lifetime of selling overpriced hoochie couture to a needy and fundamentally tacky clientele. And now that Sam Goody also wanted nothing to do with me anymore, no one tied me to this place I'd so desperately wanted to leave. I should have felt remorseless and relieved, right?

Wrong. So, so, so wrong.

I felt lower—and lonelier—than I ever had in my entire life.

Truly down in the dumps.

Or, as Zoe put it, the "dumper."

And that was when . . .

I

looked

up.

43

MALL BRAWL SHUTS DOWN
FASHION SHOW

Ocean County Observer
Sunday Edition
August 18, 1991

PINEVILLE, N.J.—An underage model for Bellarosa Boutique was assaulted at Parkway Center Mall's Back-to-School Fashion Show on Saturday afternoon.

According to Ocean County police officers on the scene, the incident began when Andrea Bellarosa, 18, of Pineville, New Jersey, tackled the model as she posed on the runway.

Dozens of witnesses report hearing Bellarosa shout an obscenity before knocking the 17-year-old victim off the catwalk and into the nearby fountain.

"She screamed, 'Die, Mono [expletive]' and charged the runway," said Bethany Darling, 18, an employee for Surf*Snow*Skate who modeled earlier in the show. "[Redacted] never saw it coming."

Because the victim is a minor, her identity is being withheld.

Tensions escalated when Bellarosa Boutique's owner, Giavanna Bellarosa, 39, also of Pineville, attempted to stop her daughter from repeatedly dunking the victim's head underwater. A team of police officers and security guards assembled to separate and remove the young females from each other and the scene. Potential criminal charges for Andrea Bellarosa included assault and disorderly conduct. However, after being treated for minor injuries, the unnamed victim chose not to pursue legal action.

"It's the craziest thing to happen here since the Cabbage Patch riot of Christmas '83," remarked Sonny Sexton, 20, a technician for Fun Tyme Arcade, referring to the infamous holiday stampede that resulted in the hospitalization of 14 shoppers and Kay-Bee Toy and Hobby employees.

It was a disturbing end to the 12th Annual Back-To-School Fashion Show, an event that has long been considered a cultural highlight of the late summer season. One observer, Zoe Gomez, 19, assistant manager of America's Best Cookie, struck a mournful tone.

"The chlorinated waters of the Wishing Well run black with mascara today."

44

STALLING

A lot happened in the six days between my bathroom revelation and leaving for Barnard.

First, I'd made it my mission to master K-turns, four-way stops, and parallel parking. I approached behind-the-wheel training with the same focus and intensity I'd always applied to my schoolwork, Mock Trial, or Odyssey of the Mind. My parents were sufficiently impressed with our practice sessions in the parking lot of Worthy Orthodontics and Pediatric Dentistry that neither objected to the use of "their" Volvo for the final driving test. I chose Dad's, but only because I knew he'd be trading it in for a midlife crisis car soon enough. Frank's Corvette was Kathy's bimbo dress. They were adults and I couldn't do a friggin' thing to stop them from making utter fools out of themselves.

I got a perfect score on the road test. I was happy, but my mouth was closed in my driver's license photo. My tooth had been broken beyond repair. It needed a full replacement.

"The other one too," Mom had said.

"Both anterior central incisors," Dad had said.

"Eight and nine," they said together.

It turned out, I couldn't just get one shiny new fake tooth and expect it to blend in with all my original old teeth. Many cosmetic dentists went too far, insisting on veneers for the entire upper row, but my parents didn't think that was necessary in my case. They only fixed the busted tooth and the one right next to it. I still wasn't used to the unfamiliar contours of my new smile. The difference was measurable in micro-millimeters, but I could feel every strange bit of it when I ran my tongue over my teeth.

I was lightly gassed during the procedure—grinding down tooth enamel with a sander wasn't painful, exactly, but it wasn't particularly pleasant. I was absolutely not whacked-out on drugs. I was lucid, if more relaxed than usual, even under the uncomfortable circumstances. I believed what I observed during those hours in the chair at Worthy Orthodontics and Pediatric Dentistry, and what I learned was this: I'd never understand why their business partnership functioned better than their marriage. But I'd always remember them—after they divorced and long afterward—working harmoniously and happily together, making two new teeth that were just imperfect enough to look like they belonged in their only child's mouth.

I pulled the Volvo into the upper-level parking area. No

one—in all my non-driving years—had ever thought to drop me off here between Macy's and Sears. Entrance four was the only one that didn't go through a major department store, but directly onto a short corridor leading to Concourse E. If you didn't know it existed, it could be easily missed. And yet, judging by the difficulty in finding a decent space, it was the preferred entrance to a whole crowd of shoppers who would never understand why anyone parked anywhere else . . .

"*Stop stalling.*"

The Drea in my head was right. My first solo drive to the mall had gone smoothly, but now I was definitely stalling. Stores closed in three hours, and I had a lot to accomplish in that time. I needed to get out of the car to make amends while I still could. I made an actual checklist because writing it down made me more accountable.

JACKET

CHEST

MIXED

TREASURE

Again, I'd called upon my Odyssey of the Mind training, by putting the easiest to-dos first. By making small, but measurable progress, I'd hopefully gain the confidence I'd need to face the final trial, the most perplexing, vexing challenge of them all.

45

JACKET

*T*he arcade was slow at this hour. Preteens, for whom the mall was de facto summer camp, had hopped on their bicycles and were pedaling home for dinner. The slightly older nighttime gamers were due to arrive in another hour or so, after finishing up their morning-into-afternoon shifts at Foot Locker or Ponderosa Steak & Ale.

Sonny Sexton would be there because he was *always* there, from opening to closing. It didn't take me long to find him, crouched in front of the coin slot of a game called *Double Dragon*. He was wearing a checkered flannel shirt to keep warm in the cranked-up AC. I not only reneged on my promise to return the jacket within twenty-four hours—I hadn't bothered returning it at all. For days afterward, a flowery hint of pomade exuded from the dingy denim. The jacket had become so inextricably linked to Sam that I'd pretty much forgotten why I'd borrowed it in the first place.

I'd kept it way longer than the lavender scent had lingered.

I'd kept it long enough to convince myself I had only imagined the traces of Sam Goody left behind.

"Hey," I said.

He stood, leaned against the machine.

"Heyyyy."

I held out the jacket by the sleeves. Without saying anything, Sonny removed his flannel shirt and knotted it around this waist. He slipped one arm in the denim, followed by the other.

"Ahhhhh . . ." He sighed as if he'd submerged himself in a warm bubble bath.

"I'm sorry for breaking my promise," I said. "I should have returned it sooner."

"A good girl like you?" He was smiling. "I knew you'd bring it back to me eventually."

"I'm not good," I replied. "It's recently come to my attention that I'm a selfish asshole."

"Well," said a soft, female voice, "too much time around Troy will do that to a person."

Even after I laid eyes on the tiny girl with the teased hair in the Casino Pier T-shirt, it still took a few seconds to connect the vision to the voice. I'd never heard Helen communicate at any level lower than a full-throated screech. I couldn't hide my terror.

"I come in peace," Helen said, showing her palms. "I owe you an apology."

"You do?" I asked timidly.

"I wasn't right in the head for a while."

"Too much time around Troy will do that to a person."

Helen rewarded me with a soft chuckle I didn't earn for lazily recycling her joke.

"My court-appointed therapist says I have anger management issues," Helen explained.

From behind her, Sonny flashed me a warning look: *Don't ask.* So as curious as I was about her legal troubles, I kept my questions to myself.

"Anyways," Helen went on, "after I called her Dr. Douchenozzle and chucked an ashtray at her head, I realized she might have a point."

Sonny opened his arms as an invitation for her to fold her body against his in a totally unsexual way.

"She's made a lot of progress already," he said. "Her parents and I are so proud."

Until that moment, I hadn't pictured Helen as someone with parents. In my mythology, she was not a normal human infant birthed on this Earth. No, Helen had emerged as a fully formed monster from the fires of Hades, a malevolent, vengeful hell-beast forged in the underworld's furnace to make my last summer in Pineville as miserable as possible.

When, in fact, she was just a girl who was hurting inside.

Helen had demons. She wasn't *a* demon.

"I shouldn't have broken up with you," Sonny said, pulling Helen closer. "I should've known something deeply fucked up was going on with you to hook up with Cookie Boy." He turned to me. "No offense."

"None taken," I insisted. "There's something deeply fucked up with me too. Unfortunately, I don't have an official diagnosis to treat it."

I was about to leave this loved-up couple alone when Helen lifted her head from Sonny's chest and gestured toward the *Double Dragon* machine.

"Wanna play a round?"

"Oh, I'm really, really bad at arcade games," I said.

"So what?" Helen asked. "Do you always have to be the best at everything all the time?"

I'd spent seventeen years trying to be the best at everything all the time. And I had only succeeded at being the worst in all the ways that truly mattered:

as a daughter,

as a friend,

as a decent human being.

"It's on me," Sonny said, squeezing two quarters out of the coin holster around his waist.

"I'm just going to die right away," I said.

"I swear I won't let you die right away." Helen held up two fingers like a Girl Scout. "I don't make promises I can't keep."

She got me on that one.

I clutched the joystick, hoping there was some truth to the word. As it turned out, one hour in arcade time was equivalent to five minutes in the outside world. I would've sworn in Mock

Court that I'd played that video game with Helen for a fraction of the time I actually did. *Double Dragon,* as Helen had explained, wasn't just a beat-'em-up game, it had a compelling story that set it apart.

"It's a classic tale of family and friendship and love and loyalty and betrayal and brotherhood," she said. "You know, all the most important shit in life."

Helen and I were twin martial artists—Billy and Jimmy aka Hammer and Spike—trying to rescue my girlfriend, Marian, who was kidnapped by a rival gang. Locations varied—city slum, factory, forest, secret hideout—but our mission never did. Helen's expert advice?

"Just kick ass!"

We'd made it through level three and were moving on to the next when Helen grumbled about having to leave the mall to start her shift on the boardwalk.

"It's almost six o'clock!" The numbers on my watch shocked me. "How did that happen?"

"There are no clocks in the arcade for a reason."

I told Helen to thank Sonny for the—ahem—fun time.

"You make a great couple," I said.

"Thank you," said Helen. "We do."

And then I found myself hugging the girl who had once tried to assassinate me.

46

CHEST

I was a half hour late for the next item on my to-do list. I ran through the Concourses to make up for lost time and was breathless when I got to Wood World.

"Sylvester!" I was panting. "I'm here!"

"Hi, there, Cassie," he replied merrily as ever.

I rested on the counter to catch my breath. His flannel shirt was the same pattern as Sonny Sexton's—a blue-and-black buffalo plaid—though Sylvester's was faded and nubby. Flannel was showing up all over the place lately and it wasn't even fall yet.

"You're a trendsetter in that shirt, you know," I said.

"I've owned this shirt for twenty years." Sylvester ho-ho-hoed. "Live long enough and everything old is new again."

That philosophy was at the core of his success, and what kept him in business all these years. By staying true to himself, Sylvester made Wood World transcend trends. Of course, it helped that he understood exactly who he was. I hadn't reached that level of self-actualization. I was closer than I was a few months ago, but hadn't arrived there yet.

"I was starting to worry I wouldn't see you tonight," he said.

"I might not have the best reputation these days, but there's no way I would stiff you like that," I replied. "Especially since this was kind of a rush job on such short notice."

"Pshaw! Wasn't anything to it. I love doing custom work. It's what I live for!"

Even if the recipient didn't appreciate this gift, I could at least feel good about bringing happiness to Sylvester.

"You ready to see it?"

"Yes!"

Sylvester laughed deep in his bowlful-of-jelly belly. I was like a kid desperate to open her first present of the holiday season. I really did want to see his creation—but quickly. I had two more to-dos before the mall closed at 8:00 p.m. Sylvester ambled out of the back office holding a wood chest, roughly the size of a shoe box. The grain was textured in various shades of purpleheart, from eggplant to amethyst to the plum lipstick I was wearing when I'd royally messed things up.

"Ohhhh," I gasped. "It's beautiful."

Sylvester had charged me far less than what the box was worth, but it still cost a shift at Bellarosa. Half a textbook. One mezzanine ticket to a Broadway show.

"Inscribed as requested."

He opened the lid on its double hinge to reveal the words he'd carved on the inside. I traced my finger along the engraving.

"What's that from, anyway?" he asked.

"Nothing."

Obviously I was lying. Nobody pays for the inscription of "nothing."

I thanked Sylvester and sped across Concourse F. I was half-way to my penultimate to-do, when I felt an unmistakable presence trailing behind me. It was perfect timing, really. It couldn't have been better if I had tried to plan it. Which is exactly why I hadn't. Why bother trying to find Zoe when I knew she would find me?

I stopped, spun around. "Boo!"

My best attempt at a scare worked well enough, even on a seasoned creeper.

"Ha!"

I'd finally beaten Zoe to it. Spooked her before she spooked me. And she was positively delighted. I was equally happy to see her wearing the velvet scarf.

"Ha! Ha! Ha!" She slapped her palms to her hollow cheeks. "Ha!"

It was a robust burst of laughter, and I loved hearing it.

"I have something for you," I said.

Her eyes saucered with surprise. "Really?"

I led her to a slightly quieter spot in the shadow of the escalators. We sat on the tiled ledge of a large planter containing a mix of real and artificial trees.

"I read these and thought of you."

I opened the flap on my knapsack and pulled out the leftovers from my stint as a co-conspirator in low-level anarchy. It was the best of feminist underground lit, zines with names like: *Bikini Kill, Chainsaw,* and *Riot Grrrl.* All made specifically by grrrls, for grrrls.

"Oh! Oh! Oh!" Zoe couldn't flip through the pages fast enough "They're . . ."

I understood why she was at a loss for words. It was impossible to fully describe the scope of these publications. Handwritten manifestos railing against "racist, classist, fattist, speciesist, heterosexist" culture. Lesbian erotica. Typed, single-spaced essays debunking "the many myths of female masturbation." Song lyrics (*"hey you think you know me but you don't"*) by bands (Bratmobile) I'd never heard of. Photo collages juxtaposing 1950s advertisements and modern pop star iconography, Disney princess and pornography. I wish I'd had such inspirational reading material when I was recovering from mono.

"Wow," Zoe finally said. "Where did you get them?"

"Someone put them in the magazine rack at the music store," I said. "There's another anarchist among us."

Specifics weren't necessary. I didn't need to mention the anarchist by name—or gender. Of course I didn't miss the irony of one boy's subversive act encouraging the radicalization of least one feminist, if not two.

Zoe closed her eyes and clutched the zines to her chest in full swoon.

"How can I repay you?"

"You already did," I said, "when you told me where to find the final clue."

When I was on Bellarosa's toilet—down in "the dumper," as Zoe had oddly and specifically put it—I looked up. And that's when I noticed for the first time that the bathroom ceiling was at least a foot lower than in the store or back office. The low height contributed to the claustrophobic atmosphere that discouraged Bellarosa employees from lingering in the bathroom for too long. The ceiling was a grid of flimsy tiles, again, unlike anywhere else in the store. I got a fluttery feeling in my rib cage, the way I always did when I knew I was on the verge of solving the unsolvable.

I climbed onto the toilet, reached up, and poked at one of the tiles with my finger. It easily gave way. And there, hidden in that secret storage space right above the commode, was not another Cabbage Patch Doll, but a taped-up Reebok shoebox.

"The treasure!" Zoe exclaimed. "What was inside?"

"I don't know."

"You don't know? You didn't open it?"

This was the most animated I'd ever seen her.

"If you're so interested, why didn't *you* open it?" I pressed. "You gave me the clue, remember?"

Zoe clicked her tongue stud against her teeth.

"It wasn't my treasure to take."

This witch certainly had a vengeful streak, but she also had integrity. And that's more than I could say about how I'd conducted myself for far too long.

"It wasn't mine either," I said. "I didn't deserve to open it."

"Cassie Worthy"—Zoe paused—"wasn't worthy."

I groaned because it was so on-the-nose and also because it was true. I was a disappointment to everyone I'd come in contact with all summer, but no one more than the person who had introduced me to the treasure hunt in the first place.

"Are you worthy now?" Zoe asked.

Not yet, but I hoped I was getting closer. I still had amends left to make.

47

MIXED

I almost expected Sam Goody to be wearing the same shirt I'd seen on Sylvester and Sonny Sexton. Didn't everyone in the Pacific Northwest wear flannel? It was a relief to see him in the same outfit he was wearing the first time I laid eyes on him: employee T-shirt, pegged black jeans, boots. It occurred to me that I'd only seen him wearing that same exact outfit, and I wondered if I'd ever get a chance to see him in anything else.

I'd chosen my own outfit with care. For the first time since I'd gotten mono, I finally filled out my favorite jeans again. I'd paired them with the cream, collarbone-baring shirt Drea had

292

designed for my disastrous date with Slade. In the weeks following that night, my stomach turned at the sight of that shirt crumpled in a ball on my bedroom floor. It might still be there if Kathy hadn't picked it up while we were packing my suitcase for school.

"What a nice top," she said, stroking the petal-soft material. "You should take better care of it than this."

My mother was right. So I handwashed the shirt in my bathroom sink and let it air dry on the clothesline in our backyard. Drea's design now smelled of fresh air and sunshine. It was even better than new. Next time, I'd complete this outfit with oxblood Doc Martens I was determined to buy before the end of first-year orientation. In our phone call over the weekend, Simone Levy had promised to take me to Eighth Street in Greenwich Village because that's where she always went to get the best deals on shoes.

Sam Goody had his back to me. He was standing in front of the Billboard 100 wall, removing CDs from some slots and returning them to others. Customers were constantly putting merchandise back where it didn't belong, and a good part of Sam Goody's day was spent correcting other people's carelessness. Freddy must've been really hungover because he was playing a deeply strange song combining Gregorian chants and French pillow talk over hypnotic rhythms. It was a hallucinogenic soundscape, and I had to focus extra-hard to stay grounded as I put one penny-loafered foot in front of the other.

I reached Sam before he turned around.

"Hi."

He pivoted away from the shelf and toward me. Conflicting emotions crossed his face in quick succession: surprise, sadness, suspicion, surrender.

I reached into my knapsack and took out a cassette tape.

"I made this," I said quickly. "And I want you to have it."

I didn't say I made it for him because that wasn't exactly true. When I was picking out all my favorite songs by all my favorite artists, I thought I was making this mixed tape for myself, to play in my dorm room. I wasn't trying to impress Simone Levy or anyone else with my tastes—I just wanted ninety minutes worth of music I loved listening to. When I found myself with under seven minutes left of tape on side two, I agonized over the final choices. Two songs ran too long—the second kept getting cut off. One song was too short and left too much dead air. Through trial and error, recordings and rerecordings, I finally struck the perfect melodramatic marathon of a song. Coming in at six minutes and forty-seven seconds, "How Soon Is Now?" left just two seconds of silence. Only after I played it back did I understand who this mixed tape was intended for all along.

Sam opened it up to read the track listing.

"*Cassie's T-shirts*," he said. "That's a good title." He paused. "Cassie."

I had brainstormed many others—*Hatchback Jams, Tunes in the Key of Sorry, Parkway Center Blues, Sturm und Drang Songs*—before settling on that one.

"I figured if I put my name in the title, you'd never forget who gave it to you."

Sam tapped the tape to his temple, then his heart.

"I'm not going to forget you," he said.

I doubted I would ever forget him either. But I still couldn't look him in the eyes. Is it any wonder *Mixed Feelings* had come in a very, very close runner-up?

"I should have gotten you a going-away gift," he said apologetically.

"You can't feel bad about that," I reasoned. "You didn't know I'd show up today."

"I didn't know, but I hoped you would," he said. "And I should've prepared myself for the most optimistic outcome. That's something new I'm trying out. Positive visualization. As an alternative to being mildly, chronically depressed."

"You don't strike me as mildly depressed," I said, before correcting myself. "Well, maybe when we first met, you did. But after that . . ."

"After that," he said, "I was trying to make up for what a jerk I was."

"You've more than compensated for that first conversation," I said. "I swear."

"Are you sure? Is there anything you want in the store? The new Marky Mark and the Funky Bunch cassingle, perhaps?"

We were joking.

We were okay.

I hugged him. Hard. Pressed my nose into his shaggy sideburns and got a good whiff of lavender. He would make a great boyfriend for someone. Maybe that someone could be me someday. Just not right now.

I would not feel any regret when we let go.

"Thank you, Sam."

His chest rumbled against mine in silent laughter. Then he pressed his mouth against my ear.

"By the way," he said, "My name is George."

48

TREASURE

"*Attention, Parkway Center Mall customers. Five minutes to closing. Please make your way to the exits. Come back again soon!*"

I had not managed my time very well. I was going against the tide of last-minute shoppers, the only person walking toward the stores and away from the doors. All the security gates were half drawn, the universal signal that you could still be let out of a shop, but would not be let in. I dipped under the shiny golden lattice, hoping Bellarosa Boutique would make an exception to the rule. Gia once told me it been Drea's idea to spray-paint the dull gray grill to match the store's opulent interior.

"If it were up to Drea, that gate would be lacquered in twenty-four-carat gold," Gia had joked.

Drea didn't deny it. "Doesn't Bellarosa deserve the best?"

Drea did deserve the best. I didn't see her, though. Had she left work early? Had I gotten there too late?

Gia was standing behind the register with a made-up, dressed-up brunette I'd never seen before. I guessed she was in her mid-twenties, but in true Bellarosa fashion, she could've been a decade older or younger.

"Cassie? What are you doing here?"

Gia practically vaulted over the counter to pull me into a deep, heavily perfumed embrace. Frank and Kathy weren't huggy people, so Gia's hands-on affection had taken some getting used to. I was back in my own clothes, so I didn't look like a Bellarosa anymore. But in her arms, I still felt like family.

"I thought you left for school already."

"Not until tomorrow." I gave Gia an extra squeeze before loosening my grip. "I'm so sorry about the fashion show—"

Gia cut me off.

"Don't worry about that, hon," she said. "All that free publicity was fantastic for business!"

"Really?"

"Really! We're up twenty percent!"

I sighed with relief. I never wanted to negatively affect Bellarosa's bottom line.

The brunette cleared her throat.

"I was just talking to Crystal here about how much easier it will be for her to track receipts with the new computerized system . . ."

I was so used to her name being preceded by "No-Good" that I almost missed it. But when the momentousness of this introduction fully hit me, I couldn't hold back.

"You're Crystal Bellarosa!"

She wrinkled her nose.

"Duh Brooze Zee."

"My brother's wife's brother's kid," Gia explained. "The D'Abruzzi cousins."

The last name sounded familiar, but in the moment I couldn't place it.

"Ohhhh," I marveled.

This was historic. I'd finally come face-to-face with No-Good Crystal. If she hadn't been so terrible at her job, I wouldn't have gotten hired by Gia, fired by Drea. I wouldn't be back in the store to bestow a possibly life-changing fortune.

"What are *you* doing here?"

All heads turned in Drea's direction. Her words were the same as Gia's, but her tone could not have been more different.

"I just need five minutes of your time," I pleaded.

"I'll give you thirty seconds," Drea countered. "But only because you're wearing one of my designs."

"Three minutes."

"Forty-five seconds."

Gia and Crystal watched us go back and forth, like spectators in a tennis match.

"Ninety seconds."

Drea sighed and rolled her eyes.

"One minute," she said. "And that's my final offer."

"Okay." I held out my hand and she refused to shake it. "I'll take it."

One minute was what I'd been shooting for. One minute was all I needed.

She glanced at the gold bangle on her wrist.

"Clock's ticking."

It was not a timepiece, but a bracelet. She was just messing with me.

"Do you insist on making this as difficult as possible?" I asked.

"After the way you disrespected my family? Abso-friggin'-lutely!"

"I didn't disrespect your fam—"

"Do you not see the name Bellarosa on the sign?"

I struck a conciliatory tone, my only chance at survival.

"You're right," I said. "And I'm sorry. And I'll be able to show you how sorry I am if you follow me to the bathroom."

"Forty-five seconds." She shook her fake watch.

I had planned this whole speech, equal parts apology and explanation for my actions leading up to the fashion show. I had practiced it at home and had gotten it down to a tight fifty-five seconds, with five seconds left for the big reveal. But Drea was making me cut through all the bullshit. I'd need to get right to the point if I had any chance of getting her to go along with me.

"That's long enough," I said, "to show you the treasure."

49

EXCHANGES AND RETURNS

*O*ur adventure began in the subbasement. It only seemed fitting for the treasure hunt to culminate on the rooftop.

"Crystal and I used to come up here to sneak cigarettes and work on our tans," Drea said. "But I've never been up here at night."

The days were noticeably shorter. Only the brightest stars bravely peeked out of the purple sky. Light pollution made star-gazing a challenge from the mall, but it would be nearly impossible once I arrived in Manhattan. Even under the best viewing conditions, Cassiopeia was too low on the horizon to be seen from anywhere on the East Coast at this time of year. On a field trip to the planetarium in second grade, I was elated to learn of the constellation with a name that sounded so much like mine. I'd always thought of the queen on her throne as "my" constellation, even though—as the story went—she chained her own daughter to a rock as a sacrificial offering to a ravenous sea serpent.

We sat facing each other on the wide ledge. Drea ceremoniously placed the Reebok shoebox between us and extracted the letter opener from her cleavage. She pointed it right between my eyes.

"I'm still pissed at you."

"Of course," I said. "Understood."

She held the box up to her ear and shook it gently, then giddily.

"Sounds like money!"

I really, really hoped she was right. If hidden treasure provided Drea with the resources to make her dream of starting her own fashion line come true, then I wanted her to have every last cent of it. I watched with eager interest as Drea cut into the lid. Vince had gone a little overboard with the duct tape, so it required more effort and less finesse than opening the Cabbage Patch boxes. After a few final jabs and stabs, the top of the box came free from the bottom. Our voices rang out over the nearly empty parking lot.

"Hooray!"

Drea placed her hands on opposite sides of the shoebox, closed her eyes, and took a deep, bracing breath. What was happening on that rooftop felt almost sacred. Drea brought a profound sense of ritual and reverence to what had started out as a silly diversion for me, but had evolved into something much deeper as we got to know each other again. I knew I might never earn her forgiveness, which is why I considered myself blessed to be the only person in the world with Drea Bellarosa when she lifted the lid and peered inside.

"What in the gawddamn hell?!"

She pulled out a grayish-green stack bound by a rubber band.

It wasn't money.

"Born in the USA Tour," read Drea in a slow, stunned voice. "Meadowlands Arena."

No, Tommy hadn't hidden thousands of dollars in Bellarosa Boutique's bathroom ceiling. He'd hidden thousands of dollars' worth of Springsteen tickets.

"Front row seats . . ." Drea fanned them out on the concrete. "For all ten nights . . ."

Our foreheads pressed together to get a better look. We simultaneously gasped at the date of the last show: August 20, 1984. Drea and I locked shocked eyes.

"We're two days too late!" Drea cried.

"Seven years and two days too late!" I cried.

We threw the useless tickets into the air like confetti. They didn't get very far in the still air and floated right back down to our feet.

"You were right all along," Drea said gloomily. "No fortune to be found."

This pessimistic prediction was the only accurate call I'd made all summer. At least I had prepared for this outcome. After how I'd betrayed her trust, I couldn't force Drea to be my friend again. But I wouldn't leave her empty-handed either.

"I have something for you."

I reached into my knapsack and presented her with the box I'd commissioned from Sylvester. She took it in her hands and stared, saying nothing.

"It's your own treasure chest," I explained.

She shook the box and unsuccessfully tried to suppress a grin at the secrets rattling within.

"What's inside?"

"Open it up to find out."

Her reluctant smile grew wider and wider as she took inventory of the booty:

* Gift certificate to Sew Amazing!

* Paperback copy of *The Vogue Guide to a Career in Fashion*

* Prepaid long-distance calling cards

Her eyes lit up when she saw the inscription carved on the inside of the lid. She read it aloud.

"Be the best possible version of yourself."

"The Bellarosa motto," I said.

Drea traced her finger across the words before quietly shutting the box. The smile faded, the mood shifted.

"Are you still mad at me?" I asked.

Drea shook her head. "No."

"Then what is it?"

She gripped the treasure chest, almost like she needed it for support.

"I let my guard down with you, Cassie. I don't do that with just anyone. I mean, I *cried* in front of you . . ."

"I know," I said. "I . . ."

She shushed me with a single sharpened fingernail.

"We were getting so close, but I knew it was only temporary. Like, you made it so clear to everyone how you couldn't wait to get the hell out of Pineville and start your new life in New York, and it pissed me off because I wanted that same dream for myself," she said.

"I'm sor—"

"Don't apologize," Drea interrupted. "You worked your ass off to get into Barnard. You should be proud of yourself."

I *was* proud of myself. And I was still excited about Barnard and New York City, about seeing what life beyond Pineville had in store for me. Yet, part of me wondered if everything I *really* needed to know—about family and friendship and love and loyalty and betrayal and sisterhood, "you know, all the most important shit in life" as Helen had put it—I had already learned that summer at the mall.

"Okay, so I won't apologize for leaving," I said. "But I am deeply sorry for making you feel . . ."

"Left behind?" she asked. "Like I did to you?"

"Exactly."

"You're so talented, Drea," I said, stroking the silk ribbon on the top she'd made me. "Please don't give up on your own fashion line."

"Who says I've given up on anything?" Drea said resolutely. "I'm going to earn my spot among the best, and that starts by proving myself at OCC this fall."

"Drea!" I threw my arms around her. "That's the best news I've heard all summer!"

Ocean County College was the local, well-regarded community college. This was the obvious first step for anyone wanting a post–high school academic do-over. It was so obvious that I was upset at myself for not suggesting it to Drea sooner. We could have avoided the fountain catfight and actually enjoyed our last week together.

Yet as Drea energetically rattled on about her schedule, I understood that this ambitious decision was meaningful because it was hers and hers alone. In addition to a figure drawing class, she had registered for core math and English courses that she could transfer to FIT or another four-year program later on. The hardest part, she said, was mustering the courage to tell Gia that she'd have to scale back her hours at the boutique. When she finally shared her short- and long-term plans, her mother burst into tears of pride and joy.

"She was so psyched for me!" Drea enthused.

"*I'm* psyched for you!"

"I'm psyched for me too!"

Now this goodbye didn't feel like the ending. It felt like the beginning. For both of us.

I looped my arm through Drea's.

"You're the best friend I've ever had," I confessed. "You know what that means?"

Drea cocked her head quizzically. "What?"

"We're both shitty at picking best friends."

Drea unleashed a raucous hawnk. I guffawed from my gut. Our shared laughter echoed for miles and miles and miles, from the mall, across the parking lot, the parkway and the turnpike, over bridges and through tunnels, until it reached the island of Manhattan.

And all the way back again.